Stuart Woods'

GOLDEN HOUR

BOOKS BY STUART WOODS

STONE BARRINGTON NOVELS

Stuart Woods' Smolder
   (by Brett Battles)
Near Miss (with Brett Battles)
Distant Thunder
Black Dog
A Safe House
Criminal Mischief
Foul Play
Class Act
Double Jeopardy
Hush-Hush
Shakeup
Choppy Water
Hit List
Treason
Stealth
Contraband
Wild Card
A Delicate Touch
Desperate Measures
Turbulence
Shoot First
Unbound
Quick & Dirty
Indecent Exposure
Fast & Loose
Below the Belt
Sex, Lies & Serious Money
Dishonorable Intentions
Family Jewels
Scandalous Behavior
Foreign Affairs
Naked Greed

Hot Pursuit
Insatiable Appetites
Paris Match
Cut and Thrust
Carnal Curiosity
Standup Guy
Doing Hard Time
Unintended Consequences
Collateral Damage
Severe Clear
Unnatural Acts
D.C. Dead
Son of Stone
Bel-Air Dead
Strategic Moves
Lucid Intervals
Kisser
Loitering with Intent
Hot Mahogany
Shoot Him If He Runs
Fresh Disasters
Dark Harbor
Two Dollar Bill
Reckless Abandon
Dirty Work
The Short Forever
Cold Paradise
L.A. Dead
Worst Fears Realized
Swimming to Catalina
Dead in the Water
Dirt
New York Dead

ED EAGLE NOVELS

Santa Fe Edge
Santa Fe Dead

Short Straw
Santa Fe Rules

HOLLY BARKER NOVELS

Hothouse Orchid

Iron Orchid

Blood Orchid

Orchid Blues

Orchid Beach

WILL LEE NOVELS

Mounting Fears

Capital Crimes

The Run

Grass Roots

Deep Lie

Run Before the Wind

Chiefs

TEDDY FAY NOVELS

Stuart Woods' Golden Hour
  (by Brett Battles)

Obsession (with Brett Battles)

Jackpot (with Bryon
  Quertermous)

Bombshell (with Parnell Hall)

Skin Game (with Parnell Hall)

The Money Shot
  (with Parnell Hall)

Smooth Operator
  (with Parnell Hall)

HERBIE FISHER NOVELS

Barely Legal (with Parnell Hall)

RICK BARRON NOVELS

Beverly Hills Dead

The Prince of Beverly Hills

STAND-ALONE NOVELS

Choke

Imperfect Strangers

Heat

Dead Eyes

L.A. Times

Palindrome

White Cargo

Under the Lake

AUTOBIOGRAPHY

An Extravagant Life: An Autobiography Incorporating Blue Water,
Green Skipper

TRAVEL

A Romantic's Guide to the Country Inns of Britain and Ireland (1979)

MEMOIR

Blue Water, Green Skipper

Stuart Woods'

GOLDEN HOUR

by BRETT BATTLES

G. P. PUTNAM'S SONS
NEW YORK

PUTNAM
— EST. 1838 —

G. P. PUTNAM'S SONS
Publishers Since 1838
An imprint of Penguin Random House LLC
penguinrandomhouse.com

Library of Congress Cataloging-in-Publication Data

Names: Battles, Brett, author.
Title: Stuart Woods' golden hour / by Brett Battles.
Other titles: Golden hour
Description: New York : G. P. Putnam's Sons, 2024. | Series: Teddy Fay novel
Identifiers: LCCN 2024030208 (print) | LCCN 2024030209 (ebook) |
ISBN 9780593331606 (hardcover) | ISBN 9780593331613 (epub)
Subjects: LCGFT: Action and adventure fiction. | Thrillers (Fiction) | Novels.
Classification: LCC PS3602.A923 S77 2024 (print) |
LCC PS3602.A923 (ebook) | DDC 813/.6—dc23/eng/20240715
LC record available at https://lccn.loc.gov/2024030208
LC ebook record available at https://lccn.loc.gov/2024030209
p.   cm.

Printed in the United States of America
1st Printing

Book design by Shannon Nicole Plunkett

Stuart Woods'

GOLDEN HOUR

1

DIRT CRUNCHED UNDER TYLER STORM AS HE
was rolled onto his back.

The brute looming above him frowned, then said over
his shoulder, "He ain't dead yet."

One of his buddies stepped next to him, then snorted.
"He's as good as."

Bloodied and bruised, Storm cracked open his eyes.
Around him stood half a dozen of Caleb Donovan's men, all
looking at Storm with disdain.

"Out of the way," a familiar voice said.

The men parted and Donovan himself stepped forward
and crouched beside Storm.

"Not your best day, is it?" Donovan said. "I did warn you
this would happen."

A smile crept across Storm's face. "You did."

Donovan narrowed his eyes. "I don't think you fully
grasp what's about to happen to you."

"You're going to kill me."

"Huh. How about that? You *do* understand."

Storm's grin widened.

"Are you smiling because you're thinking I'll do it fast and end your pain?" Donovan looked at him with pity. "Sorry, Storm, I have bad news for you."

A wet laugh slipped past Storm's lips.

"What's so damn funny?"

"It doesn't matter what you do to me," Storm said. "You're done."

It was Donovan's turn to laugh. He rose to his feet. "You got some balls. I'll give you that. But you couldn't be more wrong. I'm not even close to done. Soon everyone in this city will know who I—" He paused and looked around. "You guys hear that?"

The *whomp-whomp-whomp* of helicopter rotors began echoing off the abandoned buildings surrounding them, making it impossible to tell from which direction it came.

As Donovan twisted around looking for the source, the copter appeared above him, lighting him up with its spotlight. Dozens of police sirens could now be heard closing in.

The shot cut to Storm as his eyes fluttered closed, the smile still on his lips. The camera began to rise and the shot widened, first showing Storm surrounded by Donovan and his panicked men, then encompassing the police cars speeding in from all directions, and finally moving above the police helicopter hovering over the area.

The soundtrack hit a crescendo, and the screen went dark. After a beat, the credits began to roll.

When the film ended and the lights came on, everyone in the screening room applauded save Peter Barrington, the director of *Storm's Eye*, who was scribbling notes on a pad of paper.

"Fantastic," Ben Bacchetti said. He was head of Centurion Pictures, one of the film's producers, and Peter's best friend. "No question, you've done it again. People are going to love it."

"I couldn't agree more," Billy Barnett said. He was the other producer. "Peter, I think this is your best yet."

"You're just saying that because it stars Mark Weldon," Ben said.

Billy placed a hand dramatically on his chest. "Why, Ben, are you calling me biased?"

"Me? Never."

The others laughed.

Everyone in the room was a member of the very select club who knew that Billy Barnett's true identity was that of Teddy Fay, formerly of the CIA, and someone who, as far as most of the world knew, had perished several years ago.

They also knew that Billy Barnett wasn't Teddy's only alternate persona. He was also Academy Award–winning actor Mark Weldon, aka Tyler Storm in *Storm's Eye*.

Hattie Barrington, the film's composer and Peter's wife, eyed her husband, who was still writing in his notebook. "Why do I get the feeling you're not happy?"

Peter glanced up. "Why do you think I'm not happy?"

"That worry line on your forehead, for one."

"That obvious?"

"To me, yes."

"Well, I wouldn't say I'm not *happy*, but I could be happier," he conceded.

"You say that about all your films," Tessa Tweed, Ben's wife, said. She was an Oscar-winning actress herself and had starred as Tyler Storm's niece in the film.

"You do recall that you told us this would be the final cut, don't you?" Ben said.

Peter grimaced. "Yeah, about that—"

Before he could continue, Ben said, "And that we're already two weeks past when you were scheduled to have picture lock?"

"I do, but—"

"And, most importantly, the final film must be in the can before you leave for Europe in a few days."

"It's only one scene," Peter said quickly.

"Which one?"

"The confession at the house."

"I loved that part," Tessa said. "I wouldn't change a thing."

Peter shook his head. "The pacing's off."

To Billy, Ben said, "Thoughts?"

Billy considered it for a moment, then said, "It's a good scene, but if Peter thinks there's room for improvement, then I trust him."

"You're supposed to be on my side," Ben said.

"I'm on the movie's side, always and forever. Besides, there's still time for him to work his magic. And we *are* under budget."

"For which I thank you," Ben said.

"It's what I do."

"I promise I'll be done before we get on the plane," Peter said.

"The day *before* you get on the plane," Ben said.

"You don't trust me?"

"Oh, I trust you. But I also know that if the deadline is right before you board, you'll find some way to keep tweaking it during the ride to the airport."

Peter opened his mouth to argue the point, then shrugged. "You know me too well."

On that coming Sunday, Peter, Billy, Tessa, and Hattie were departing on a European press tour to promote *Storm's Eye*'s upcoming release, finishing with the film's world premiere at the inaugural World Thriller Film Festival in Berlin. Adriene Adele, one of the film's other stars, would also be joining them.

"Question," Hattie asked, raising a hand like she was in school. "What about Tom Norman's new movie?"

Peter looked at her, confused.

"The premiere is in two nights," she reminded him. "You're taking me, remember?"

He winced. "Right. Um, sorry, sweetheart. Not sure I'll be able to make it."

She sighed. "It wouldn't be the first time."

"I have an idea," Billy said. "I was going solo, but if you wouldn't mind the company of an old movie producer, I would be honored to be your date."

"Billy, are you hitting on my wife?" Peter said.

"I wouldn't dare."

"I happily accept," Hattie said.

Peter grinned. "Thanks, Billy. If I were to choose anyone to stand in for me, it would be you."

"Excuse me, but your best friend is sitting right here," Ben said, pointing at himself.

"You'd be on that list, too. Just a few slots farther down."

"A few *slots?*"

Peter shrugged and stood. "Now, if you'd all excuse me, I need to get back to work."

2

OWEN PACE TUGGED DOWN ON THE BRIM OF
his baseball cap and adjusted his wool scarf so that it covered
his mouth and nose. Once satisfied, he exited the Saint-
Michel Notre-Dame Metro station.

As he'd hoped, the sidewalk was packed with a mix of
tourists and Parisians on their way home from work. Meld-
ing into the crowd, he entered Paris's Latin Quarter unnoticed.

He maintained his vigilance as he made his way through
the quarter's warren of narrow, cobbled roads, and reached
his destination without any of his internal alarms going off.

Bar Dupuy was in the basement of a centuries-old building. Owen had been there many times and knew the layout
well, which was why he had suggested it as a meeting place.
The long, dimly lit room was about twice as wide as the narrow alley above. Booths ran down the wall on the right, and
stools lined the bar on the left. At the back was a shadowy

hallway, where the restrooms and an emergency exit were located.

The only customers were all sitting at the bar. Owen ordered a whiskey and carried it to the booth closest to the back hallway, sitting so that he faced the main entrance.

The meet was set up for ten p.m., but that time came and went without the other party showing up. This was not unexpected.

Tonight was to be Owen's first meeting with a potential source. The person in question worked for the embassy of a former Soviet republic. Owen had learned that the man had become disillusioned by the corruption in his government and his president's rapid turn toward authoritarianism. Owen's hope was that he could persuade him to become an inside source for the CIA.

Cultivating these kinds of connections was Owen's specialty, so he was well aware that an aborted first meeting was not out of the ordinary.

He nursed his whiskey, giving the man extra time in case he was only running late. His stomach began to rumble, and he cursed himself for not picking up something to eat earlier.

He checked his watch. It was nearly ten-thirty. He'd waited long enough. He tipped back the rest of his whiskey and pushed himself out of his booth.

But the moment he stood his bowels twisted into a knot. He doubled over and grabbed the table to keep from falling.

"You all right, my friend?" the bartender asked.

"Something I ate, I think." Owen tried to recall what that could have been, but he was having a hard time concentrating.

"Do you want some water?"

Owen shook his head. "I just need to—"

He was hit with a cramp so intense he had to sit back down.

The bartender hurried over. "You don't look good."

Owen could feel the sweat beading on his forehead as he tried to ride out the cramp. Gritting his teeth, he whispered, "Toilet."

The bartender helped him to his feet and guided him into the back hallway.

Owen shuffled forward, unable to focus on anything but the pain in his gut.

A door opened, and he assumed they'd reached the men's room. But then another pair of hands grabbed him and pulled him forward. The next thing he knew, he was moving up a set of stairs.

He tried to look around and see what was happening, but between the darkness and his inability to open his eyes beyond slits, all he could see were shadows.

With as much strength as he could muster, he whispered, "What's . . . going on?"

Someone leaned next to his ear and said, "Payback."

Owen felt a prick in his arm, and within moments, his world went black.

The sedan pulled in behind the row of police vehicles, and the driver killed the engine.

"Would you like me to check first?" he asked.

Rick La Rose shook his head. "I've got this."

The CIA's Paris Station Chief climbed out and made his

way toward a group of floodlights set up at the edge of a pond, thirty yards from the road.

An officer near the front of the park put up a hand and said, "I'm sorry, sir. This area is currently closed to the public. Please return to your vehicle."

Rick flashed his ID and said in French, "I'm expected."

"One moment." The officer spoke softly into his radio, then waved Rick through.

Several cops were huddled in conversation near the pond. As Rick approached, a woman broke from the group and intercepted him.

"Monsieur La Rose," she said. "I am Ann de Coster, DGSI." DGSI was the acronym for France's internal security agency.

They shook hands.

"Sorry to have you come out in the middle of the night like this," she said.

"Not your fault. Part of the job. The body?"

"This way."

She led him to a body bag that lay on the grass.

"Shall I open it?" she asked.

"Please."

She unzipped it halfway but hesitated before pulling it open. "It is not pleasant."

"Death seldom is."

"More than usual."

"I understand."

She separated the halves, exposing the body from head to stomach.

While bruises and cuts vied for space on the man's torso

and face, it was the slice across his throat that undoubtedly ended his life. Even with all the damage, however, there was no question that the victim was Owen Pace.

"One of yours?" de Coster asked.

"He is."

"I am sorry."

"Thank you. Was he searched?"

"He was."

"May I see?"

"Of course."

She led him to a portable table on which sat a clear plastic bag holding Owen's belongings. Without opening the bag, Rick pushed the items around so that he could see everything—a thin wallet, some coins, a few hundred euros, keys, and a business card.

It was this final item that caused his jaw to tense. The only thing on the card was a stylized letter *T* printed in black.

Rick had been right to come here himself.

He turned back to de Coster. "Thank you."

"The police will have to process the body," she said.

"I understand. If you could ask them to contact my office as soon as it's released, I'd appreciate it."

"I will."

When he returned to his car, his driver asked, "Home?"

"I'm afraid my day's begun already."

"The office, then."

"Please."

Rick raised the privacy divider and called CIA Director Lance Cabot.

"Is it Pace?" Lance asked.

"Yes."

"And?"

"The business card was there."

"So there's no chance his death is a coincidence."

"None whatsoever."

"Then we have a serious problem."

———————

After hanging up with Rick La Rose, Lance pondered how to proceed. A conventional route, using only Agency resources, would be the safest bet. But safe meant slow, and in this case, slow meant more deaths, likely many more.

There was a potentially quicker way of ending the assassinations of his people. If successful, it could drastically cut down the number of dead. The only problem was it would mean involving someone no longer associated with the CIA, a man who might not be keen on working with Lance.

Lance would need help convincing him, and as luck would have it, he knew just who to call.

The man answered on the first ring. "Stone Barrington."

"Stone, it's Lance. Do you have a moment?"

3

"TESSA! TESSA! OVER HERE!"

Tessa paused and waved at the gathered press as they took pictures.

"Tessa! This way!"

A red-carpet pro, Tessa swiveled smoothly from side to side so everyone could get a perfect shot of her in her Veronica De Piante dress.

"Over here! Hey, Tessa!"

"We may be here a while," Billy whispered to Ben and Hattie.

They were standing several feet away to give Tessa the spotlight. While they, too, were award-winning celebrities in their own right, the press would take a superstar actress over a composer, a producer, and a studio head any day of the week.

After a few more shots, one of the publicists working the line ushered the trio over to Tessa for a few group pics.

Another PR person then guided them farther down the carpet to a reporter from Glitter Entertainment, who was just finishing up interviewing one of the costars of *Not on My Watch*, the movie they were here to see. Behind the reporter was a roped-off area filled with excited fans.

"Thanks, everyone, for your support!" the actor said.

He waved and the fans cheered, then the Centurion group took his place at the mic.

"The Glimmer live stream continues with Oscar winners Tessa Tweed and her husband, Ben Bacchetti, head of Centurion Pictures," the reporter said. "And with them are producer Billy Barnett and composer Hattie Barrington. What? No Peter Barrington or Mark Weldon tonight?"

"Peter's putting the finishing touches on his next film," Ben said. "And Mark is out of town and couldn't make it back in time."

"Would that next film be the highly anticipated *Storm's Eye*?"

"You are well informed."

"Tessa, there are rumblings that your performance will have you in line for another Oscar."

"I don't know about that," Tessa said. "But we're not here to talk about *Storm's Eye*. Tonight is all about Tom Norman and *Not on My Watch*, which we are all very excited to see."

"Of course, but could you give us a little taste of what—"

There was a disturbance behind Billy and the others, then Tom Norman—the reigning action-movie box-office champion—popped up between Tessa and Ben. "Did someone mention my name?"

"Ladies and gentlemen, Tom Norman!" the reporter said.

The crowd roared with excitement.

Tom waved and smiled his megastar smile. "Thanks for coming, everyone! I expect you all to see *Not on My Watch* when it opens on Friday!"

More cheers and excited shouts followed.

Tom put arms around Tessa's and Ben's shoulders. "I can't tell you how much I appreciate you coming tonight."

"We wouldn't have missed it," Tessa said.

"I'm looking forward to seeing *Storm's Eye* at the World Thriller Film Festival."

"You're going to Berlin?" Ben said.

"Made sure there was a hole in my schedule so I could attend. Say, when's Peter going to put me in one of his movies?"

The interviewer's eyes lit up. "I think we all want to know that!"

Billy jumped in. "That's an interesting idea. Perhaps we should set up a meeting for when we're all back in town."

Tom swung his arm out from behind Ben and pointed at Billy, his smile even broader than before. "You're on!"

"A potential Tom Norman–Peter Barrington pairing?" the reporter said. "Remember, you heard it here first!"

There were a few more questions about Tom's movie, then the Centurion group moved on so that Tom could have the spotlight to himself.

After they were in the theater lobby, Ben said to Billy, "You really want to meet with Tom Norman?"

"He would be a huge get for the studio," Billy said.

"We don't do big-budget action films."

"Which is likely why he wants to work with us."

"You think he's entering his action-star-doing-something-artsy phase?"

"It *is* a thing."

Ben sighed. "I know. I'm just thinking about the circus we'd have to deal with if we did cast him in something."

"I don't know," Tessa said. "It could be fun."

"Peter's interested," Hattie said.

They all turned to her.

She held up her phone. "I texted him."

Ben glanced at Billy. "The meeting was your idea. So, you're in charge."

"Oh, no," Billy said. "Any discussion with a megastar like Tom is definitely head-of-the-studio-level stuff."

"How about I appoint *you* temporary head for the meeting?"

"Nice try, but I do not believe the corporate bylaws allow that."

"I'll double-check just to be sure."

They reached the theater door and an usher said, "Allow me to show you to your seats."

As they walked down the aisle, Ben whispered to Billy, "This conversation is not over."

"It is as far as I'm concerned," Billy said.

"Perhaps you two should flip a coin," Tessa suggested.

"Even better," Hattie said, "arm wrestle!"

Tessa grinned. "I'd pay to see that."

"A lot of people would."

"They could do it as a fundraiser," Tessa said.

"I *love* that idea."

"Okay, okay," Ben said. "I'll do the meeting."

"Thank you, ladies," Billy said. "Your help is much appreciated."

"Here we are," the usher said.

The first four seats were empty. Standing up, from where he'd been sitting in the fifth, was Stone Barrington.

"Stone," Billy said. "I didn't realize you'd be here."

Stone stepped out and hugged his daughter-in-law, then Tessa, before shaking Ben's and Billy's hands.

"Came into town at the last minute," he said. "Peter's assistant arranged for me to use his spot."

"I'm so glad you could join us," Hattie said.

"As am I."

"We should probably sit," Ben said, noticing another group being led down the aisle.

Billy went in first so that Stone would be next to Hattie.

"How was the latest screening of *Storm's Eye*?" Stone asked Billy once everyone was settled.

"I told Peter this already, but I think it's my favorite of his yet."

"And yet he's still working on it."

"Your son, the perfectionist."

Stone chuckled.

It wasn't long before the rest of the guests entered and took their seats.

———

The movie was two hours of sweat and explosions and death-defying stunt work. In other words, a typical Tom Norman film.

After it was over and Billy and Stone were rising from their chairs to leave, Stone said, "Are you free after this?"

"I need to drive your daughter-in-law home, but after that I will be."

"Join me at the Arrington for a drink?"

"I can do that."

"In the interest of full disclosure, someone else will be joining us, too."

"Who?"

"Lance."

"As in Cabot?"

"The very same. He would like to talk to you about something."

"And that would be what?"

"Something that is not my place to say."

"But you know what it is."

Stone nodded. "I've been briefed."

"So I'm the reason you're in L.A.?"

"You are."

"What if I say no to drinks?"

"Then you drop Hattie off, go home, and we never discuss this again."

"And Lance would be okay with that?"

Stone grimaced. "I'll make him understand. Though there is one thing that I can tell you that might help you decide."

"I'm listening."

"It concerns Operation Golden Hour."

Billy was seldom caught off guard, but he was at that moment.

"Should I expect you?" Stone asked. "Or should I tell Lance you're not coming."

"I'll be there."

4

BY THE TIME TEDDY ARRIVED AT THE AR-
rington Hotel—still in his Billy Barnett guise—it was nearly
eleven. He gave the valet his keys, climbed into a waiting
golf cart, and was driven to Stone's house, located behind
the hotel's main building.

Stone opened the door and let Teddy in. "You made it."

"Did you think I wasn't coming?" Teddy asked.

Stone smirked. "I thought there was a chance."

"I can't deny that the thought of going home crossed my
mind, but . . ."

"How about something to drink?"

"Macallan?"

"The twelve- or the eighteen-year-old?"

"Eighteen. A double."

Stone led Teddy into the living room, then headed over
to the bar.

Lance Cabot rose from where he'd been sitting on the couch. "Good evening, Teddy. You're looking good. Hollywood obviously suits you."

"I like to think so."

Lance gestured to the chair on the other side of the coffee table. "Please, sit."

Stone joined a few moments later, handed Teddy his drink, and sat in the chair next to him.

Teddy thanked him, then said to Lance, "Stone said the craziest thing to get me to show up here. He said that you wanted to talk to me about Golden Hour."

"That's correct."

"Golden Hour happened over two decades ago." Teddy knew this because he'd been part of the mission.

"There has been some recent fallout."

"What kind of fallout?"

"The terminal kind," Lance said. "Someone is killing the agents who were assigned to Golden Hour."

"And this is recent?" Teddy asked. "That makes no sense."

"It started one month ago."

"How many have been killed?"

"Three. Marcus Rendon, Laurel Nguyen, and Owen Pace."

Teddy had known all of them, of course, but Nguyen's loss was particularly painful. She had been a good friend when Teddy had still worked at the CIA.

"I thought Nguyen and Rendon had left the Agency years go," he said.

Lance nodded. "Both retired, seven and ten years ago, respectively."

"But they were still targeted?"

"They were. Rendon was first. Nguyen was executed two weeks ago. And Pace last night while on assignment in Paris."

"Just because all three were part of Golden Hour doesn't mean they were killed because of it. If memory serves, there were twelve of us on the operation. Have any of the others been targeted?"

"Not yet," Lance said.

"Then I assume there's something else that makes you believe the murders are tied to Golden Hour."

Lance opened a manila envelope and slid out two business cards. Printed in the middle of each was a logo featuring the letter *T*. The cards were otherwise blank. "One was found on Rendon and the other on Nguyen."

Teddy's jaw clenched. "The Trust?"

"The Trust," Lance said. "There was a card on Owen, too, but it's in transit."

"It can't be the Trust. They're all dead."

Run by a man named Tovar Lintz, the Trust was the organization Operation Golden Hour had been created to take down—a task the CIA accomplished with great success.

Disguised as a legitimate financial institution, the Trust's true purpose had been to fund terrorist operations around the world. Anyone who got in the organization's way usually ended up dead, with a business card, exactly like those on the table, left in the victim's pocket.

Teddy picked up one of the cards, studied it, then set it back down. "It's been decades. If there was anyone left who wanted revenge, they would have done it years ago. At most, this is a copycat."

"A copycat who has been killing agents involved in Golden Hour."

Teddy picked up his whisky and finished it off.

"Can I get you a refresh?" Stone asked.

"Please."

Stone picked up Teddy's glass and walked over to the bar.

Teddy waited until he returned before he said to Lance, "How does anyone outside the CIA even know who the agents on the mission were? Unless procedures have changed, those kind of records are locked away."

For the first time, Lance looked uncomfortable. "I'm dealing with that issue, so you don't have to worry about it."

"You have a mole, don't you?"

For a moment, it looked as though Lance wasn't going to respond, but then he said, "It *is* possible that someone is helping from the inside."

"I would say it's more than possible."

"As I said, I am dealing with it."

"All right, then what is it you want from me?" Teddy asked.

"To find out who's doing this to my people."

"You have a whole agency of operatives who can do that for you."

"But none with your unique qualifications."

"Unique in what way?"

"You were one of the planners of Golden Hour and know more about it than any of the other agents still alive."

Teddy had created a device that was the centerpiece of

the operation. He'd been on the mission to make sure it worked correctly.

"I'd hardly call that unique. You could easily bring any of the other agents up to speed."

"I'm not finished."

"I apologize. Please, continue expounding on my uniqueness."

"You are about to embark on a press tour in Europe, where all the assassinations have occurred, and where we believe this new threat is based. The trip is the perfect cover."

"The trip isn't a cover. It's my job. One that will be keeping me very busy."

"Naturally, I would never ask you to shirk your responsibilities."

"Then what are you asking?"

Lance shared a glance with Stone.

"You know my feelings on this," Stone said. "I only agreed to host this meeting if *you* told him."

"Told me what?"

"Very well," Lance said. "I believe the best chance we have to draw out whoever's behind this is if we use you as bait."

Teddy folded his arms over his chest and leaned back. "I'm going to need a few more details than that."

"As far as whoever's behind this knows, you're dead. If you weren't, they'd be coming after you, too. I propose we seed a few well-placed rumors saying Teddy Fay might not be as dead as reported. Not long after, we leak more rumors that you may have a connection to the film festival you'll be attending in Berlin. Or perhaps even to your press tour.

Mind you, without pointing a finger at Billy Barnett or Mark Weldon."

"How kind of you," Teddy said. "You do realize doing this could put innocent people in danger, several of whom are close friends of mine."

"We believe the chances of others being harmed are minimal."

"And that would be because . . . ?"

"Because whoever's doing this has been isolating their targets before killing them."

"So far, you mean," Teddy said. "That pattern could change."

"Unlikely, but I'll grant that the possibility exists. To guard against that, there will be a team keeping an eye on you and your colleagues. Covertly, of course."

"And without your mole knowing about them."

"We may not know who it is yet, but we've uncovered enough to know he or she works at Langley. I will simply use resources outside of Virginia, and make sure all communication goes directly through me."

"That seems a little—"

Lance held up his palm, silencing Teddy. "I am fully aware that it is not the perfect plan."

"Thank God for that," Teddy said wryly.

"The problem is we're on the clock here. The longer this takes, the more people will die. People you and I know and have worked with. If you have a better idea, I'd love to hear it."

Lance's words struck Teddy in his weakest spot, his sense of loyalty to his former colleagues. And as much as he didn't like it, the plan made sense.

"If I do this," he said, "I'm in charge. That means I do things my way. My people. My methods. No interference."

"With the exception of my people there for protection."

"And if I need to use them, I can."

"Agreed," Lance said. "Also anyone I can send your way who might have information that will help you."

"Only if you really think they can help."

"I wouldn't waste your time."

"Fine," Teddy said. "One more thing. You pick up the bills."

"Of course, but let's not buy any airplanes or mansions you might take a fancy to."

Teddy pointed his thumb at Stone. "That's him, not me."

"I'll have you know I've added neither plane nor home to my portfolio in quite some time," Stone said.

"Which only means you're due," Lance noted. "So, Teddy, do we have a deal?"

Teddy hesitated a moment, then nodded. "Deal."

Stone saw Teddy out, then returned to the living room.

Lance had moved to the back window and had his phone to his ear.

"The specialist I told you about is on board," Lance said into the device. "He'll have a contact embedded in a press tour for Centurion Pictures' new film. I want a team in place to watch over everyone on the tour. I want nothing to happen to any of them." He listened. "Good, then that's settled. I'll forward you the info on the tour and the contact." He hung up.

Stone poured himself a Knob Creek and took a sip. "I told you it was better to let him know you'd be leaking the rumors than him finding out later."

"Yes, yes. You were right, and I was wrong. Does that make you feel better?"

"It warms my heart."

"I think that might be the Knob Creek."

"Huh. You may be right." Stone saluted him and took another drink.

5

FELIX BRAUN, PRESIDENT AND CEO OF BRAUN
Logistics and Security, was in his office in Berlin the next
morning, going over a proposal for a new client, when his
intercom rang.

"Yes?"

"Mr. Wenz to see you," his assistant said.

"Send him in."

Wenz was a former German special forces member and
Braun's right-hand man. Listed as a security consultant on
BLS company records, his true role was to run an off-the-
books operation they referred to as the special projects
division.

The division's purpose was to take on jobs that the legitimate side of BLS could not touch. For instance, the removal
of an unwanted rival or the pressuring of a politician with
things like kidnapping family members. Necessary things
that the governments of the world did not look kindly upon.

Wenz entered and walked up to Braun's desk.

"Good morning, Dieter," Braun said. "I hope you bring me good news."

"A little yes, and a little no," the man said, his perpetually calm demeanor revealing nothing.

Braun frowned. "Start with the good."

"Our contact at the CIA has confirmed that the Agency knows the body was that of Owen Pace. He was identified by the Paris station chief."

"Did our calling card catch his attention?"

"That our contact was unable to confirm, but it would have been hard to miss."

"We need to know for sure that they are getting our message," Braun said.

"I agree, and we're working on it."

"And the not good news?"

"Schmidt lost his target."

"You have got to be kidding me."

"I wish I were."

If anyone else had delivered the news, Braun would have chewed their head off. But Dieter was the only one who always gave him the unvarnished truth. He respected that.

Braun took a breath. "Explain."

"According to Schmidt, he followed Rogers to the agent's hotel, gave him enough time to fall asleep, and then sneaked into the room to take care of him. Only Rogers wasn't there, and it looked like he never had been. The room was untouched."

Braun squeezed his eyes shut for a moment. Then,

through clenched teeth, he said, "Please tell me Schmidt is attempting to locate him."

"He is."

"And?"

"When I talked to him right before I came here, he said he has a promising lead."

"Promising but not concrete?"

"Correct," Wenz said.

Braun grimaced. "This is my fault."

"I didn't say that."

"You didn't have to. I'm the one who decided to give Schmidt a chance, even with your warnings."

Braun and Schmidt had both lost their fathers for the same reason, and he'd let that blind himself to Schmidt's deficiencies.

Braun thought for a moment, then said, "Let him play out his lead, but whether he finds Rogers or not, when he's done, he's done with special projects. I'll send him over to security where he can play bodyguard for some heiress."

"Understood," Wenz said.

"And remind him, if he *does* succeed, not to forget the card."

"I will."

The business cards with the Trust's logo on them had been part of Braun's plan from the beginning. A little souvenir left behind to make sure the CIA knew why this was happening to them. Braun had been a child when the Trust was around, so there was no way the Agency could use the cards to tie him or his company to the assassinations.

"Anything else?" Braun asked.

"I've dispatched a team to check out the rumor of another Golden Hour agent in Romania. But that's all for now."

Braun's mood lifted slightly. "Let me know if anything changes."

Wenz bowed his head and exited the office.

As soon as the door was closed, Braun woke his computer.

Unlike other jobs the special projects division took on, the one to eliminate CIA agents who had been part of Golden Hour had no client. Or, rather, Braun was his own client. He'd been planning his revenge since he was a preteen, when his father—and Schmidt's—had been murdered as part of Golden Hour.

He opened the list of Golden Hour agents his CIA mole had obtained for him. On it were twelve names, all current or former members of the Agency, and every one of them a murderer.

Four of the names had been struck through—the three recently dispatched by Braun's people, and a fourth who'd died years ago in a plane mishap over the East Coast of the United States.

Teddy Fay's premature death angered Braun every time he thought about it. Fay had been the prime architect behind the mission and had designed and built the device used to murder most of Golden Hour's victims, including Braun's father.

If Braun had been limited to killing just one person on the list, it would have been Fay. But the spy's early demise had denied him that privilege.

His intercom rang again. "Yes?" he barked, thoughts of the missed opportunity still spinning in his head.

"Mr. Helman from Regent Swiss Bank on line one," his assistant said.

Braun took a breath to regain his composure, then switched lines. "Gunther, how are you?"

"I'm good, Felix. And you?"

"Never better. I assume you're calling about security for the bank's anniversary gala."

"I am."

6

AT 11:00 A.M. ON SUNDAY MORNING, A DRIVER
picked up Billy from his home in the Hollywood Hills and
drove him to the Van Nuys Airport, where Centurion Pictures' Gulfstream G-700 jet awaited.

A man in a black polo shirt and khaki pants met him at
his car. "Good morning, Mr. Barnett. I'm Kyle and I'll be
your flight attendant today."

"Good morning, Kyle. Are we waiting for anyone else?"

"No, sir, you are the last. Luggage in the trunk?"

"It is."

While Kyle handled the bags, Billy boarded the plane.

"Finally," Tessa said. She was in a seat close to the door.
"We were beginning to think you'd found some way to
weasel out of the trip."

"Me?" he said dramatically. "I would never."

"So, you *did* think about it."

The passenger area had single seats running down each side with an aisle in between. Peter and Hattie had taken a row toward the back of the cabin, while Stacy Lange—Billy's personal assistant—sat across from Adriene Adele, the actor who had played Tessa's sister in *Storm's Eye*. The final passenger was Lizzie Franks, the Centurion Pictures PR person who would be riding herd on everyone throughout the trip. She was seated directly behind Stacy.

The seat across from Tessa was empty, so Billy gestured toward it. "May I?"

"I'd be insulted if you didn't."

Kyle climbed on board a few minutes later, closed the door, and approached Billy. "A mimosa before the flight?"

"It's like you're reading my mind. Thank you."

The drink arrived as the pilot's voice came over the intercom.

"Good morning, ladies and gentlemen. This is Captain Chisholm. We've been cleared to taxi. If you haven't already, please take your seat and buckle in."

Takeoff was textbook, and in short order, Captain Chisholm's voice came over the intercom again. "Folks, we've just reached cruising altitude. Feel free to move around, but for your safety I advise keeping your belt fastened when seated."

The intercom had barely switched off when Stacy jumped out of her seat and knelt in the aisle, next to Billy.

"Here," she said, thrusting a stack of papers at him.

He eyed the pages without taking them. "What's all this?"

"Location reports, latest revised budget, and new schedule for *The Scapegoat.*" *The Scapegoat* was Peter's next film, which would begin shooting in a few months.

Billy raised an eyebrow. "Are you familiar with email? It's a very efficient way of sharing information without killing trees."

"Bless your heart, trying to be the funny guy." Stacy's expression turned annoyed. "I did email them to you, but *you* didn't respond."

"When?"

"Yesterday morning."

"I don't recall seeing—"

"Before you finish answering that, tell me. Did you even check?"

Saying he hadn't had time because he'd spent the last day prepping for the mission Lance had given him was not an option. So he chuckled and said, "It must have slipped my mind."

Stacy studied him. "That is very unlike you. Are you sick? Should I arrange for a doctor to meet the plane?"

"I'm perfectly fine. I was just busy."

Her eyes narrowed. "What were you doing that kept you so occupied? I know I blocked out plenty of time on your schedule."

"Perhaps the things I was doing were none of your business."

"Unlikely. Everything you do is my business. I'm your assistant, remember? But we can discuss that later." She held out the papers again. "Lucky for you, I printed everything out. And since you'll be sitting here with nothing else to do for a while, what better time to go over all of it?"

"You do remember that you work for me, not the other way around."

"If I were your boss, you would have already dealt with all this to avoid my wrath."

"Wrath?"

"What? It's a perfectly acceptable word."

"For a nineteenth-century robber baron perhaps."

She stood, said, "You have until we land," and headed for her seat.

"Don't work for you, remember," he said to her back.

"Not listening," she retorted, then sat and promptly put earbuds in her ears.

Across the aisle, Tessa looked like she was about to burst out laughing.

"You have something you'd like to say?" Billy asked.

"Not a word."

"That's what I thought."

"It's fun watching someone keeping you in line, though."

"That's nine words."

"Huh. I guess I did have something to say, after all."

It took a bit more than twelve hours to reach Rome, Italy, where they landed on Monday, at 9:10 a.m., local time.

Passport control was handled on board by an airport official, after which they deplaned and walked to the luxury van that would take them to their hotel.

Before Billy could climb into the vehicle, Stacy stepped in front of him. "Well?"

"Well what?" he asked.

"Your assignment?"

STUART WOODS' GOLDEN HOUR

"What about it?"

"Did you finish?"

"I did."

"Do you have notes?"

"I do."

"Can I get them so that I can forward them to the studio?"

"Why, Stacy, don't you check your email?"

"What?" She opened her phone and tapped the screen. "Got it. Thanks, Billy."

"Do I get an A?"

She snorted. "Absolutely not. You get a B minus, at best. Points deducted for not turning it in on time."

"You're going to make an excellent producer someday."

She grinned. "I know."

A mixed group of fans and paparazzi were waiting in front of the hotel when the van arrived. Because of the vehicle's tinted windows, those outside couldn't see the Centurion Pictures group, but that didn't stop them from shouting excitedly.

"Are they here for us?" Adriene asked.

"Of course they are," Lizzie said.

"To be fair," Hattie said, "they're not here for *all* of us. They're here for Tessa, Peter, and you."

"Me?" Adriene said. "No one knows who I am."

"Are you sure about that?" Billy asked, pointing at a person in the crowd holding a sign that read: BENVENUTA A ROMA, ADRIENE.

Her cheeks reddened. "Oh my."

Having only been cast in bit parts before her costarring role in *Storm's Eye*, she'd never been part of a press tour.

Tessa smiled. "I did tell you your life was going to change."

"You did. It's just . . ."

"Hearing it and experiencing it are two different things?"

"Exactly that."

"Get used to it. You've earned it."

"Everyone, hang tight here," Lizzie said. "I'll be right back."

The noise of the crowd intensified as she opened the door and slipped out, but the shouts quickly turned to groans of disappointment when those waiting realized she wasn't who they'd come to see.

Billy's cell vibrated. "This is Billy Barnett."

Lance Cabot's voice came over the line. "I take it you're not in a place you can talk freely."

"That's correct."

"No problem. I just wanted to let you know that I've arranged for an old friend of yours to meet you in Rome."

"Is that so?"

"Do you remember Samuel Rogers?"

"I do." Rogers had been another one of the agents on Golden Hour.

"He'll contact you within the next twenty-four hours. I believe he might have some information that could prove useful."

"Good to know. I'll keep an eye out."

"You do that. I also wanted to let you know that we've begun seeding the rumor we discussed."

"Wonderful," Billy said, less than thrilled.

"Rogers will likely not have heard the rumor when you meet, so it may be best if he continues to believe Teddy Fay is dead. But you decide how you want to handle it."

"What *did* you tell him?"

"That he's meeting with the specialist I've sent."

"Okay. Any update on your rodent problem?"

"Still working on it."

"So, the problem remains."

"For the moment."

"Is there anything else I need to know?"

Lance gave Billy an identification code to use when meeting Rogers, then they ended the call.

"Was that something I need to know about?" Stacy asked.

Billy shook his head. "Just a friend who wanted to send me something."

"A friend with a rodent problem?"

"Moles in his yard."

"How awful for him."

"More than you know."

Lizzie exited the hotel followed by three bellhops and several people in suits. The latter had to be the security team from Strategic Services' European office, which had been specifically hired for use by the press tour group when necessary.

As soon as the bodyguards created a clear path through the fans to the hotel entrance, Lizzie climbed into the van and handed out room key cards.

When she was done, she said, "The elevators are on the

left side of the lobby. All the rooms are on the fourth floor, except for Stacy and me. We're on five."

Adriene glanced out the window at the crowd. "Do we just ignore them?"

"You can if you want. You can also give them a wave as you walk by. Or, if you're up for it, you can sign a few autographs."

Tessa caught Adriene's eye. "What do you say? I'm game if you are."

Adriene couldn't hide her excitement. "Are you sure?"

"Of course."

"I'd love that."

"Peter, Hattie, do you want to join them or go to your room?"

"Room for me," Hattie said.

"Me, too," Peter said.

"Then the four of you go first," Lizzie said, glancing at Billy and Stacy to include them. "I'll stay back with Tessa and Adriene."

"To make sure we're not out there all day?" Tessa asked.

"You know me too well," Lizzie said. "All right. Put on your smiles, everyone. Here we go."

7

THE ELEVATOR DINGED AS IT REACHED THE
fourth floor.

"Lobby at six?" Billy asked Stacy as he, Peter, and Hattie
exited.

"Yep. See you then."

The door closed.

Peter looked at the sleeve that held his and Hattie's
key cards. "We're in four-oh-four. That's . . ." He looked at
the directional sign on the wall. "To the right. Billy, where
are you?"

"Four-oh-one. Same direction."

Billy dropped Peter and Hattie off at their suite, then
continued to his, which was at the end of the hall, next to a
set of emergency stairs. This was thanks to Lance, who had
used a trusted contact to manipulate the room assignments,
giving Billy a quick and discreet way in and out, if needed.

As Billy stepped inside, he stilled. Something felt off.

He crept through the entryway and peered into the living room.

Standing at the window, looking out at the city, was a woman dressed in black skintight pants, a black leather jacket, and a black baseball cap, through which looped her long, dark ponytail.

Sensing him, she turned, a smirk on her lips. But as soon as she caught sight of him, her smile slipped, and her hand moved smoothly under her jacket.

"Hello, Vesna," Billy said.

Vesna Martic blew out a breath and withdrew her hand from where it had no doubt been resting on a gun in a shoulder holster. "Teddy, Teddy, Teddy. I must say, you're not looking yourself these days."

She was an ex–Bosnian intelligence officer and current freelance operative who'd worked with Teddy several times in the past. Most recently, she'd lent a hand in dealing with a particularly nasty Serbian crime boss.

"And you look your same lovely self. Though I wasn't expecting you to be here waiting for me."

"*You* were the one who asked to meet."

"Yes, but I assumed you'd knock first."

She waved her hand dismissively. "I arrived early and got bored. You don't mind, do you?"

"As long as you don't make a habit of it. Something to drink?"

"Isn't it a little early for that?"

"I was thinking coffee."

"Ah. In that case, I would love a cappuccino."

Teddy called room service and gave his order. As he hung up, the suite's doorbell rang.

"Now, that's what I call fast service," Vesna said.

"Too fast," Teddy said. "Perhaps you should step into the bedroom."

She raised a provocative eyebrow. "I didn't realize it was one of those kinds of meetings."

"You know me better than that."

"True. You are always the gentleman." She disappeared into the other room.

Teddy answered the door to find a bellboy with his luggage. He had the man set the bags in the entryway, tipped him, then sent him on his way.

"All clear," he said toward the bedroom.

After he and Vesna were settled in the sitting area— Vesna on the couch and Teddy on a brown Chesterfield chair—she said, "So, this is you as Billy Barnett."

"You are one of a very select group who knows that."

"And if I tell anyone else, you'll put me in a deep, dark cell and do terrible things to me."

"I'm glad we see eye to eye."

"I don't know. It sounds kind of fun."

"Believe me, you wouldn't think that if it happened."

"Maybe, maybe not. Are there any other versions of you?"

"We'll bridge that topic when needed."

"So, that's a yes."

"You've always been one of the smartest people I know."

"I suppose you want a report?"

"If you don't mind."

Not wanting to rely solely on his CIA security detail, Teddy had hired Vesna to both watch his back and help with the investigation. Her contacts in Europe ran much deeper than Teddy's these days. What he hadn't done yet was fill her in on any details. That was something better done in person.

"I've been watching the hotel since yesterday, and other than the group of fans by the entrance and the team your CIA friends sent, I haven't seen anything unusual."

The team she mentioned was made up of the agents Lance had promised to provide, though she was unaware of the director's personal involvement in the mission.

"How many in the team?"

"Ten. They've been here since last night and are based out of five rooms on the third floor."

"Have they been in this suite?"

"They're CIA. Of course they've been in here. How could they resist?"

She pulled several audio bugs from her jacket pocket and tossed them onto the coffee table.

"Apparently, they were hoping to overhear some Hollywood secrets," she said. "Don't worry. These are deactivated."

"And you're sure you found all of them."

She gave him a what-do-you-think look.

"I had to ask," he said. He picked up one of the bugs, looked it over, then dropped it with the others. "Give me a second."

He went into the bedroom and called Lance.

"Do you have something for me already?" Lance asked.

"I do. But a request, not an update."

"And that is?"

"To tell the people you have watching over me that if they try to bug my suite again, I'm off the job."

"Someone bugged your room?"

"I wouldn't be telling you this if they didn't."

"Are you sure it was my people?"

"One hundred percent."

"I'll have a conversation with them. Just so you know, doing that was not part of my instructions."

"Goodbye, Lance."

Teddy hung up and returned to the living room.

"In theory, it won't be happening again," he said.

"Just in case the theory proves false . . ." Vesna pulled out a device about the size of a standard smartphone and set it on the table. "I'll leave the detector with you, and you can scan at will."

"Much appreciated."

"I have also left a bag in your room with the items you requested."

"And I thank you for that, too."

While he might have been able to smuggle weapons into the country on Centurion's jet, he hadn't wanted to take a chance that they'd be discovered. Hopefully, he wouldn't need to use the ones she brought, but he'd rather have them and not need them than need them and not have them.

"Can you tell me what this is all about now?" she asked.

"That deep, dark cell you mentioned earlier? There's an even deeper and darker one waiting for you if you share anything I'm about to tell you without my okay."

Though he trusted Vesna more than nearly anyone else in the intelligence world, it was best to lay out the consequences of breaking that trust in clear terms.

"What is that phrase you once taught me?" She thought for a second, then her face brightened. "Ah, yes. The bowl of silence."

"The cone of silence."

"I understand and accept," she said.

Teddy laid it out for her, omitting names that she didn't need to know, the possibility of a mole at the CIA, and the fact that his mission had come down from the director personally.

When he finished, she said, "So, you're trying to smoke out whoever is behind these murders by using you as bait."

"Precisely."

"Bold. I like it."

"That makes one of us."

She raised an eyebrow.

"Don't get me wrong," he said. "It's the best plan for the job."

"But you would rather not be the piece of meat sitting in the trap."

"I couldn't have said it better myself."

"I'm guessing that in addition to me keeping you safe, you'd like my help in figuring out who these people are."

"Correct."

"Well, I do prefer you breathing than in a pine box."

"Why, thank you."

"I'll poke around and see what I can find out. I assume the sooner we figure this out, the better."

"You assume correct," Teddy said.

"Understood. I have a question."

"And that is?"

"If we *do* draw them out, then what? Do we detain them? Or do we terminate them?"

"Hopefully, neither."

"Your CIA watchers will handle that?"

"As I said, hopefully."

"And if they don't?"

"Then we do what needs to be done."

8

A FEW MINUTES BEFORE 6:00 P.M., BILLY JOINED
Stacy and Lizzie in the hotel lobby.

"Ladies, you look lovely."

Lizzie, dressed in a Black Halo sleeveless jumpsuit, gave
him an exaggerated bow, while Stacy, decked out in an em-
erald green Elliatt cocktail dress, smiled sheepishly and said,
"Thank you. You're not so bad yourself."

"My thanks in return." Billy was wearing a gray Empo-
rio Armani suit, a black shirt, and a gray tie that had a hint
of red running through it.

"Good, I'm not the first," Adriene said, joining them.

"Is that a Ramy Brook?" Lizzie asked as she checked out
Adriene's dress.

Adriene spun around. "You like it?"

"Not like. Love."

"How did it go with your adoring fans earlier?" Billy
asked.

"Exhilarating and surreal," Adriene said.

"You should have seen her," Lizzie said. "She took to it like a real pro."

"She *is* a real pro," he said. "No problems with anyone?"

While most fans were well-behaved if a little excited when meeting a star, a few crossed the line into dangerous. There had been one in particular during the filming of *Storm's Eye* who had taken it all the way to murder.

"Not a one," Adriene said. "They were all so nice. I was just sorry I couldn't sign something for everyone."

"I take it the little general had you moving right along."

"'Little general'?"

Lizzie raised a hand. "That's me. I have a bit of a reputation."

"Well deserved," Billy said.

"I'd like to think so," Lizzie said. "But don't worry, I save my true bite for unruly members of the press."

The elevator opened and Peter, Hattie, and Tessa stepped out. Like the others, they were dressed to the nines: Peter in a black Prada suit, and Hattie and Tessa in dresses by Versace and Dolce & Gabbana respectively.

Lizzie waved over the Strategic Services detail—a group of three men and three women, all dressed in black suits.

"Ready to depart?" one of the women asked.

"We are."

"Any more fans out there?" Adriene asked.

"It was down to three when we checked a few minutes ago," the woman said. "If you will all follow me."

The woman took the lead, while her colleagues made a loose circle around the Centurion Pictures group.

It turned out only a single fan remained in front of the hotel. Tessa, Adriene, Peter, and Hattie signed autographs for her and took selfies, then the group departed in three SUVs.

The party they were bound for was being throw by Cineteca Paoletti—the company that handled the distribution of Centurion's releases in Italy. The fete was a yearly event, attended by a who's who of Italian entertainment. Tonight, Billy, Tessa, Peter, and the others were to be the guests of honor.

Thirty minutes after climbing into their rides, they pulled up in front of the Di Loreto Museo di Antichità, the museum where the party was being held.

Like most entertainment industry events, a step and repeat backdrop was set up outside the entrance so that paparazzi could photograph attendees. Lizzie and Stacy hung to the side while the others smiled and posed for the cameras.

Once that was done and the group had moved inside, an attendant directed them to a hallway that took them to an impressive set of wooden doors. In front of the doors was a podium behind which a trio of women stood.

"*Benvenuto*," the woman in the middle said.

"We're with Centurion Pictures," Lizzie said.

In English, the woman said, "Angelica will show you in."

The woman on her right dipped her head and smiled. "If you would follow me."

The third woman pulled the doors open, and Angelica led Billy and the others into a large, high-ceilinged room where a couple hundred people were already in attendance.

From somewhere deeper in the space, a string quartet

began playing music from Hattie's Academy Award–winning soundtrack to *Desperation at Dawn*, which had also won the best picture Oscar for Billy, Peter, and Ben.

"Sweetheart," Hattie said to Peter, "if you're wondering what you can get me for my birthday, live musicians playing my music every time I walk into a room would be nice."

"I bet it would," Peter said.

"I was looking more for 'Of course, dear. What a lovely idea.'"

"Of course, dear. What a lovely idea."

She wrapped her arm in his. "I knew there was a reason I married you."

"Ah! There you are!" a voice boomed from several feet away.

The crowd parted, and Marcus Paoletti strode out, arms open wide. He was a tall, barrel-chested, bald man, blessed with an abundance of charm and charisma, which served him well as founder and president of Cineteca Paoletti.

"I was afraid your plane wouldn't arrive in time," he said, then wrapped Billy, who happened to be closest, in a bear hug.

"We wouldn't have missed it for the world," Billy said as they parted. He motioned to Adriene. "This is Adriene Adele, costar of *Storm's Eye* and a rising talent."

Marcus wrapped her in a hug and air-kissed her cheeks. "Miss Adele, it is an honor to meet you."

"I should be the one saying that to you," she said, beaming.

"And you know Tessa, Peter, and Hattie, of course," Billy said.

"Everyone knows the glamorous Tessa Tweed." Marcus gave her a hug. "And the talented Barringtons." He hugged Hattie first, then Peter, then stage-whispered to Hattie, "Did you enjoy the little musical surprise I arranged for you?"

"I was just telling Peter what a wonderful treat it was!"

"Thanks, Marcus," Peter said. "I have a feeling I'm going to be paying for that for a long time."

Marcus laughed. "My apologies, my friend. But how could I not have done something to honor someone who creates such lovely music?"

"You got me there," Peter admitted.

Marcus's gaze landed on Stacy and Lizzie. "And who are these lovely ladies?"

"Elizabeth Franks, Centurion Pictures PR, and Stacy Lange, my assistant," Billy said.

"Welcome," Marcus said and gave Lizzie a hug.

When he turned to Stacy, she stuck out her hand before he could put his arms around her, and said, "Nice to meet you."

He looked at her hand and chuckled. "Of course." They shook, then he said to everyone, "Your trip was good, yes?"

"Very good," Tessa said.

"I'm happy to hear that. We are so excited to have you in Italy." Marcus sucked in a breath. "How rude of me. Your hands are empty. We must remedy this."

He led them through the room until they found a waiter carrying a tray of champagne flutes.

Marcus handed a glass to each of them, then took one for himself and raised it in the air. "To Centurion Pictures. I hope your time in Italy exceeds your expectations."

Glasses were touched and drinks were had.

"Come, come," Marcus said. "There are many people here you should meet."

Thirty minutes later, Billy was in conversation with a small group of Italian filmmakers, discussing the day-to-day struggles of getting a movie made, when a hand pressed against his back.

"Pardon me," a female voice said. "You are Billy Barnett, *sì*?"

Billy turned to find a stunning woman with dark hair, brown eyes, and tanned skin standing beside him. "I am."

"Mr. Barnett, I am—"

"*You* are Bianca Barone."

"You recognize me?"

"How could I not recognize the queen of Italian cinema."

"You are being too kind, Mr. Barnett."

"Please, call me Billy."

"And you must call me Bianca."

"I'm honored to meet you, Bianca. I'm a big fan of your work."

"Stop. My head is already too big. Your compliments will make me insufferable."

"And yet I only speak the truth."

She slipped an arm through his. "Then the least you can do is get me a drink while you fill my head with these truths."

"Happily."

He excused himself from the others, and he and Bianca made their way to the nearest bar.

The bartender smiled as they walked up. *"Buonasera,"* he said, then continued in Italian.

Billy's Italian had been passable once, but it was rusty now. "*Buonasera.* You wouldn't happen to speak English, would you?"

"Ah, *si.*" The man held his index finger and thumb about two inches apart. "Little bit. How can I help?"

Billy turned to Bianca. "What is your pleasure?"

"Prosecco would be nice."

"For prosecco, we have La Marca, Ruffino, or Cinzano," the bartender said.

"Cinzano, *per favore,*" Bianca said.

"And for you, *signore?*"

"Make it two," Billy said.

Billy and Bianca found a quiet spot to enjoy their drinks and each other's company.

"Your first time in Italy?" she asked.

"Not first. But it's been a while, so I'm sure a lot has changed."

"Do you like what you've seen so far?"

"Very much."

Her eyes lingered on his. "I like what I see, too."

"I get the sense you're not talking about the city sights."

"I am not. Were you?"

"I was not."

She stepped closer and ran a finger down his chest. "It's good that we think the same, *si?*"

"*Si.*"

Into his ear, she whispered, "When you've had enough of this party, perhaps we could go someplace not so crowded, where we could get to know each other better."

"How about now? I happen to know the perfect place."

"You do?"

"My suite."

She grinned. "See? Thinking the same again."

Billy put an arm around her waist, and they turned toward the exit.

Before they could even take a step, a red-faced man who looked to have had a bit too much to drink blocked their way, then puffed out his chest and bellowed, "Where the hell do you think you're going?"

9

IGNORING THE MAN, BIANCA SAID TO BILLY, "I
believe we were leaving, yes?"

She tried to guide Billy around the obstacle, but the man
moved back into their path.

"Eduardo, get out of our way!" she said.

Eduardo swayed slightly as he eyed Billy up and down.
"Who is this . . . person? I do not know him."

At the bark of his voice, several of the nearby partygoers
turned to see what was going on.

"Why would you need to know him?"

"Because I would like to know who is talking to my
wife!"

"Wife?" Billy said.

"*Ex*-wife," Bianca said. "We divorce nine months ago."
She glared at Eduardo. "Someone is having a hard time getting over it."

"You are making a big mistake," Eduardo said. "How do you know he will not try to take advantage of you?"

"Oh, you poor delusional man. Taking advantage of me is exactly what I'm hoping he'll do." She glanced at Billy. "You will do this for me, *si*?"

"That and more, if you desire," Billy said.

She snuggled against him. "I knew you would be accommo . . . accommo . . ."

"Accommodating?"

"Yes. Such a nice word."

Eduardo stepped forward to separate them, but before he could lay a hand on Billy, Billy moved himself and Bianca out of the man's path.

Eduardo tried to veer after them but ended up tangling his feet and stumbling into a table, upon which sat several glasses.

Alcohol spewed out of the flutes and onto him as he and the table crashed to the floor.

Now, everyone in the room was looking in their direction.

"Come," Bianca whispered, taking Billy's hand. "He can figure out how to get up on his own."

They exited the room, walked quickly down the hallway, and nearly ran into Stacy as they entered the museum lobby.

"Oh, there you are," Stacy said to Billy. "I was just coming to look for you."

Bianca raised an eyebrow and checked Stacy out. "And who is this?"

"This is my personal assistant, Stacy Lange," Billy said. "Stacy, this is Bianca Barone."

"Ms. Barone, a pleasure to meet you," Stacy said. She was used to dealing with celebrities and knew how to show respect without coming across as a fanatic.

"Nice to meet you, too," Bianca said, then glanced at Billy. "How personal?"

Stacy looked as if she'd just bitten into a lemon. "Not *that* kind of personal. First, that would be inappropriate. And second, Billy's old enough to be my—"

"No need to finish that sentence," Billy said.

Bianca looked embarrassed. "My apologies. My ex-husband was a little too personal with his personal assistant. I am, how do you say . . . oversensitive on this issue."

"No need to apologize," Stacy said. "And sorry your ex was such an asshole."

"Not was, still is."

Stacy laughed.

"You said you were looking for me?" Billy said.

"Right." She held out an envelope. "For you."

He took it. On the front was written BILLY BARNETT, but nothing else. "Who's it from?"

"No idea."

"Then how did you get it?"

"A motorcycle courier brought it to the party entrance. The staff sent someone to find you but saw me first."

"What did the courier look like?"

"Like a courier," she said, as if it were the most obvious answer.

"Did you see his or her face?"

"His, and no. He kept his helmet on the whole time, and its visor was tinted."

Billy slipped the envelope in his pocket. "Thank you, Stacy."

"Do *you* know who it's from?"

"I have an idea."

She waited, but when he didn't elaborate, she said, "Another detail about your life I don't need to know?"

He smiled and said, "Enjoy the rest of the party."

Stacy headed down the hallway, and Billy called the car service the Centurion team was using in Rome. While he and Bianca waited, he opened the envelope and pulled out the message.

Written on the paper was a Rome address and five a.m. There was no name, but Billy didn't need it. The sender had to be Samuel Rogers.

The car pulled up a few moments later. Billy opened the back door and let Bianca get in. Instead of climbing in after her, he leaned inside and said, "Give the driver your address and he'll take you home."

She looked at him, confused. "I thought we were going to your hotel."

"As did I." He held up the envelope. "I have some business to take care of, I'm afraid. So, I'll have to take a rain check."

The early morning meeting meant tomorrow was going to be even busier for Billy than originally planned.

Bianca's mood darkened. "It is another woman, I assume. You men, you are all the same."

"You assume incorrectly."

Her eyes locked on his. "You are telling me the truth?"

"I am." He flashed the envelope again. "Purely business.

No pleasure involved. If you are free tomorrow evening, might I suggest dinner alone in my suite?"

"Are you sure you will not find more business to keep you away from me?"

"I cannot promise that, but I will do my best to make sure that doesn't happen."

She thought for a moment, then nodded. "Give me your phone."

Billy did so. She called her own phone on his, hung up both, and handed his cell back.

"There. Now you have my number. Text me what time we will meet."

"It may be a little late. We have a lot of press to do to-morrow."

She shrugged. "I'm Italian. Your idea of late is still early for me."

10

AROUND THE SAME TIME THE CENTURION crew walked into the party in Rome, Braun's assistant stuck his head into Braun's office in Berlin. "Mr. Lawrence is here."

"Send him in."

"Yes, sir. Also, you'll need to leave in ten minutes to make your dinner appointment."

Braun checked his watch. It was 6:45 p.m. "Tell Dieter to meet me in the garage."

"Yes, Mr. Braun."

The assistant disappeared and a moment later Kelvin Lawrence entered. He was the head of Braun's research department, and the one who'd been tracking down members of Golden Hour for Braun and Dieter.

"I only have a few minutes," Braun said. "Where are you with the list?"

"It's taking more time than I hoped," Lawrence said.

"I'm working as fast as I can while still running the department at the same time."

"This needs to be your focus. I don't want this to drag on."

"Then, may I suggest adding someone to assist me?"

"Increasing the number of people who know about what we're doing in not an attractive option."

"I realize that, Mr. Braun. But I do have someone in mind, and she already works here."

"*She?*"

"Jillian Courtois."

"Who?"

"The new girl. She's been here two months now."

Now Braun remembered. Some hotshot computer geek that Lawrence had snapped up.

"Frankly, her skills are vastly superior to anyone else in the department, including me," Lawrence said.

"I don't recall her working on any of our previous special projects."

"Not officially. She did do a bit on that job for the Russians but wasn't aware what it was for."

"What bit?"

"She's the one who located Alexis Komarov."

Braun arched an eyebrow. "Is that so?"

Braun's special projects unit had delivered the now-deceased Komarov into the hands of an oligarch Komarov had been bad-mouthing to the Russian president—apparently, with Courtois's help.

"And she had no interest in knowing the reason we needed the information?" Braun asked.

"She's completely data focused. That's all that's important

to her. You give her a task, and she does it—and doesn't ask why." Lawrence paused, then added, "She's not what you would call a people person."

"I don't know. I still don't like the idea of bringing someone new on to this."

"I think you would change your mind if you met her."

Braun took a breath. "Fine. Talk to my assistant and find time in my schedule."

"I thought this might come up, so I brought her with me. If you have a moment now, she's right outside."

Braun looked at his watch again. "I'm leaving in three minutes."

"I won't even need that long."

Lawrence exited the office and returned with the woman. She was slight with dirty blond hair pulled back into a messy bun. Behind her too-large glasses, her eyes bounced around as if she'd never before been in an executive's office. Perhaps she hadn't.

"Mr. Braun," Lawrence said. "May I present Jillian Courtois."

"Hello, Ms. Courtois," Braun said.

She bowed her head and mumbled something, without ever looking directly at him.

"I'm sorry?" he said.

"H-h-hello, Mr. Braun," she said, just marginally louder.

"Mr. Lawrence tells me you are very good at your job."

With more confidence than her previous uttering, she said, "I am."

"He wants to put you on something he's been working on for me. Do you have a problem with that?"

She shook her head. "W-w-why would I?"

"It's a rather sensitive job."

Her brow furrowed. "I'll just be providing information, right?"

Braun nodded. "But I can't have you talking about it to anyone."

"Who would I talk to?" she asked, genuinely mystified.

"I see what you mean," Braun said to Lawrence. "Try her out. But if she can't keep up, take her off the project."

"You won't be disappointed," Lawrence said.

Lawrence and Jillian left, and Braun went down to the garage, where he found Dieter waiting for him in the back of the company's Mercedes-Maybach.

While the chauffeur drove them to dinner, Braun told Dieter about the addition of Jillian. "If you have any problems with her, let me know."

"Will do," Dieter said.

They soon arrived at the restaurant and were ushered into a private room in the back. Their potential client, an Uzbek national named Orif Kim, joined them a few minutes later.

Introductions were made, and soon they enjoyed a lovely dinner of pork loin and white asparagus.

Once the dishes were cleared, Braun instructed the staff to give them some privacy, then said to Kim, "I understand you might be in need of our services."

Kim looked around the room. "Is it safe to talk here?"

"You can rest assured that it is," Braun said. "I happen to be one of the restaurant's main investors, and had this room built to specifications that prevent anyone outside from listening in. In addition, it was scanned for bugs before you arrived, and none were found."

"You are very thorough."

"It's our job to be thorough."

"That's good. What I'm about to say is purely fictional, of course."

"Of course."

"Perhaps there's a country very much like my own, where a group of citizens have found someone who they would like to put in a prominent position. The only problem is that position is already held by someone who has become adept at abusing his power. A transition is desired, but . . ."

"But there are things that need to be done," Braun said, "that your group of concerned citizens would rather not touch with their own hands."

"Not *my* group of citizens. This is merely a story. But the gist of what you say is correct."

"When would this removal hypothetically need to occur?"

"Soon, I would think. Perhaps even to coincide with our Independence Day holiday at the end of August."

"A kind of celebration."

"You could call it that. Of course, the group would still need to come to a final decision that it is the right thing to do, and then that they choose the right people to carry out the task."

"In regard to the latter point, I would say they should look for a fictional company identical to my own. Such an organization would have the wherewithal to properly deal with the job."

"I would think it important that they have experience in this area," Kim said.

"I agree."

Kim smiled. "I would also think that any potential clients would want to see proof of such experience."

"Ah, that could be tricky but not impossible."

"I'm sure it would be a requirement."

"Then proof would be provided."

"How quickly?"

Braun laughed good-naturedly. "Anyone who deals in this kind of business would want to make sure the client is serious first. You mentioned making a final decision. When do you think that will happen?"

"At a meeting to be held in three weeks, I would think. Fictionally, of course."

"Then that's when proof would be presented. Fictionally, of course."

———

Thirty minutes later, Braun and Dieter were back in the Mercedes.

"That went even better than I expected," Braun said. "But you know what this means."

"We need to complete both phase one *and* phase two of our current mission in the next twenty-one days."

"Not twenty-one. Fourteen. We need at least a week between the end of phase two and when we meet with Mr. Kim again."

After eliminating the Golden Hour agents in the first phase of the operation, phase two would be a strike at the very top of the U.S. government. While the current leader-

STUART WOODS' GOLDEN HOUR

ship hadn't been the ones to allow Golden Hour to proceed, they did now represent that government.

Braun would then use its successful completion to secure the job Mr. Kim had dangled in front of them.

"I hope this Jillian woman is good at her job," Dieter said.

"Lawrence says she's the best."

"If that's true, then we should be able to make your deadline, no problem."

"That's what I like to hear."

To Jillian Courtois's surprise, the new assignment came with a private office. It was a definite step-up from the cubicle she'd been in. Now she could close the door and not be bothered by anyone.

It wasn't that she didn't like other people, she just didn't understand most of them. Isolating herself was always her preference.

Her computer dinged with the arrival of an email from her boss, Mr. Lawrence. In it was the list of people he'd told her to look into, along with several outside contacts he thought might help her.

She read the list. It consisted of twelve names, four of which were highlighted in gray. She sent her boss a message asking what the highlighting meant.

Instead of messaging her back, as she would have preferred, he knocked on her door and stuck his head in.

"You can ignore the highlighted ones," he said. "They're deceased."

"Oh."

"Concentrate on the others, find out their locations, and whatever else Mr. Braun may need of you."

"Got it."

"Jillian, I can't stress what an excellent opportunity this is for you. You play your cards right, and you could be moving up very quickly."

"I see," she said. Then she tentatively added, "Thank you," when he seemed to be waiting for her to say more.

He smiled. "Be yourself and you'll do fine. And get cracking on that list. Mr. Braun will want results soon."

He exited and closed the door behind him.

She stared after him, confused.

She'd been hired by BLS straight out of university. One of her professors was an acquaintance of Lawrence's, and when he heard the man was looking for new talent, he'd recommended Jillian.

At the time, she'd thought herself lucky as she'd been dreading looking for work. Imagining all the interviews she'd have to go through had made her skin crawl.

Now, thanks to overhearing the conversation between her boss and Braun, she was beginning to wonder if maybe she hadn't been so lucky after all. It almost sounded like the results of the work she'd been assigned would be used in unethical ways. And what was that bit about the Russian she'd located?

She almost googled him on the spot to see if there was any news but stopped herself. She was being paid very well to do something she was good at. She couldn't just throw that away.

Besides, Lawrence had been right when he'd said she

wasn't a people person. Which likely meant she'd misread Lawrence and Braun's conversation.

That had to be it.

Feeling slightly less anxious, she focused back on the list. The first name was Danielle Verde.

She copied it and began a search.

11

TEDDY ARRIVED AT THE MEET LOCATION JUST
before 5:00 a.m.

It was a restaurant on a narrow side street, not far from
Piazza Navona. When he tried the door, he found it unlocked.

He had made the decision not to let Rogers know that
Teddy Fay was still alive and had transformed himself into a
bland-looking middle-aged man, with graying blond hair,
before leaving the hotel.

This also helped him evade his CIA minders, as he preferred that they concentrate their efforts on keeping his
friends safe. Besides, he didn't need them watching his back.
He had Vesna for that.

He removed his pistol from his shoulder holster, then
eased the door open and stepped inside.

There was just enough light from a nearby streetlamp

coming in through the windows for him to see that the room was unoccupied.

He crossed to a set of swinging double doors at the back. Each had a dinner-plate-sized window in the top half, through which dim light streamed into the hall.

He peered through one of them.

Leaning against a stove and facing the door was Samuel Rogers, a gun held loosely at his side.

Teddy scanned the rest of the room to make sure Rogers was alone, then announced, "I'm coming in."

After holstering his own weapon, he opened the door and stepped inside, holding out his palms to show they were empty.

"Lance sends his regards and said that he hopes you had a nice time in Malta," he said. This had been the identification code Lance had given him.

Rogers relaxed and put his gun away. "So, you're Lance's specialist?"

Teddy sneered. "I'm not Lance's anything."

"All of us in the Agency are Lance's something or other."

"Good thing I don't work for the Agency then."

"You don't?"

"I'm more of an outside consultant."

"I see." Rogers studied him anew. "All right, Mr. Consultant, what is it you want from me?"

"Did Lance not tell you why we are meeting?"

"The only thing I was told was that I have information you need. I was not told what that information is."

"How very Lance of him."

Rogers snorted. "Are you sure you don't work for the Agency?"

"I'm sure," Teddy said.

"How can I help you?"

"I understand you were part of an operation called Golden Hour."

Rogers's brow furrowed in surprise. "That's not a name I've heard in a long time. Yes, I was. But how can that possibly be of interest now?"

"Because someone is killing the agents who were assigned to that mission."

"Are you messing with me?"

"I assure you, I'm not."

Teddy briefed him on what had been happening, without mentioning the names of those killed.

"Owen Pace was part of Golden Hour. He was one of the victims, wasn't he?"

Teddy nodded. "The latest."

"Now I know why Lance wanted us to meet. I was one of the last people to talk to Owen."

"In person?"

"On the phone."

"What did you talk about?"

"He was cultivating a new source. Said it was someone with knowledge of the dark money funding of terrorist operations. Owen knew I've dealt with a lot of that, so he wanted to know if I'd ever heard of the guy. When I said I hadn't, he asked me if I could look into him."

"What did you find?"

"Just generic stuff. Felt off to me."

"Did you pass that on to Owen?"

He nodded. "The last time we spoke, I warned him that there was a good chance the guy wasn't who he said he was.

I told him he shouldn't do anything until he could be sure one way or the other."

"How did he respond?"

"He said he'd think about it. The next morning, he was dead." Rogers shook his head. "It's hard to believe this has something to do with the Trust, though. Stopping those involved was the purpose of Golden—" Rogers sucked in a breath. "Oh, shit."

"What?"

"A few days ago in Prague, I was followed to my hotel. I gave the guy the slip, but I have no idea who he was or why he was interested in me."

"Were you working on anything that would have warranted that kind of attention?"

"That's the thing. I wasn't. But if he was following me because of Golden Hour . . ."

"That would explain his interest."

Rogers nodded, then ran a hand through his hair. "That means he probably was there to kill me."

"Do you have any guesses as to who could be behind this? Maybe someone associated with the Trust you remember from back then?"

After considering the question, Rogers shook his head. "Sorry. No one comes to mind. I do know a few people who *might* have heard something. I can contact them and report back."

"That would be very helpful. How long do you think that will take?"

"I don't anticipate any problems reaching them, so maybe by this evening. Tomorrow, latest."

"Sooner is better. The longer whoever is behind this is allowed to operate, the more people will die."

"I understand. Do I contact you directly or . . . ?"

"Go through Billy Barnett," Teddy said.

"He's a movie guy, though. Unless he's also with the Agency."

"Not with, more a friend of. And his position provides the perfect cover to pass messages. No one will suspect his involvement with us."

"I'll do as you say."

"One thing, though. He's leaving tomorrow morning on the 7:55 a.m. train to Venice."

"I'll try to be in touch before then, but no promises."

12

BY 8:00 A.M., TEDDY HAD CHANGED INTO BILLY
Barnett and was in the hotel restaurant, having breakfast
with Tessa, Peter, Hattie, Adriene, and an entertainment
writer from one of Italy's foremost entertainment news
outlets.

Tessa, Adriene, and Peter regaled their guest with tales
from the set, while Hattie discussed her approach for the
soundtrack. Billy was thrown a few softball questions
throughout the meal, for which he made sure to highlight
the contributions of other members of the production staff.

At precisely ten a.m., Stacy approached the table and
gave Billy a subtle nod.

"This has been a wonderful way to start our day," he
said to the reporter. "But unfortunately, we have another
appointment we need to get to."

They said their goodbyes, then the Centurion group headed out to a waiting van.

On the drive to Cineteca Paoletti's studio lot, Billy checked for messages from Rogers. He knew it was unlikely there would be any this soon, and he was right.

Lizzie was waiting for them when they arrived. After escorting everyone into a conference room, she said, "I hope you're excited for press junket day!"

"Is anyone ever excited for press junket day?" Peter asked.

"I am," Adriene said.

"Only because it's your first," Tessa said.

"It's really not that bad," Lizzie said to Adriene. "You each get your own room. Journalists will come in, interview you for ten minutes, then cycle to the next room."

"How many journalists?" Billy asked.

"Fifteen."

"At ten minutes each? That's what?" Adriene asked.

"Two and a half hours," Billy said.

"Whoa."

"And that's not counting the five minutes between for moving around."

"*And* the fact that there's always a few that go long," Lizzie added. "To be safe, figure it will take four hours."

Instead of looking excited, Adriene now looked like the proverbial deer in the headlights.

"Four hours is nothing," Lizzie assured her. "Some press junkets can last all day."

"All *day?*" Adriene said.

"Don't worry," Billy said. "The time will fly by."

"And the questions are almost always the same from

reporter to reporter," Hattie added. "After the third or fourth interview, you'll be running on autopilot."

"Just be yourself, and you'll do fine," Billy said.

Several offices had been converted into interview rooms, with comfortable chairs, beautiful flowers, and the film's logo mounted on a backdrop. Once all of the film's principals were in their assigned rooms, the reporters began rotating in and out.

Billy had done many events like this before, and easily charmed his way through what turned out to be three and a quarter hours of repeating himself over and over.

When the last reporter had left, Stacy stuck her head into the room and said, "That's a wrap."

"Next time someone suggests I come on one of these trips, please remind me to fire them."

"Ah, come on. It wasn't that bad."

"Wait until you have to sit in this chair."

"I *am* waiting."

"I have a feeling that day will come sooner than later, and when it does, then we'll talk."

"I look forward to it."

"What's next?" he asked.

"Tessa, Peter, and Adriene are off with Lizzie to appear on an afternoon talk show. You and Hattie have nothing on the schedule until the cocktail party this evening."

"You mean I'm free?"

"You are *not* free. You have several dozen emails awaiting your responses."

"That doesn't sound fun."

She flashed a cheeky smile. "Finish first, then you can have fun."

Between dealing with his emails and occasionally check-
ing to see if Rogers had made contact, Billy was kept busy all
afternoon. If Stacy hadn't called him at five p.m. and reminded him to get ready for the cocktail party, he would
have still been sitting in front of his laptop.

By six p.m., he was just stepping out of the elevator into
the lobby when his phone vibrated.

He checked the screen, hoping for a text from agent
Rogers, but it was from Stacy, asking if he was on his way.

The best thing about tonight's party was that Billy and
the others didn't have to travel anywhere. The event was
being hosted by Centurion Pictures and thrown in a ban-
quet room at their hotel. The invited guests were mostly
journalists and film people from countries near Italy that
the *Storm's Eye* press tour would not be visiting.

There were already quite a few people present when Billy
entered. He greeted and schmoozed and made sure the attendees were having a good time. About forty minutes after
the party began, the lights dimmed, and selected scenes from
Storm's Eye played on a large screen at one end of the room.

From the enthusiastic applause that broke out after the
last clip had finished, it was obvious the crowd genuinely
enjoyed what they'd watched.

No question about it. Centurion had another hit on its
hands.

As the lights came back on, Billy sensed someone move
next to him.

"*Buonasera,*" Bianca said.

"*Buonasera.* I hadn't realized you were coming to this."

"I may have used some of my influence to obtain an invite. Though you *could* have given me one yourself."

"You're right. My apologies. I should have thought of that."

"Yes, you should have." She pouted and playfully tapped his arm. "Please tell me you have not also forgotten about our date."

"Of course not."

Her smile returned. "Good. I would not have taken being rejected two nights in a row well."

"Rest assured. No rejection will be forthcoming."

She played her fingers across the front of his jacket. "That is exactly what I wanted to hear."

He gestured toward the screen. "Did you enjoy what you saw?"

"How could I not? It looks fantastic. I cannot wait to see the entire film."

"Peter will be happy to hear that."

"This Mark Weldon, he is a very good actor. So much talent. He did not come on this trip with you?"

"He'll be joining us at our next stop."

"That is too bad. I would have liked to meet him."

"You could always come to Venice and meet him there."

"That is an intriguing idea. Perhaps I will. For now, though, all I want to think about is you."

"Then I believe I'm starting to feel hungry. Shall we go to my suite and order dinner?"

She pressed her body against his. "To your suite, *si*. But I think we should wait to order until we've worked up an appetite."

13

BIANCA DIDN'T EVEN STIR AS BILLY SLIPPED
off the mattress at dawn and padded into the bathroom.

He checked his phone. Still no word from Rogers, which
probably meant the agent hadn't been able to find out anything useful. That was disappointing.

He sent a text to Vesna, asking if her sources had come
up with anything yet, and received an immediate response.

Not yet, but soon I hope.

He texted back.

Any way to speed that up?

His phone buzzed again.

**I see someone woke up on the wrong side of the bed
this morning. I'll crack the whip.**

He shot another message to her.

That's all I ask.

Twenty minutes later, Billy was showered, dressed, packed, and in the middle of writing a note to Bianca, when he heard the sheets rustle.

"Leaving already?" she asked, her voice heavy with sleep.

He sat beside her and threaded a lock of her hair behind her ear. "I'm afraid the train waits for no one."

"There are trains to Venice all day. Take a later one and play with me some more."

"Tempting, I assure you. But you know how these tours are. I wouldn't want to give our PR person a heart attack."

"True," she conceded. "Then I must settle for a memory of what was."

He leaned down and kissed her. "And what a memory."

She laughed and kissed him back. "I hope we can do this again. In Venice, perhaps?"

"The invitation is open." He stood. "Get some more sleep, then order breakfast. I'll tell the desk the room will be occupied until noon."

She stretched and yawned. "What a wonderful idea."

"Take care of yourself, Bianca."

"Safe travels, Billy."

———————

The others were in the lobby by the time Billy arrived. With them was the six-member team from Strategic Services. Instead of wearing suits that would draw attention, they were dressed casually. Their job today was to make sure Billy and the others made it onto the train with little fuss and hopefully unnoticed. A new team would meet the travelers when they arrived in Venice.

Billy had a quick word with the receptionist, then Lizzie led the group out to a pair of waiting vans. The Centurion people climbed into one, the Strategic Services team into the other, then they were off.

"I wish we'd had time to do a little sightseeing," Adriene said, looking wistfully out the window.

"That's why they call this work and not a vacation," Peter said.

"You'll just have to settle for attending parties and rubbing elbows with Europe's elite for now," Tessa said.

Adriene shrugged dramatically. "Well, if I must."

Lizzie put a hand to the side of her mouth and stage-whispered, "You want to know a secret?"

"Of course," Adriene said.

"Tessa and Mark will be the only ones working during the day tomorrow. You don't have anything on your schedule until the evening, so you'll have plenty of time to roam Venice."

"Seriously?"

"Would I lie to you?"

"Then consider me a tourist! Stacy, if you're not doing anything, you want to come with?"

"As long as Billy won't need me," Stacy said.

"I will not," Billy told her.

Stacy smiled in excitement and said to Billy, "Thank you! Hey, you and Hattie will also be free. You should come, too."

"That's a great idea," Adriene said.

"Count me in," Hattie said. "But, Billy, didn't you say something about visiting a friend?"

"I did," Billy said, feigning disappointment. "I'm afraid I'll have to pass on your Venetian adventure. But I'm sure you ladies will have a great time without me."

"What friend?" Stacy asked. "You didn't mention anything to me."

"I'm mentioning it now."

She frowned. "You really need to work on your communication skills."

"I'll put that on my to-do list."

"See that you do."

When she turned away, he mouthed *thank you* to Hattie. Her comment had help him cover the fact that he would be busy all day as Mark Weldon.

In short order, they arrived at the train station.

Tessa, Peter, Hattie, and Billy donned sunglasses and face masks to avoid being mobbed by fans.

Tessa then handed a spare mask to Adriene. "You should wear one, too."

"No one's going to know who I am."

"You may be surprised. But even if that's true, they will someday, so it's good practice."

Adriene put on the mask and her sunglasses.

"Everyone, wait here for a moment," Lizzie said.

She hopped out and was immediately approached by three porters pulling luggage trolleys. She directed them to the back of the van, and they began transferring everyone's bags to their carts. As this was happening, the Strategic Services team exited their vehicle.

Lizzie had a quick conversation with the bodyguards,

then she reopened the van door. "All right, we're set. Remember, act casual, and try not to do anything that will draw attention."

When Billy climbed out, he whispered to Lizzie, "When we get back home, remind me to talk to Ben about getting you a raise."

"Do not even joke with me about that."

"I never joke about money."

"Then expect that reminder," she said, trying to stifle a grin.

As they headed inside, the security team fell in around them in a way that made it appear they weren't all traveling together.

The station was a jumble of commuters and tourists rushing this way and that.

Lizzie did her best to keep the Centurion group away from the densest populated areas and was able to steer them nearly all the way to the platform before someone in the passing crowd shouted Tessa's name.

Heads turned and several people began moving toward them. Before things got out of control, three of the Strategic Services team closed ranks around Tessa, Adriene, and Peter, and moved them quickly toward the platform, with Lizzie following right behind.

Billy, Hattie, and Stacy continued at the more leisurely pace. No one knew who Stacy was yet, and Billy and Hattie were seldom recognized in public. In case something did happen, the three remaining Strategic Services bodyguards stayed nearby.

"It's times like this I'm glad I have no desire to be an actor," Stacy said.

"I couldn't agree more," Hattie said, then glanced at Billy, a twinkle in her eye. "How about you? Any thoughts of working in front of the camera instead of behind it?"

"Me?" he said. "Not a chance."

When they reached the platform, they saw a couple dozen people standing by the last car, craning their necks to peer through the windows. One of the bodyguards stood by the nearest door, and another at the entrance at the far end of the car, preventing any unauthorized boarding.

Excited shouts rang out as Tessa and Adriene appeared at one of the windows, maskless. The crowd coalesced just outside, and the two stars waved.

While this was going on, Billy, Hattie, Stacy, and their security team climbed quietly onto the train a few cars back and made their way toward the last car. On the way, Billy picked out members of the CIA team assigned to watch his back, sitting in the car two away from the end. They studiously avoided his gaze.

Vesna sat in the last row of the same car.

As Billy neared, she glanced up from her magazine, then returned her gaze to the periodical, acting like she had no idea who he was.

A sign on the door to the final car read NO ENTRY BEYOND THIS POINT in Italian.

Instead of open seating, like in the passenger cars Billy and the others had just passed through, the last car was divided into eight private cabins off a hallway that ran the length of the car.

Lizzie stepped out of one of the rooms. "Sorry to have deserted you like that. Did you have any issues?"

"Not a one," Billy said. "Good call on the security."

"Yeah," she said. "But they're done when we pull out. Now I'm wondering if I should have hired them for the full trip."

"Problems?"

"Not exactly, but did you get a look at the fans outside?"

"Just a glance."

"Some of them have signs with Tessa's name or picture on them. They were prepared." She frowned. "Which means someone tipped them off."

"How many people knew about our travel plans?"

"I thought only a handful."

"Could it have been someone at the hotel?" Hattie said.

"That's what I'm thinking. You don't need to worry about any of that, though." Lizzie smiled. "We have the whole car. Tessa and Adriene are in that cabin." She pointed to the door she'd stepped through, then at the one next to it. "And Peter's in there. You can join them or use one of the others."

Billy and Stacy took the empty one on the other side of Peter's, while Hattie joined her husband.

Once he was settled, Billy checked his phone again. While there was still nothing from Rogers, there was a message from Vesna.

> **Heard from one of my contacts who may have a lead on Paris assassin.**
>
> **Should know more by tonight.**

Finally, some good news. Billy tapped out an acknowledgment and hit SEND, then settled in as the train began to move.

"Do you mind if I check on Tessa and Adriene?" Stacy asked. The trio had formed a tight bond during the filming of *Storm's Eye*.

"Why would I mind?"

"I didn't want you to feel like you were being abandoned."

"I think my fragile ego will adapt to your defection."

She snapped up her purse, gave him a wave, and hurried out.

The door had barely slid closed again when Billy's phone vibrated. It was a text from Rogers. Billy had all but given up on him.

I have something for our mutual friend.

I'm guessing you left Rome already?

Teddy messaged back:

Yes. Just.

Rogers texted:

The 7:55 to Venice?

Teddy replied in the affirmative.

Nearly half a minute passed before his phone vibrated with Rogers's response.

Will meet you en route.

Teddy sent a message to Vesna, letting her know about Rogers's plan.

14

THERE WAS A KNOCK ON JILLIAN'S OFFICE
door, and before she could say anything, it opened and her
boss strode in.

"Drop whatever you're doing," he said.

She blinked. "What?"

"Something's come up that you need to discuss with Mr.
Braun."

The hairs on her arms began to prickle. "*I* do?"

"Yes, you. You're the one heading up research on Golden
Hour."

"W-w-what do I need to talk to him about?"

"It concerns one of the names on the list."

"Oh, um, okay. I guess that makes sense."

"A rumor has come to my attention that Mr. Braun will
be very interested in hearing. I want you to inform him and
ask him what he wants to do. If he'd like us to follow up, you
will handle it."

He handed her a thumb drive.

"The rumor is on here?" she asked.

He shook his head. "That's an encryption key that will allow you to communicate with several of our special contacts, including the person who passed the rumor to me. Their username is marked with an asterisk."

"'Special contacts'?"

"People in sensitive positions who help us with our research but need to keep a low profile."

"I guess that makes sense. But what's the rumor?"

He gave her a piece of paper. "Read, it then put it in your burn bag." Every member of the research department had burn bags that were picked up at the end of each day and taken to an incinerator.

Jillian's eyes widened in surprise as she read the paper. "How sure are they?"

"Like I said, it's a rumor, but the contact says it's from a trusted source."

"When should I tell him?"

"Now would be good."

Dieter knocked on Braun's office door and stuck his head inside. "Schmidt has an update. I thought you might want to listen in."

"Absolutely," Braun said, waving him in.

Dieter set his cell on Braun's desk and activated the speaker. "So, what is this news?"

"I've found Rogers," Schmidt said. "I told you I would."

"Where?" Dieter asked.

"In Italy."

STUART WOODS' GOLDEN HOUR

Before Dieter could respond, Braun pushed out of his chair and leaned toward the phone. "Could you be a little more specific, Mr. Schmidt?"

"Mr. Braun? I-I didn't realize you were—"

"A location, if you don't mind."

"Right. Um, I tracked him down in Rome and followed him to Florence."

"Are you looking at his corpse? Because that's what I'm expecting you to say next."

"Well, no, sir. N-not yet."

"Why not?" Braun snapped.

"I-I-I haven't been able to get close enough. But I will. You don't need to worry about that."

"Funny," Dieter said, his tone neutral. "That's almost a direct quote of what you said when you found Rogers in Prague."

"T-t-this time it's different. I promise."

"You're right about that," Braun growled. "Would you like me to explain what will happen to you if you don't get it done?"

"No, sir. That won't be necessary."

"I thought not."

"Is there anything else?" Dieter asked.

"No, Mr. Wenz. The next time you hear from me, I promise it will be good news."

"We look forward to it," Dieter said, then tapped the disconnect button.

"I swear to God," Braun said. "If he fucks this up, too . . ." He shook his head and began pacing behind his desk. "Does he not understand how important this is to me?"

Dieter remained silent as his boss walked back and forth.

Finally, Braun stopped. "Schmidt has become too much of a liability. Where's our closest team?"

"In Rome."

"Put them on standby and keep tabs on Schmidt. If it's not done within the hour, send the team to deal with Rogers."

"Understood."

Braun's desk phone buzzed. He hit the intercom button. "Yes?"

"Jillian Courtois would like a moment," his assistant said.

"Send her in." He clicked off the phone and said to Dieter, "You should stay for this."

Like before, Jillian entered as if she wasn't sure she should be there.

"Come, come," Braun said, waving her to his desk.

"S-s-sorry, Mr. Braun," she said and hurried over.

"Well?" Braun said.

She swallowed nervously, then said, "Something came up concerning one of the names on your list."

"Which name?"

"Teddy Fay."

"Teddy Fay is dead," he said, eyes narrowing in annoyance at being reminded that his father's killer had escaped justice.

"That may not be true, Mr. Braun."

He stared at her, not sure he'd heard correctly. "Say that again."

"It-it-it's possible that Teddy Fay is still alive."

"Explain."

"It's only a rumor, but the source is credible. M-M-Mr.

Lawrence wanted me to tell you and ask if you'd like me to look into it further."

Braun stared at nothing, not wanting to believe it could be true for fear of his hopes being dashed, but unable to stop himself. If Teddy Fay was alive, then Braun would have his long-desired chance to squeeze the life out of the son of a bitch.

"M-M-Mr. Braun?" Jillian said.

He blinked and focused back on her.

"What would you like me to—"

"Do it," he said, cutting her off. "Find out if it is true, and if it is, find him."

15

BILLY RECEIVED ANOTHER TEXT FROM ROG-
ers as the train departed Florence.

I'm on board. Where are you?

Billy replied:

Last car, through the door that says no entry. Cabin 6.

Several minutes later, Billy heard someone sprinting down the hallway.

Instinctively, he grabbed his silencer-equipped pistol and reached for the door. Before he could pull it open, he heard the soft metallic spit of a sound-suppressed gunshot followed by the *thud* of something hitting the floor.

He shoved the cabin door open. Sprawled on the floor just outside was Rogers, his body unmoving.

Billy leaned out. Running down the hallway toward him was man in a suit.

As soon as he saw Billy, he skidded to a stop and raised his pistol.

Before either he or Billy could pull their triggers, Tessa's cabin door slid open, and Stacy leaned out.

"Go back!" Billy yelled.

The assassin grabbed Stacy's arm before she could do anything and yanked her toward him. At the same moment, Vesna appeared at the other end of the hall.

In the split second before Stacy would have become the assassin's human shield, both Billy and Vesna fired their guns.

Billy's bullet punched through the assassin's forehead, and Vesna's caught him in the back, heart high. The man was dead before he hit the floor.

Billy motioned for Vesna to make sure no one else could enter the car, then rushed to Stacy, who had stumbled into the outside wall, where he positioned himself to block the bodies from view.

"W-w-what's going on?" she asked, her voice shaky.

"Do you trust me?"

"Yes. Of course."

"Close your eyes."

"O-okay."

Tessa stuck her head out of her cabin. "What's all the—" She gasped as she caught sight of the assassin's body. "Is he . . . ?"

Billy walked Stacy to her. "He is. Please, take Stacy inside. She's going into shock." He passed Stacy to her.

"She's not the only one."

"I'll explain everything in a bit. For now, keep her and—" He looked into the cabin. "Where's Adriene and Lizzie?"

"Lizzie went to get something to eat, and Adriene was sleepy, so she went to one of the other cabins to take a nap."

"Do you know which one?"

"Next door, I think," Tessa said. "Go, I'll take care of Stacy."

Billy peeked into the neighboring cabin and was relieved to see Adriene stretched out across the seats, sound asleep. He hurried back to Rogers and checked for a pulse, but as he feared, the man was dead.

He could hear music and what sounded like the roar of a jet coming from inside Peter and Hattie's cabin. As much as he was loathed to involve anyone else in this, he had little choice.

He tapped on their door. The noise inside cut off, and Peter slid the door open.

"Hey, Billy. What's up?"

"I could use your assistance."

"Sure, what do you need?" He caught sight of Rogers's body. "Is he dead?"

"Yes."

"Did *you* kill him?"

"Not him." Billy nodded his head toward the assassin.

Peter gaped at the second body, then said, "Well, this isn't great."

"What's not great?" Hattie asked, then peeked into the hall from behind Peter.

"We had an uninvited guest," Billy said.

Hattie leaned forward enough to see Rogers. "Is that a body?"

"Yes, but *he* was invited."

She noticed the assassin. "Oh."

"I need both of your help," Billy said.

"Just tell us what to do."

"Hattie, Lizzie went to the restaurant car. If you could find her and keep her away until I give you the all-clear, that would be great."

"No problem." She hurried down the hallway.

"You're not going to ask me to help you move them, are you?" Peter said.

"I think I've scarred you enough as it is. What I need you to do is go to the entrance of our car. You'll find a friend of mine there. Dark hair, looks like the kind of person you don't want to mess with. Send her to me, then you stay there and make sure no one else comes in."

"Got it."

Peter followed his wife's route out of the car. A few seconds later, Vesna returned.

"Dead?" she asked, eyeing Rogers's body.

Billy nodded.

She pointed at the assassin. "Who is this asshole?"

"Never seen him before."

"Sorry I couldn't stop him before he got here. Some idiot thought I was going to get to the toilet before him and got in my way."

"You arrived in time to stop him from killing one of my friends. For that, I'll be forever grateful."

"What do we do with them?"

"That's a question for someone else. Wait here. I'll be right back."

He walked to the end of the car and called Lance.

As soon as the director was on the line, Billy explained what had just gone down.

"That's four dead now," Lance said.

"Not my biggest concern at the moment."

"I apologize. Of course not. That would be the body."

"The bod*ies*."

"Right. One moment." Lance returned half a minute later. "I have your position as approximately twenty minutes outside Bologna, still in the mountains."

Billy looked out the window. "That sounds right."

"I have a cleanup team that can meet you en route. Bologna is too soon, so probably in Ferrara. They'll take Rogers and clean up the mess."

"What about the assassin?"

"Do you have anything you can grab fingerprints with?"

"I do."

"Get prints and take pictures, then give those to the cleaners. The area you're currently in is rural, correct?"

"Very."

"Then it seems to me it's the perfect location for the assassin to get off the train. I'll have my watchers deal with that."

"You mean the watchers who have yet to notice that anything happened?"

"They aren't with you now?"

"No. As far as I know, they're still in their seats, oblivious."

"I see," Lance said, not sounding pleased. "I'll have them there in a few moments."

"Don't," Teddy said. "I have someone I trust who can help me. We'll take care of it."

"That wasn't an offer. Their job is to—"

"Lance, let me make this perfectly clear. Not only was one of your agents killed, but my friends were put in danger because *your* team was not doing their job. My colleague was in the same car as they, and realized something was up, so they have no excuse. Per our agreement, I'm in charge, and I make the calls. My call is that I never want to see any of them again."

"I can't say I wouldn't feel the same in your shoes. Very well. I'll have them replaced as soon as you arrive in Venice."

"Only if the replacements are competent. Otherwise, don't bother. Even then, I'm not sure I would trust them."

"I'll make sure it's a team of our very best."

"Why weren't they your very best from the start?"

"I don't know the answer to that question, but I promise you will not have similar issues with the new team."

"This doesn't have anything to do with your mole, does it?"

"No. I can guarantee you that."

"Fine. If you'll excuse me there are a few things that need my attention."

Billy hung up and rejoined Vesna.

They wrapped Rogers in a blanket and moved him into an empty cabin. Billy then took photos of the assassin and used the fingerprint kit he kept in his makeup box to take a full set of prints.

A check of the man's pocket turned up a couple hundred euros, a mobile phone, and a business card that had the Trust's logo printed on it.

Billy grabbed the man's arms and Vesna the legs, and

they carried the assassin out the door at the back end of the car. The remainder of the walkway was capped off by three metal chains meant to prevent anyone from walking off.

They lifted the assassin over the chains and dumped him off the back. The body fell onto the tracks, bounced over one of the rails, and rolled to the side.

"Still a lot to clean up," Vesna said.

"Being handled by others. I'd like you to take over for Peter and keep any train personnel away until the car's been sanitized, if you don't mind."

She nodded and turned to leave.

"Vesna?"

She glanced back.

"Thank you."

"This is why I am here, is it not?"

"That doesn't mean I don't appreciate it."

"Don't worry. You will pay me back someday."

"Count on it."

16

AS PROMISED, THE CIA CLEANUP TEAM
boarded in Ferrara.

While two of the four agents set to work removing any signs of the encounter from the hallway, Billy took the other two into the cabin where Rogers's body lay.

The leader surveyed the situation, then said, "Okay. We've got it from here."

Billy went down to Tessa's cabin and knocked before sliding the door open.

"Mind if I join you?"

"Please do," Tessa said.

With her were Peter and Stacy, who looked less off-kilter than earlier.

Hattie was in the cabin next door, keeping Lizzie and Adriene occupied.

Making sure Adriene remained in the dark about the

events had been simple since she'd slept through everything. Getting Lizzie back to her cabin without her finding out had been accomplished by the art of distraction. When she and Hattie had returned from the restaurant car, Billy, Peter, and Tessa had staged an animated conversation about a scene in Peter's new script, and in the process blocked Lizzie's view of the blood on the floor.

Stacy was another matter entirely. She had seen too much.

"How are you feeling?" Billy asked her.

She snorted. "Like I just stepped into one of Peter's movies."

"I can imagine."

"Did you actually *shoot* the guy that grabbed me?"

"I did."

She made several aborted attempts to ask a follow-up question but couldn't find the words.

"If you're wondering if I had a choice, the answer is no," Billy said. "It was either I shoot him or let him shoot you."

She mulled it over for several seconds, then said, "Can I ask a question?"

"You can."

"Please don't think I don't appreciate you saving my life because I do. I *really, really* do. But why did any of that happen in the first place?"

"That is an excellent question."

"And the answer?"

He winced. "Well, it's complicated."

"You need to tell her," Tessa said to Billy.

"Tell me what?" Stacy asked, confused.

Billy knew Tessa was right. He'd known it since the moment Stacy looked into the corridor. But knowing it and actually bringing her into the fold about his big secret were two different things. But try as he might, he could not come up with an alternative. "There's something you don't know about me."

"Really?" she said exaggeratedly. "I would have never guessed."

"It's something that *very* few people know. If I tell you, you must agree never to talk about this to anyone who doesn't know."

"Why?"

"Because people could die."

"You—you'd kill me?"

"Of course I wouldn't kill you. But there are a lot of people out there who would love to kill me, and since you and I work together, you might become collateral damage."

"I'm not sure I want to know now."

Tessa put a hand on her shoulder. "It'll be better if you do, I think."

"You already know?" Stacy asked, confused.

"Both Peter and I do."

"Hattie, too," Peter said.

"And Ben," Tessa said.

"But Adriene and Lizzie don't," Billy said. "And it needs to stay that way."

Stacy chewed her lower lip and after a moment seemed to come to a decision. "All right. Whatever you're about to tell me, I won't share with anyone else."

"I have your promise?" Billy asked.

"Do you want me to sign my name in blood somewhere?"

"Now there's a thought."

"I was kidding."

"So was I."

She frowned. "I used to know when you were kidding."

"You still do. You're just a little on edge at the moment."

"You think?"

He smiled reassuringly.

"So, what's your big secret?" Stacy asked. "Are you Superman or something?"

"Or something," Peter said.

"Are you going to tell me he's the Hulk, then?"

"You're intertwining comic book universes."

Exasperated, Stacy said, "Is that really what's important right now?"

"Don't worry, I'm not a superhero," Teddy said. "You told me once that you'd be better at your job if you knew everything I was up to."

"I've told you more than once."

"Not the point I was trying to make, but yes, you have."

"And . . . ?"

"Billy Barnett is just one of my identities."

"What do you mean? You have multi-personalities like that old movie? What was it called?"

"*Sybil?*" Peter offered.

"Never heard of it."

"You mean *Split*," Tessa said.

"That's it."

"I believe the character in that movie had dissociative personality disorder," Peter said. "That's not what Billy's talking about. Think more *Mr. & Mrs. Smith.*"

"Donald Glover and Maya Erskine or Brad Pitt and Angelina Jolie?"

Peter shrugged. "Either one."

"Because I like the Donald and Maya one better."

"Me, too."

"For me, it's Brad and Angelina," Tessa said.

"Only because of your childhood crush on Brad Pitt," Peter said.

"I feel like we're getting off topic," Billy interjected.

"So, not like *Mr. & Mrs. Smith?*" Stacy asked.

"That's not what I—" Billy stopped himself, took a breath, and said, "You're probably too young to remember this, but many years ago there were news reports about a rogue former CIA agent."

Stacy's mind spun for a moment. "I vaguely remember that. He killed some people who turned out to be not so great themselves. At least, I think that's what my mom said."

"Your mother is a very intelligent person."

"Tommy something, right?"

"Teddy."

"Right. Teddy . . ."

"Fay."

"Yes! Teddy Fay." She looked happy at making the connection, but her smile waned as Billy continued to stare at her. "What?"

"Nice to meet you, Stacy. I'm Teddy Fay."

She laughed. "Right. The one thing I do remember is that Teddy Fay is dead." When she noticed no one else was laughing with her, she said, "He is dead, isn't he?"

"He is not," Peter said, shaking his head.

"Billy's Teddy Fay?"

"He is," Tessa said.

"How long have you two known?"

"Since about the same time we came to Hollywood," Tessa said.

"He saved our lives, too," Peter said.

She looked back at her boss. "If you're Teddy Fay, why aren't you in prison?"

"Another excellent question," Billy said. "I'm pretty good at hiding, but more importantly, I have a presidential pardon."

"You have a pardon?"

"I'd show it to you, but as you probably can imagine, I don't carry it around with me."

"So, the guy who grabbed me . . . ?"

"Was sent to kill the man with whom I was going to meet."

"And that man was the other dead guy," she guessed.

"Correct."

"Why were you meeting him?"

"Because I'm doing something for the CIA."

She stared at him. "*The* CIA? The same agency you went rogue from?"

"I'm certainly not talking about the Culinary Institute of America." Billy motioned at the door. "There's a team of agents in the hallway right now cleaning everything up."

She narrowed her eyes for a moment. Then she moved to the window and pulled the curtain away enough to peek into the corridor. "My God. You weren't lying."

"I haven't lied about anything."

She turned back to him. "You mean you haven't since we started this conversation. Because clearly—"

Billy held up a hand, stopping her. "Yes. As of this conversation."

"And if I hadn't seen what happened, I'd still be in the dark, wouldn't I?"

"Today, for sure. Though chances are, it would have eventually become necessary to tell you."

She looked at Peter. "Totally *Mr. & Mrs. Smith*."

"Right?" Peter said.

She whipped her head around to look at Billy again. "Hold on. Is it just Billy and Teddy? Or do you have more identities?"

"About that . . ."

She snorted. "So, what? Are you going to tell me you're Mark Weldon, too?"

"Whoa," Peter said, impressed.

"Good guess," Tessa said, clapping.

With a roll of her eyes, Stacy said, "I was *joking*."

"Have you ever seen Billy and Mark in the same place?" Peter asked.

"I'm sure I have." Stacy's face scrunched up in thought. The longer she stayed quiet, the more worried her expression turned. She looked skeptically at Billy. "You can't be Mark. You don't even sound like him."

Adjusting his voice to that of Mark Weldon, Billy said, "Are you sure about that?"

Stacy slammed back against the seat. "Oh. My. God."

"Believe me now?"

She hesitated, then nodded. "How many others?"

"Those are the main ones."

"How many people know about this?"

"Less than twenty."

She looked at him for several seconds, then said, "Is it too early to have a drink?"

Just outside of Padua, traffic control ordered the passen-ger train to stop for five minutes, ostensibly to allow a freight train to pass through the area ahead of them.

The actual reason for the stop was so that the CIA cleanup team could disembark with Rogers's body, the delay arranged by Lance through his counterpart in Italian intelligence.

When the train began moving again, no evidence of the short but deadly encounter remained.

17

IN CASE ANOTHER MOB AWAITED THEM AT
Venice's Santa Lucia train station, Billy and the others
changed their clothes, donned face masks, hats, and scarves,
then gathered in the corridor.

"Okay, everyone," Lizzie said. "Like in Rome, the plan is
to blend into the crowd."

"I hesitate to point this out, but that didn't work so well,"
Peter said.

"It worked well enough for some of us," Billy said.

"Peter's not wrong," Lizzie said. "Which is why the Strategic Services team who'll be watching over us is twice as
large as the one in Rome. We're also going to move up three
cars and exit from there."

Peter gave her a thumbs-up.

"If you get separated from the rest of us, follow the signs
to the Grand Canal," she said. "I'll find you there."

When the platform came into view, Billy whispered to Stacy, "How are you doing?"

"Oh, I'm great. Never better."

"Happy to hear that."

"I was being sarcastic."

"Really?" he said drolly. "I wouldn't have noticed if you hadn't said so." His tone turned serious. "When we leave, stay close."

Stacy's expression turned wary. "Are you expecting trouble?"

"I doubt that we'll be in any danger, but it would be a mistake not to remain vigilant."

"That's not as comforting as you may think it sounds."

The train finally stopped, and the line of people waiting to disembark began moving.

When Billy stepped onto the platform, he casually glanced back toward their private car. Sure enough, a crowd of gawkers were gathered there, waiting to catch a glimpse of the movie stars.

As his gaze swung back, he scanned the crowd and spotted a watcher. The man was standing to the side and had a phone pressed against his ear. Others might have thought he was in the middle of a conversation, but Billy saw it for the ruse it was. What the man was really doing was observing the passengers leaving the train.

Billy touched Stacy's arm. "How about we get a photo of you?"

"Here?"

"Say yes," he whispered.

"Um, yes, Billy. I would love a photo."

He guided her to the spot he wanted, then positioned himself so that the watcher was visible over her shoulder.

He raised his phone. "Smile."

He snapped off a couple of close-ups of the man, then a few wider pictures of Stacy.

He showed her one of the latter. "How's this?"

"Oh, that's good," she said, surprised. "Can you text it to me?"

By the time they exited the station, he'd identified and photographed three more watchers.

"There you are," Lizzie said, jogging up to them. "I thought we lost you." She pointed at a boat tied to one of the docks. "That's ours. Everyone else is on board. We're just waiting for the luggage."

As she said this, a pair of attendants exited the station, pushing carts piled high with their bags.

"And I guess we're set," Lizzie said. "Follow me."

Once they and the luggage were aboard and the ropes untied, the boat motored into the wide canal.

Billy kept an eye on the station the whole time. Just before it disappeared from sight, two of the watchers raced out and started searching the crowd.

Neither man looked in the boat's direction, however.

"Billy," Stacy said. "What are you looking at?"

"Just a couple of rodents, scurrying around."

"More moles?"

"Rats, I believe."

She shivered and sucked in a breath. "Yuck. Keep them away from me."

"I will do my best."

18

BRAUN WAS IN HIS DASSAULT FALCON 2000-
LXS jet, heading for a meeting in Geneva, when Dieter
called.

"I just heard from our freelancers in Venice," Dieter
said. He'd been forced to use local talent to watch the station, since their Rome-based team wouldn't make it to Venice before Schmidt's train arrived. "Neither Schmidt nor
Rogers were on board."

"Not on board?" Braun scoffed. "That doesn't make any
sense. They had to be."

"The watchers were in place when the train arrived, and
when neither man got off, they even searched inside."

"They must have checked the wrong train!" Braun insisted.

"I thought so, too, but have confirmed it was the correct one."

"Then where is Schmidt?"

"He must have left at an earlier stop. I'm assuming with Rogers. It's the only thing that makes sense."

"Have you tried calling him?"

"Numerous times but only got his voicemail. I contacted our Rome-based team. They were still an hour out of Venice, so I've told them to check security footage at the stops between where Schmidt boarded and Venice. We should know soon where he and Rogers got off."

"Dammit, Dieter! The longer this takes, the more likely Rogers slips through our hands. I will not stand for that!"

"I understand."

Braun stewed for a moment, his annoyance at Schmidt's incompetence reaching a breaking point. "I want you to go to Italy and oversee this in person."

"I'm already on the way to the airport."

This was why Braun liked Dieter. The man had a way of reading his mind and doing what needed to be done. "Good. And one more thing."

"Yes?"

"I don't ever want to see Schmidt again."

"Understood."

―――――

Per Dieter's instructions, the team from Rome that had been heading to Venice split into groups of two. Each group took one of the three stops between where Schmidt had told Dieter he'd boarded the train in Florence and where he was supposed to get off in Venice.

Dieter was boarding his flight to Italy when the team leader texted him that neither man had left the train at any of the stops.

That didn't make any sense. Schmidt had been clear about boarding that specific train in Florence. Had he lied? Or had he and Rogers hopped off between stops for some unknown reason?

He shot off a text, telling the team leader to send someone to Florence to see if Schmidt had lied about catching the train.

The two men sent to Florence used the same "we're searching for an underage relative who ran off with an older man" ruse they'd used in Bologna. The sympathetic security chief took them straight to the surveillance room, where it took only a few minutes to find video of both Schmidt and Rogers boarding the Venice-bound train.

Just as they were about to leave, the security officer helping them received a phone call.

"*Pronto?*" The man listened for a moment. "Where?" As the person on the other end spoke, the man glanced at Dieter's men. "Can you give me a description?" Another pause, then, "I may know something. I will call you back." He hung up and looked at the men again. "The person who is with your cousin, do you know what he looks like?"

"We do. Why?"

"It's possible he has been found."

Dieter switched his phone on the moment his plane was on the ground at the Venice Marco Polo Airport and was greeted with several message alerts.

He worked through them, his jaw tensing.

Upon exiting the plane, he called Braun. "Schmidt is dead."

"You've dealt with him already?"

"Not me. I just arrived. His body was found along the tracks in the hills outside Bologna."

"What are you saying? He fell off the train?"

"No. According to our men on-site, he was shot."

Silence.

Dieter had to check his phone to make sure his boss was still on the line.

Finally, Braun said, his anger barely contained, "Who did it? Rogers?"

"Likely, but I don't know yet."

"And where is *he*?"

"Unknown. The only video we have of either of them is when they boarded the train in Florence. It's likely Rogers hopped off after killing Schmidt."

"Have you rechecked the video?" Braun demanded.

"Already in process."

"The video in Venice, too. By *our* people, not your deadbeat freelancers."

"Also happening," Dieter said, as calm as always. "I do have some good news."

"Well, that would be a nice change."

"I had a message from Jillian. She's heard from a second source, who has no connection to the first, that Teddy Fay is alive."

"Rumors are one thing. Has she found any proof yet?"

"Not yet."

Braun swore under his breath. "You don't understand how much I want it to be true!"

"Perhaps not, but I know it's important. I'll work with Jillian on it. If there's proof, we'll find it."

According to Jillian, the second source had also claimed that Fay was currently in Europe. But Dieter thought it best not to share that information with his boss just yet.

Dieter's phone beeped with another call. He glanced at the screen and saw that it was Hilgard, the man he'd sent to shadow the CIA's Paris station chief.

"Sir, I need to take this call. If there's nothing else . . . ?"

"Just get things back on track!" Braun said and hung up.

Dieter answered the other call. "Yes?"

"Rick La Rose is at Orly Airport," Hilgard said.

Given that La Rose was the CIA's highest-ranking representative on the continent, Dieter thought it prudent to watch him while they carried out Braun's revenge on the participants of Golden Hour.

"Is he picking someone up?"

"No. He's waiting at a gate for a flight."

"Alone?"

"Yes."

"Where is he going?"

"Venice, Italy."

A smile spread across Dieter's face. "Can you get on that flight?"

"I can try."

"Do it. If you can't, get on the next one."

"Yes, sir."

Dieter hung up and shot off a text to the men who'd been checking the train stations.

Meet me in Venice ASAP

19

AFTER CHECKING INTO HIS HOTEL SUITE, Billy turned himself into Mark Weldon, then went down to the lobby, where everyone was to meet for their next event.

"Mark!" Adriene ran over and gave him a hug. "When did you get in?"

"Arrived this morning," he said.

"We missed you in Rome."

"You'll have to tell me all about it."

Tessa, Peter, and Hattie came over.

"There he is," Peter said. "Glad you could find room in your busy schedule for us."

"Oh, you know, I was in the area, so I thought, why not?"

"How was the flight?" Tessa asked.

"Smooth and drama free."

"Sounds like our train ride," Adriene said. "I slept most of the way."

"Glad to hear it."

Lizzie and Stacy joined them.

"Hey, Mark," Lizzie said. "You ready to join our circus?"

"I've been told by Ben Bacchetti that I don't have a choice."

"My husband *can* be a taskmaster," Tessa said.

Lizzie looked around. "Where's Billy?"

Stacy had been hanging back, studying Mark, so it took her a moment to register the question. "Oh, he said that since he wasn't really needed for this, he was going to stay here and get some work done."

"Too bad," Lizzie said. "I hear the location is beautiful."

"His loss," Mark said.

"All right," Lizzie said. "Everyone, follow me."

A boat took them to a four-century-old house where the actors of *Storm's Eye* would be doing a photo shoot for *Vogue Italia*. The photographer was the world-renowned Flavio Cee, and the pictures would accompany an article about the movie.

Mark and Peter were photographed individually in a variety of suits, while Tessa, Hattie, and Adriene changed into and out of at least a dozen dresses each for their time in front of the lens. The shoot finished up with several group shots on the roof, with the city in the background.

After Flavio clicked his camera for the final time, he said, "I think I have everything I need. Thank you, everyone."

"Can we see?" Adriene asked.

"Of course. Come, come."

They gathered around the monitor, and Flavio flipped through the shots.

"These are fantastic," Tessa said.

"They make me look like a fashion model," Adriene said.

"Adriene," Peter said. "These *will* be in *Vogue Italia*, so you are a fashion model."

"Huh. I hadn't thought of it that way."

"Thank you, Flavio," Mark said. "These are marvelous. Your reputation is well deserved."

Flavio put a hand over his heart and gave a slight bow. "If I may ask, what are your plans this evening?"

Mark looked around until he spotted Lizzie and then waved her over. "What's on tap for tonight?"

"We don't have anything on the schedule until the morning," she said. "Tonight, you're free."

"In that case," Flavio said, "it would be my pleasure to treat you all to dinner at Kampa's."

"I read about Kampa's on the train," Tessa said. "It sounds wonderful. But can you get a reservation this late?"

Flavio smirked. "If I cannot, no one can. I am one of the owners."

"In that case, you can count me in," Tessa said.

Hattie put her arm through Peter's. "Us, too."

"*Signorina* Adele?" Flavio asked.

"Call me Adriene, and are you kidding? I wouldn't miss it for the world."

"If Lizzie and Stacy can join us, too, I'll make it unanimous," Mark said.

Flavio clapped his hands together in delight. "*Bene, bene.* Shall we say eight p.m.?"

———

When the group returned to the hotel, one of the desk clerks called Stacy over and handed her an envelope.

"Do you have a secret admirer we don't know about?" Tessa asked when Stacy caught up to everyone at the elevators.

"If only. It's for Billy." She started to hold the envelope out to Mark, then realized what she was doing and yanked it back. "Sorry. Too much sun today."

"Quite all right," he said.

An elevator car arrived, and they stepped inside. Lizzie exited on the floor where she and Stacy were sharing a room, while Stacy stayed on until they reached the floor where everyone else's suites were located.

As was normal when both Mark and Billy were staying at the same hotel, adjacent rooms had been procured. Tessa, Hattie, Peter, and Adriene went down the hall, toward their rooms, while Stacy followed Mark in the opposite direction.

Mark reached his room first and pulled out his key. Stacy continued to the door to Billy's suite, then looked at it, confused.

"What am I supposed to do now?" she whispered.

"I believe knocking would be appropriate in this situation," he said.

"Well, yeah. But Billy's not home."

"And how would you know that?"

"Because—" She stopped herself. "Oh, right. I wouldn't."

He entered his room as she rapped on Billy's door. He waited several seconds, then stepped back into the hall and checked to make sure Adriene had gone into her room. "You can relax. We're alone now."

Stacy expelled a breath and let her shoulders sag. "Oh, thank God."

He opened Billy's door. "After you."

She hurried inside and he followed.

As she dropped onto the couch, he said, "You look like you could use a drink."

"Is it that obvious?"

He poured her a glass of Castello Monaci Artas Primitivo zinfandel and handed her the glass.

"Thank you," she said and took a drink.

"Better?"

"Too early to tell." She lolled her head back against the cushion. "This multiple ID thing is exhausting, and I've only been dealing with it for less than a day. I can't imagine how tiring it is for you to change who you are all the time."

"Not exhausting at all. Remember, I've been doing it for years."

"And you've never tripped up? Acted like one person while looking like another?"

"Not once."

"No wonder you won an Oscar."

Mark returned to the bar and poured himself a glass of wine, then took the seat across from her.

She studied him for a moment. "Is it difficult to live like this?"

"Like what?"

"Leading a double life. Wait. Triple life?"

"I lead it very well, thank you very much."

She snorted. "Sorry. It's just all so . . . weird."

"It'll take some getting used to, but I have every faith in you."

"Thanks, but I'm not sure how I'm going to keep everything straight."

"What do you mean?"

"Are you Mark? Are you Billy? Are you Teddy Fay?"

"That part's easy. When I look like this, I'm Mark Weldon. When I look like Billy, I'm Billy Barnett. And when I look like Teddy, I'm Teddy Fay."

"I don't even know what Teddy Fay looks like."

"I'll introduce you to him someday."

She huffed again and took another drink.

"Simple rule of thumb," he said. "Act like you always have."

"Easy for you to say, Mr. Man of a Thousand Faces."

"That was Lon Chaney."

"Who?"

"Never mind. I believe you have a message for me."

"I don't know what you're talking about. I have a message for *Billy*, not Mark."

"See, you're getting the hang of it already." He held out his hand. "Hand it over."

She gave him the envelope.

Written on the note inside was 10:00 p.m., an address, and instructions for a meeting with Rick La Rose, the CIA's Paris station chief.

"Spy stuff?" Stacy asked.

"Spy stuff."

She finished her wine and stood. "I think I'll take a walk around and clear my head. Don't forget. Meet in the lobby at eight, for dinner."

"Actually, I need you to make excuses for me."

"You're not coming?"

He waved the envelope she'd given him.

"Ah," she said. *"Urgent* spy stuff."

"The world of secrets never sleeps."

"I assume I'm making excuses for Mark *and* Billy."

"You assume correctly."

"I'm really going to hate this, aren't I?"

"You might, but honestly, I'm starting to wonder why I didn't tell you long ago. It's so much easier for me."

She rolled her eyes and left without another word.

He then called Lance.

"Good afternoon." In the background of the CIA director's voice was the muffled drone of helicopter rotors.

"Not catching you at a bad time, am I?"

"Perfect, actually. I'm on my way to New York for brunch with my Japanese counterpart. How can I help you?"

"By not setting up meetings for me without checking with me ahead of time."

"I take it you've heard from Rick La Rose."

"I have."

"I thought it best he touch base with you after today's unpleasantness. He's also the one who's been overseeing the investigation into Owen Pace's death, so he might have information that could be useful to you."

"Which brings us back to why I called."

"Yes, yes. Clear it with you first. I'll keep that in mind for next time."

"Does La Rose know about Golden Hour?"

"He does. He's been assisting me since I first started suspecting something was up."

"He left his note for Billy Barnett. Is that who he's expecting to see?"

"No. I told him Billy is just an intermediary and would pass the message on."

"Then who *does* he think he's going to meet?"

"I haven't told him your secret, if that's what you're asking. I used the same cover story I did with Rogers, that you're a freelancer with knowledge of Golden Hour."

"And if he does figure it out?"

"Handle it however you think appropriate, short of killing him, of course. I'd rather not have to replace him."

"How trustworthy is he?"

"There are few I trust more."

"Correct me if I'm wrong, but you don't trust anyone."

"True. Like I said, handle it how you want."

"What I want is not to be dealing with any of this and just enjoy the PR tour."

"Please, we both know no one enjoys those tours. Besides, your conscience wouldn't let you do nothing."

That was true, though it didn't help him feel any less annoyed. "It's always a pleasure, Lance."

20

BEFORE LEAVING THE HOTEL FOR HIS MEET-
ing with Rick La Rose, Teddy altered his appearance to look
as unmemorable as possible. He then donned a pair of jeans,
a black hoodie, and a black New York Yankees baseball cap
that he wore low over his eyes.

He sent Vesna a picture of what he looked like with a
text that read:

Heading out

She replied with a thumbs-up.

As he walked through the hotel lobby, he passed right by
a pair of his new CIA protection agents. Neither realized
who he was.

He took a train across the lagoon to the mainland, then
grabbed a rideshare that dropped him off in the industrial
area surrounding the port, a couple of blocks from the building that Rick had chosen for the meet. Teddy slipped his

right-side ear pod in as the car drove away and activated the radio app.

"Check, check," he whispered.

"Read you," Vesna said. "Route clear."

"Copy."

Keeping to the shadows, he made his way to the unoccupied manufacturing facility where Rick had directed him.

"Any backup?" he whispered.

"If there is, it's not close by," Vesna said.

"Copy."

Teddy found the unlocked side door through which he'd been told to enter. "Going in and putting myself on mute."

"Copy," Vesna replied.

He stepped into a dim, cavernous space that was all but empty.

Per instructions, he climbed a metal staircase anchored to the wall to a mezzanine walkway. On one side was a half wall overlooking the open space, and on the other were several office doors.

Light leaked out around the partially opened door to the first office. Inside, Rick La Rose leaned against a desk, his phone lying next to him, its flashlight on. He was not holding a weapon.

After the recognition code was dealt with, Rick said, "I heard Lance didn't tell you I was coming. I'm sorry about that."

"Lance's faults are neither yours nor mine," Teddy said. "No apologies necessary."

"Agreed." Rick held out his hand and they shook. "Rick La Rose."

"John," Teddy said.

"There is one thing I really do need to apologize for. I heard about trouble on the train this morning, and that the team sent to protect your colleague and his friends was—"

"Oblivious? Useless?"

Rick winced. "Both of those. The new people are all top-notch. If there are any problems, contact me directly. I'll fix it right away." He pulled out a business card and handed it to Teddy.

"You're asking me to bypass Lance?"

"Technically, but the response will be quicker because he'd likely just call me anyway."

"Noted." Teddy slid the card into his pocket. "I understand you've been dealing with Owen Pace's murder."

Rick's expression darkened. "I have."

"Any leads on who did it?"

"Sadly, no. We have security footage that shows Pace entering the Latin Quarter that evening, but none of him leaving, mainly because the CCTV system in the area experienced an outage."

"How convenient."

"Very," he said.

"Hacked?"

"That's the leading theory, but it's still under investigation." Rick paused, then asked, "Were you present when Rogers was killed today?"

"I may have been in the vicinity."

"He was one of my mentors when I started out. We lost a good man."

"I'm sorry."

Rick nodded grimly, then removed a picture from his pocket and handed it to Teddy.

"What's this?" Teddy asked.

"I don't know if you know this or not, but Rogers was almost killed in Prague before he came to Italy."

"He told me."

Rick jutted his chin at the picture. "That's a still from security footage of the man who was following him."

Teddy looked at the photo. The man was standing on a sidewalk, his face in three-quarter profile.

"I know where you can find his body," Teddy said.

"Let me guess, he's the guy who killed Rogers on the train."

"One and the same. Have you ID'ed him?"

"Check the back."

Teddy flipped over the picture. Written there was the name Oscar Schmidt, followed by a list of aliases.

"What else do you know about him?"

"Born outside Vienna," Rick said. "Spent a couple years in the Austrian armed forces and has been bouncing between mercenary outfits ever since. His last known employer was a Bulgarian group. I made some inquiries and found out he left there for eighteen months ago. I haven't found anyone who knows where he went next."

"Too bad. If you had, then my mission would be finished."

"Sorry to disappoint. My people are still looking into it, but don't hold your breath."

Teddy glanced at the picture again, then said, "May I keep this?"

"It's for you."

Teddy slipped it into his pocket. "Any guesses as to who might—"

Vesna's voice popped into Teddy's ear. "You have company."

He unmuted the radio. "Explain."

"Two men. One is at a door on the north side and appears to be picking the lock. The other man is positioned at the east corner, near the street. He's the lookout."

"Copy."

Before Teddy could say anything else, Rick asked, "Who are you talking to?"

"A friend."

"You didn't come alone?"

"It's been that kind of day," Teddy said. "You did?"

"I have two agents on standby a mile away, though they don't know who they're backing up. No one knows I left Paris."

"You might want to recheck your definition of 'no one.'"

"What do you mean?"

"Someone's trying to sneak into the building. We should get out of—"

"He got the door open," Vesna said. "He's coming in armed."

Teddy pulled out his pistol and began attaching his silencer to the barrel. "Too late to leave. One's entering right now with a weapon."

Rick retrieved his gun while Teddy crept to the office door.

"Would you like me to deal with his lookout?" Vesna asked.

"If it wouldn't be too much trouble," Teddy said.

"No trouble at all."

21

TEDDY CROUCHED BEHIND THE MEZZANINE'S
half wall and rose just high enough to peek over the top.

Below, the shadowy form of the intruder was moving toward the stairs.

Teddy ducked back down and whispered, "Is there someone who wants you dead?"

"I *am* the CIA's Paris station chief, so . . ."

"Hazard of the job?"

Rick nodded. "As far as I know, there's no one actively pursuing me at the moment."

A faint groan of metal drifted up from the stairs.

Teddy scanned the mezzanine. Jammed against the wall between the first and second offices were a pair of old file cabinets. They would work for what he needed.

"How do you feel about being bait?" he asked.

"Not my favorite role, but what do you have in mind?"

Teddy told him.

"If this doesn't work and I get killed, I'm not going to be happy about it."

"I'll be sure to convey your sentiments to the appropriate people."

Rick smirked, then reentered the office they'd met in and quietly shut the door, while Teddy repositioned himself to the other side of the discarded file cabinets.

Several seconds later, the stairs groaned again, this time from much closer to the top.

When Teddy heard the gentle tap of a shoe stepping onto the mezzanine, he sent Rick a text that read:

Now

A moment later, Rick began talking at a normal level, his voice muffled but understandable through the office door. "I'm not sure how feasible that'll be. I'll have to check with Washington to see if we can make it work."

As the Paris station chief droned on, Teddy listened to the faint sounds of the intruder creeping along the mezzanine. When the steps reached the office door, they stopped.

Teddy waited another moment, then leaned out until he had eyes on the intruder. The man had his ear turned toward the door, listening to Rick. After several seconds, he reached into his jacket.

Teddy raised his gun, ready to take him out if he was going for a weapon. But when the man's hand reappeared, the item he was holding was too small to be a gun.

He stuck it to the top of the doorframe, where it stayed, inspected his work, then headed toward the stairs.

Teddy sneaked out from cover and silently halved the

distance between them before the intruder sensed he was there and looked back.

"Hi," Teddy said. He nodded his head at the office Rick was in. "Let's go inside for a chat."

The intruder bolted toward the stairs. Hoping to freeze the guy in place, Teddy fired a warning shot over the man's head.

The intruder jerked down at the sound, then tripped over his own feet onto the top step of the stairs, and tumbled down, out of sight.

Teddy raced over just in time to see the man bounce off the last few risers and come to rest on the concrete floor in a disjointed heap.

Rick ran up behind him. "What the hell happened?"

"He decided to take the fast way down."

"I thought the idea was to capture him."

"I forgot to send him the script."

"Clearly."

Teddy jogged back to the office doorway and pried off what the intruder had stuck there. As he'd thought, it was a listening device.

He tossed it to Rick, who looked it over and said, "If my people can find a serial number, they might be able to track where this came from."

"Even better if they find out who bought it."

"No promises."

Teddy unmuted his radio as he and Rick headed down the stairs. "Vesna. Status?"

It took a moment before she came on. When she did, she was breathing heavily. "In pursuit."

"Pursuit? I thought you were sneaking up on him."

"Can we discuss this later? I'm a little preoccupied."

"We can."

Teddy and Rick reached the ground level and crouched next to the intruder. One look and they could tell the man was dead.

Rick stepped away to make a phone call while Teddy searched the body.

He found a Glock 9mm subcompact pistol in a shoulder holster; a silencer; three more listening bugs; a phone; a set of car keys; and a wallet holding nearly a thousand euros, two credit cards, and an Italian ID that Teddy was sure was fake. He laid them on the floor next to the body.

"I'll be waiting," Rick said, then hung up and rejoined Teddy. "Thanks to your exploits on the train earlier today, we have a cleanup team in the area. Should be here in thirty minutes."

"You want me to stay with you till they arrive?"

"No. My backup can be here in a few minutes."

Vesna's voice came over the radio. "I have bad news. The watcher got away."

Teddy unmuted his mic. "What happened?"

"Someone picked him up in a car, and they raced off. Sorry."

"No apology necessary. But I am curious: how did the guy know you were after him in the first place?"

"As I was sneaking up on him, something started banging inside the building. The watcher turned and saw me. The rest was a lot of running. I don't suppose you had anything to do with the noise."

"Our guy decided to use the stairs as a slide instead of as intended."

"So, it was *your* fault."

"It was his fault, for which he paid the ultimate price."

"That's unfortunate."

"Very."

22

"YOU WANT TO TELL ME WHAT HAPPENED?"
Dieter asked, his normally smooth tone somehow sounding
more menacing than it would if he were yelling.

He had pulled the BMW to the side of the road and was
staring into the back seat at Max Gruber, who was still pant-
ing from being chased.

"I'm sorry," Gruber said between breaths. "Someone
must have been watching us."

"Really? What gave you that idea?"

"Well, I mean, she had to—"

"Obviously, someone was watching you," Dieter cut
him off. "What I'm wondering is why you didn't spot them
earlier?"

"I swear we did a thorough search. There was no one."

"And yet there was. Which means your thorough search
was not thorough enough, don't you think?"

Gruber reluctantly nodded.

"And where is Hilgard?" Dieter asked.

"I'm not sure. He was still inside when I was, um, spotted."

"Perhaps you should tell me what happened from the beginning."

"Um, sure. I can do that." Gruber ran a hand through his hair. "We did exactly what you told us to do. We followed the CIA agent to the building, then we searched the area to make sure he hadn't brought anyone else with him."

Dieter arched an eyebrow.

"Which we failed at," Gruber added quickly. "Then we waited to see what would happen. About thirty minutes later, another guy showed up and went inside."

"Was the new guy alone?"

"He was when we caught sight of him."

"Did you recognize him?"

"No. But I got a photo."

"Show me."

Gruber did so. The image was of a man walking down a dimly lit sidewalk.

Dieter zoomed in to get a look at the man's face, but it didn't help. The man was wearing a baseball cap low on his forehead and a face mask that covered everything except his eyes.

The photo was practically useless.

"Continue," he said to Gruber.

"Right. We, um, gave the new guy a few minutes inside, then Hilgard went in to bug the meeting."

"Did he succeed?"

"I don't know. Not long after he entered, I heard several loud thumps, like something hitting metal over and over. That's when I spotted the woman sneaking up behind me and ran."

"Have you tried calling him?"

"I couldn't. I was running."

Dieter pulled out his phone, but his call to Hilgard was sent to voicemail. He tried twice more, but the response was the same.

He turned the car around and headed back toward where he'd picked up Gruber.

"Which building was the meeting in?" he asked.

Gruber leaned between the two front seats and frowned. "You can't see it from here. It's three or four streets up, I think."

Dieter scanned the area until he spotted a building taller than the others, then drove toward it and parked.

"Come on," he said to Gruber as he climbed out.

After he picked the lock and disabled the alarm, they took the stairs to the roof.

"Point it out," Dieter said.

Gruber looked around, then said, "There."

They watched the building for twenty minutes without seeing anyone going in or out. Dieter was just starting to think that they could go investigate it themselves, when the headlights of a delivery van turned onto the road the building was on and then entered the building's parking lot.

As the vehicle stopped, a man stepped out of the building. Dieter used the zoom on his phone to get a better look at him. It was Rick La Rose, the CIA's Paris station chief.

Several men dressed in dark coveralls piled out of the van and followed La Rose inside.

Fifteen minutes later, they exited carrying a body bag.

"Well, that isn't good," Dieter said.

"Do you think that's Hilgard?" Gruber asked.

Dieter didn't answer. Of course it was Hilgard.

He watched the men put the bag in the back of the van, then everyone, including La Rose, climbed in and the van drove off.

Dieter pulled out his phone to call Braun.

Teddy and Vesna sat together at the back of a mostly empty train car on the return ride across the lagoon.

"Did your friend have any useful information?" she asked.

Teddy handed her the photo.

"This looks like the guy we helped off the train," she said.

"That's because it is."

"Does he have a name?"

"Several, actually. Check the other side."

She looked at the list of names on the back of the photo, and her brow furrowed.

"Don't tell me you know him," Teddy said.

"Oscar Schmidt," she said, rolling the name over her tongue. "It sounds familiar. Do you know anything else about him?"

Teddy relayed what Rick had told him. When he mentioned the guy had worked as a mercenary for a Bulgarian outfit, she smirked.

"That's it," she said. "Horne Solutions."

"Never heard of them."

"You know these groups. They come and go. Horne was swallowed up a year or so ago by a German company. Maybe Schmidt moved with them."

"Do you know the name of the company?"

"Unfortunately. It's called Braun Logistics and Security."

"Never heard of them."

"You wouldn't have. They popped up about ten years ago or so. Until they purchased Horne Solutions, they concentrated solely on event and personal security."

"Why do I get the feeling you don't like them."

"Where in the world did you get that idea?" she asked in mock innocence.

"The use of 'unfortunately' was a bit of a tell."

She chuckled. "It's not that I don't like the company. I am not a fan of one of the men in charge."

"Who's that?"

"Dieter Wenz."

"Now that name sounds familiar," Teddy said.

"Only because you've heard me cursing him."

It took Teddy a few seconds to connect the dots. "Is he the guy with the neck fetish? The one you were with in Cyprus on that—"

"He is. And please, let's not talk about it any further."

"Consider the topic shelved."

Among Wenz's many storied traits was his penchant to inject a knockout drug to the base of an abductee target's neck to subdue them.

During the mission in Cyprus, Vesna had become

romantically entangled with him until it ended in spectacular form when it turned out Wenz was working both sides and nearly got the whole team killed.

"Is there anyone you can check with to see if Schmidt made the transition to Braun Logistics?"

"If you are asking me to contact Dieter, that is not happening."

"I was thinking someone who you'd be less likely to kill on sight."

She thought for a moment before nodding. "There are a few people who might know. I can try them."

"I appreciate it."

"Thank me if it pays off."

As they were nearing the station, Teddy remembered her text from that morning.

"You said you had info about Owen Pace's murder."

"I said *might*. And that hasn't changed." She pulled out her phone and shook her head. "Still nothing. I'll give them a nudge." She sent off a text.

No reply arrived by the time they reached their stop. Acting once more like they didn't know each other, they caught separate boats.

Teddy was almost to the hotel when his phone vibrated multiple times. He opened the cell and was greeted with three messages from Vesna. The first two were photos and the last a two-word text, which read:

You're welcome

Teddy waited until he was inside Mark Weldon's suite before he looked at the images.

They both appeared to be grabs from security footage.

But unlike the middle-of-the-road image quality of standard CCTV cameras, these were taken at a much higher resolution.

The first picture was of two men sitting in the cab of a delivery van. The second was the back of what he presumed to be the same van. Its doors were open, and three men were standing near it, facing in the camera's direction.

Two of the men were propping up the third, who was none other than a clearly unconscious Owen Pace.

Teddy called Vesna.

As soon as she answered, he asked, "Where were these taken?"

"Specifically, I can't tell you because I don't know. What I can tell you is that the van was at a facility owned by a Paris crime organization, though the men in the photo are not Paris locals."

"The crime org sent you these?"

She snorted. "Of course not. These were taken by their rivals, who have been keeping an eye on the facility."

"Do you recognize any of the men?" he asked.

"Funny thing that. Earlier this evening, I would have said the only one I recognized was Owen Pace."

"And now?"

"The guy in the van's front passenger seat is the same asshole I chased this evening."

Teddy brought up the picture of the cab and zoomed in on the man's face.

"You know what this means?" she asked.

"It means that they were trying to bug my meeting tonight because of Golden Hour. Are you sure they didn't follow us there?"

"I would bet your life on it."

"That's not how that idiom goes."

"I stand by what I said."

Teddy looked at the pictures again. "If I give these to the Agency, and the people you received them from find out, will there be any blowback on you?"

"I am not an amateur. Do whatever you need to do. They have no idea who I am."

"Thank you, Vesna. This is better than I'd even hoped."

"You asked for my help, so I am helping. But I do need you to do one thing for me."

"What's that?"

"Go to sleep so I can go to sleep."

"Good night, Vesna."

"Good night, Teddy."

Before going to bed, he sent copies of the photos to Lance and Rick, with a message about the man in the van being connected to that evening's activities.

He then used his back door into the CIA's computer system to upload the images of the four men from the van into the facial recognition program. Lance and Rick would likely do the same, but he didn't want to wait for them to give him the results.

With that done, he finally lay down. Within seconds, he was out like a light.

23

IT WAS JUST A LITTLE AFTER FOUR A.M. WHEN
Jillian used the encryption key Lawrence had given her to
check the message inbox. At the top was a message from
one of the contacts who claimed Teddy Fay might still be
alive.

Have heard that Fay is potentially involved in
upcoming World Thriller Film Festival in Berlin,
under an assumed identity. No word on type of
involvement or what name he is using.

Now here was something with which she could work.
Before she could open her secure browser, a voice in the
back of her mind spoke up, asking why Braun would be interested in a man who was supposed to be dead but now was
living a different life.

Before she could follow that thought any further, her phone rang.

"Hello?" she answered.

"Ms. Courtois," Braun's assistant said. "Mr. Braun would like to know if there's been any progress concerning finding Teddy Fay."

"Mr. Braun's here?" She had thought that other than the night security staff, she was the only one at the office.

"He is. And your answer?"

"Uh, well, there is one new development, but—"

"Good. Please come up."

"Right now?" she asked, but Braun's assistant had already hung up.

She popped a couple of mints in her mouth, ran a hand through her hair, and hurried to the elevator.

Braun's assistant motioned for her to go straight into Braun's office when she arrived.

She opened the door and stepped inside.

Braun was at his desk, his phone to his ear. When he noticed her, he waved her over.

"It's beginning to be a pattern," Braun said into the phone. "I need you to get us back on track." He glanced at Jillian, who was now standing in front of his desk. "I need to go. Keep me posted."

He hung up.

"I can come back if this is a bad time," Jillian said.

Ignoring her offer, he said, "What's this new development?"

She told him about the message.

"A film festival?" He frowned. "Why would Teddy Fay have anything to do with a film festival?"

"He might not," she said. "But it's something I can check."

He thought for a moment, then nodded. "Agreed. But there's also something else I need you to look into."

"Of course."

"That was Dieter on the phone." He gave her a sanitized version of what had happened in Venice, portraying it as a job for a client. "He got a photo of an unknown man who tried to cause some problems. I'll forward it to you as soon as I receive it, and I want you to find out who it is."

"I'll do my best."

He eyed her. "I pay you very well for what you do. I expect results. Is that understood?"

"Of course."

"Good. I'd rather not have to replace someone who had as much potential as you did."

"Did?"

He smiled but said nothing more.

That's when it hit her. As far as Braun was concerned, her job was for life, and it was up to her how long either would last.

"I understand," she said.

"That's a good girl. Now hop to it."

She left as fast as she could without actually running.

24

THE SUN WAS ALREADY SHINING WHEN TEDDY
woke on Thursday morning. Today would be a Mark
Weldon day, which is why he had spent the night in Mark's
suite.

Since there would be a food component to the activity
he and Tessa would be participating in, he ordered a light
breakfast of fruit and yogurt and then took a quick shower.
By the time his food arrived, he'd turned himself back into
Mark Weldon and donned a stylish yet relaxed outfit.

He checked his email while he ate. Both Lance and Rick
had responded to the photos of Owen Pace's kidnapper. He
opened Lance's first.

Who's your source?

Teddy's answer was a short and sweet: *Nice try.*

Rick's email read:

This is fantastic. I'll run them through the system and will let you know if we get any hits.

Not having to wait for Rick, Teddy logged onto the CIA system and checked the results of his own search. Hits had come back on all four men who'd been with Pace.

The two men propping him up were former Russian special forces personnel who had transitioned to freelance mercenary work. The driver had a similar story, though his military service had been in the U.S.

The man in the front passenger seat—the same man Vesna had chased the previous evening—was identified as a German national named Max Gruber. Gruber had bypassed the traditional military route and had gone straight into mercenary work.

All four men had been working for Horne Solutions when it had been taken over by Braun, and it was assumed they had remained.

Teddy was about to see what information the Agency had on Braun Logistics when someone knocked on his door.

When he looked through the peephole, he saw Lizzie standing in the hall, scrolling through her phone.

He opened the door. "Good morning, Lizzie."

"Mark! Good, you're up."

"I didn't know it was an option not to be."

"It's not. But you've only been here a day, and I wasn't sure how you'd react to jet lag."

"Not something I ever worry about."

"Lucky you. I'm here to remind you to be in the lobby in ten minutes."

"I'll be there with bells on," he said.

"No bells, please. It'll interfere with the mics."

"I'll be there with no bells on, then."

"If only all talent was as accommodating." She looked him up and down.

"Something wrong with my outfit?" he asked.

"Nope. Looks great."

"I'm pleased to have your approval."

"You should be. I have a very discerning eye." Her phone vibrated. "I need to take this. See you in a bit."

After she departed, he texted Stacy to remind her to cover for Billy.

Then he texted Vesna.

About to leave.

Anything on Schmidt?

Vesna replied:

Working on it. Anything on the men with Owen Pace?

There was no time to get into it now, so he texted her:

Yes. I'll fill you in when I have a moment.

She sent another reply.

Always the tease.

BTW, who are you today?

He stopped, took a picture of himself, and sent it to her with a message that read:

Hi. I'm Mark. Pleasure to meet you.

She replied with a rolling eyes emoji.

Mark and Tessa rode down one of the canals in a gondola.
With them was Javier Coma, the host of *Food Coma* on EDC,
the Eats & Delights Channel. Javier had started off as a You-
Tuber before being tapped by EDC to be their next big star.

The lead actors of *Storm's Eye* were Javier's guests for a
day of exploring and eating in Venice. The show was scheduled to air the weekend before the movie came out.

True to Javier's roots, parts of the show were shot vlog
style, with either his cameraman or, as he was doing at that
moment, Javier himself wielding the camera.

In this case, he held a GoPro at the end of a selfie stick,
the lens aimed so that it captured him, Tessa, Mark, and the
gondolier.

"Riding a gondola through the canals of Venice is like
traveling through history," Javier said. "This city has en-
dured sieges, military takeovers, and the Black Death, and
it's still here for all to enjoy."

He swung the camera around dramatically, then stopped
recording.

"Okay, you can relax," he said, his infectious smile still
as bright as it had been when taping. "I'll get a few B-roll
shots of the water and the boat, then take a few more of us
as we near our stop."

"Sounds good," Mark said.

"I can't believe I'm sitting here with the two of you. It's
like a dream. Thank you so much for joining me today."

"Are you kidding?" Tessa said. "I'm a big fan. I was
watching you long before EDC snapped you up!"

"You were?" Javier said, genuinely surprised.

"Absolutely. Every time my husband and I plan a trip, I check to see if you've been there, and if you have, what restaurants you recommend."

Javier put a hand over his heart. "I'm having a bit of an out-of-body experience at the thought that superstar Tessa Tweed watches my show."

"Oh, stop it. I'm just like anyone else."

"You are most definitely not just like anyone else."

"You know what I mean."

"If I may interject," Mark said. "Maybe you should save the fangirling and fanboying for when the camera is rolling. The viewers will love it."

"Good idea," Tessa said, then smiled at Javier. "When I say it again later, pretend it's the first time and react the same."

"I won't have to pretend anything to react the same," Javier said.

Tessa reached forward and squeezed his arm. "Aren't you a charmer."

Mark peeked ahead. He could see the film crew waiting at the edge of the canal, fifty yards away. "I think we're almost there."

Javier twisted toward the front. "Oh. Then I need to get back to work."

The host busied himself with camera duties, then as they neared their disembarkation point, he, Tessa, and Mark smiled for the camera that was taping their arrival from the walkway.

After exiting the gondola, Javier led them over a bridge and down a side pathway toward the home of a chef friend of his, who would be making them lunch.

Though the area wasn't one of the higher-trafficked parts of the city, there were still plenty of locals and tourists walking around. The locals mostly ignored the cameras, while the tourists craned their necks to see what was going on. A few appeared to recognize Tessa and Mark, but production security did a good job of keeping them from getting too close.

While they were passing through a particularly narrow section, Mark noticed Vesna walking toward him. As she passed him, she slipped a folded piece of paper into his hand, which he promptly put in his pocket.

It was another twenty-five minutes before he was able to excuse himself to use the restroom, where he could finally read the note.

Check your messages

His phone had been on silent while they'd been taping, so he'd missed several texts from Vesna.

The first read:

Heard back about Schmidt.

The second had been sent five minutes later.

Hello? Are you even seeing these?

The penultimate text read:

How do you Hollywood people put up with being unreachable like this?

The final one was simply two words:

Call me

He left the restroom and tracked down one of the producers. "Is there somewhere I can make a private call?"

"One moment, Mr. Weldon. I'll check for you."

When she returned, she directed him to a home library on the second floor. Once there, he called Vesna.

"Finally," she said.

"I'm touched that you missed me so much."

"Do not flatter yourself. I miss no man."

"I will note that in your dossier."

"See that you do."

"You mentioned Schmidt?"

"According to my sources, he was still working for BLS, in something they call the special projects group."

"That's quite a coincidence," he said. "According to *my* sources the men in the pictures you sent me work for BLS, too. No mention of which division, but I'd guess it's the same."

"I'm shocked," she said, not sounding shocked at all.

"If you're curious, the man you chased is named Max Gruber."

"Now I know what to call him when I run into him again. I do have a question."

"Yes?"

"Does this mean we're done?"

"Does what mean we're done?"

"The job was to find out who was behind the assassinations, right? Obviously, it's BLS."

"The only obvious thing is BLS's involvement in

carrying out the assassinations through their special projects unit. What we still don't know is who hired them. If Braun Logistics is taken down before we find out, it's highly likely the client will go to ground, then resurface later and pick up where they left off."

"That's a valid concern. So, we continue as is?"

"Actually, I'm thinking it would be a good idea to send you to Berlin to find out what you can about BLS. I'll join you as soon as the press tour gets there in a few days, and we can decide our next move."

"Are you okay with no one watching your back until then?"

"I still have the new team of CIA minders. Unless you think they're not up to it."

She made a noncommittal grunt, then said, "I'll admit, they're better than the last group."

"See, I'll be fine."

"I said nothing about being fine."

"It's what I heard. Now, get out of here. The sooner you're in Berlin, the better."

"Oh, very well. I'll let you go back to your little TV show. I'm sure this acting thing will pan out for you someday."

25

JILLIAN FINISHED OFF ANOTHER RED BULL
and tossed the can in the rubbish bin with the half dozen
others she'd already consumed.

She had decided to work the Teddy Fay problem from
two directions. The first was to look for any hints that Fay
had still been alive after his reported death. To that end, she'd
set up several autonomous searches that were even now ri-
fling through news and record databases around the world.

Her second direction was looking into his potential involvement in the World Thriller Film Festival.

For this, she took a more hands-on approach. She hacked
into the festival's computer system and obtained a list of every employee and volunteer. She then hunted down photos
of each male on the list and discarded individuals who were
too young, too tall, and too short to be Fay. That left her
with eight men.

The only confirmed image she had of Fay was a decades-old screen grab pulled from security footage taken when Golden Hour had been active. The quality of the picture was less than ideal, but it was good enough that she could confidently conclude that even with extreme plastic surgery, none of the eight were Fay.

Frustrated, she clicked through the film festival's website, hoping for inspiration. It wasn't until she was perusing the synopses of films that would be showing when she realized she'd overlooked something obvious.

It could be said that the people who made each of the films were also associated with the festival. Perhaps not all would be coming to Berlin, but some would be.

The task would mean drilling deeper, but this was the kind of thing for which she lived. The task had the added benefit of needing her complete focus and thus kept her from hearing the questions that were swirling in her head about Braun, if only temporarily.

She grabbed a fresh energy drink, downed half, then cracked her knuckles and set to work.

26

"THANK YOU, TESSA AND MARK, FOR JOINING
me on a delicious day touring one of my favorite cities in the
world," Javier said.

"We should be thanking you," Tessa said. "So much
fun!"

"I say we do this again someday soon," Mark said.

"I'm going to hold you to that!" Javier said. He turned his
smiling face to the camera. "And thanks to all of you for
watching another episode of *Food Coma*. Don't forget to go
out and see *Storm's Eye*! Until next time, this is Javier Coma."

With a signal from the off-camera assistant director, the
gondolier pushed the boat holding Javier, Tessa, and Mark
into the middle of the canal. The trio waved at the camera
and then talked with one another as if they were heading off
on another adventure.

Once the director determined they had enough video,
he shouted, "Cut. That's a wrap!"

The gondolier guided the boat back to the walkway, and a crew member helped everyone climb ashore.

"Thanks again," Javier said to Tessa and Mark. "That was a blast."

"I wasn't lying about doing it again," Mark said.

"And I wasn't lying about holding you to it." Javier gave each of them a hug. "Best of luck with the film. I'm sure it will do great."

The producer and director came over and shared their thanks.

As they were saying goodbye, a motorboat pulled in behind the gondola, with Lizzie in back.

"Ready to go?" she said.

By the time they reached the hotel, it was almost seven p.m.

"I don't suppose either of you are up for dinner," Lizzie said after they'd stepped off the boat.

Tessa put a hand on her stomach. "I doubt I'll be eating again until we're back in the States."

"Not sure I'll hold out that long," Mark said, "but I'm definitely done eating for today."

Tessa's phone buzzed with a text. "Peter, Hattie, Adriene, and Stacy are in the bar. Do you want to join them?"

"A drink I can do," Mark said.

"Me, too," Lizzie said.

They entered the hotel and took the elevator up to the rooftop bar.

Peter spotted them as they entered and waved them to their table overlooking the canal. A waiter appeared as soon as they sat and took their drink orders.

Once he left, Adriene asked, "How was the shoot?"

"Forget about the shoot," Hattie said. "I want to know about the food."

Tessa and Mark traded off describing their day. Tessa was in the middle of recounting the tiramisu they'd had at Pasticceria Tonolo when a familiar figure walked up to their table.

"My *Storm's Eye* friends!" Bianca Barone said, beaming. "So good to see you again."

"Bianca, what a surprise," Tessa said. "I didn't know you were coming to Venice."

"I had a few days free, and Billy mentioned you'd be here. So, I thought, why not see you all again before you leave my wonderful country." She looked around. "Is Billy not with you?"

"Visiting with friends, I think. Not sure when he's due back."

Bianca looked at Stacy. "You are his assistant, yes? I'm sorry, I don't remember your name."

"Stacy. And I am." Stacy looked as if she'd been hoping not to be pulled into the conversation.

"Ah, yes, Stacy. Do you know when he'll be back?"

Stacy tried very hard not to look at Mark as she said, "Sorry, he didn't say. Late, I think."

"I'm sure he will come back if he knows I'm here. Can you contact him?"

"Sure. I'll, um, I'll send him a message." She pulled out her phone and began composing a text.

"Are you here alone?" Peter asked Bianca.

"I am."

"Then, please, join us." He retrieved a chair for her from an empty table. "Mark, can you move over a bit?"

Mark glanced at him, and Peter gave him a wink that Bianca couldn't see.

"Of course," Mark said, then created room.

As Bianca sat, she took her first good look at Mark. "You are Mark Weldon."

"So I've been told."

"We missed you in Rome. Fortunately, I had the opportunity to watch several clips from your new movie. You are *very* talented." She smiled coyly and pressed her arm against his for a moment.

"Thank you."

"I am so sorry," she said. "I should have introduced myself."

"No need. I've seen several of your films."

"You have? And?"

"And you are very talented, too."

She leaned into him again, the contact lasting longer than the last time. "Which movie is your favorite?"

"I liked them all, but if I had to choose one, I'd say *Marcella*."

She placed a hand on her chest. "This is my favorite, too."

"It's a classic," Peter said. "That opening shot, just wow."

"Would you believe we did that in only three takes?" Bianca said.

"You're kidding?"

The sun went down and the light of the city began reflecting off the canal as the group talked.

Finally, Lizzie yawned and said, "I hate to be the killjoy,

but we have to leave for the airport at seven a.m., so I'm going to get some sleep."

"I could use some shut-eye, too," Mark said.

The rest of the Centurion group echoed the sentiments and chairs started moving away from the table.

"But it's still so early," Bianca said.

"My apologies," Mark said. "It was a long day, and I'm still a bit jet-lagged."

"But, Mark," Lizzie said, "didn't you say earlier that—"

"Lizzie, there's something I wanted to ask you about the schedule," Stacy said as she grabbed Lizzie's hand and started leading her away.

Bianca gave Mark her best puppy-dog eyes. "Is there nothing I can say to convince you to stay up a little longer?"

"I wish there were, but if I don't leave now, I'll fall asleep right here at the table."

"I suppose it cannot be helped." She sighed. "If you change your mind, you can always call my room."

"You're staying here?" Tessa asked.

Bianca smiled and kept her eyes on Mark as she said, "Room six twenty-three."

The group exited the bar together, and Lizzie, Adriene, and Stacy grabbed the first elevator down.

Before the doors could close, Bianca put out a hand to keep them open and said to Stacy, "Still no word from Billy?"

Stacy made a show of checking her phone. "Sorry, no."

"Tell him his loss."

"I'm sure he'll feel the same."

Bianca removed her hand, and the elevator left. When the next one arrived, the rest of them entered the car.

They reached Bianca's floor first. Mark held the door open while she hugged Tessa, Peter, and Hattie, and kissed their cheeks.

Peter took over door duties when she said her goodbyes to Mark. For him, the kisses were more corner of the mouth than cheek. Before she pulled away, she whispered in his ear, "Remember, six twenty-three."

"How could I forget?"

As soon as the doors closed, Tessa, Peter, and Hattie stifled laughs.

"Not a word out of any of you," Mark said.

"Can I just ask a question?" Peter said.

"No."

"Please?"

Mark grimaced. "If you must."

"Have you ever had to compete with yourself for a woman?"

"If you were paying attention, *she* was coming on to *me*, not the other way around. So I was not competing with anyone."

"I wonder what would have happened if you'd given in," Tessa said. "When the two of you were alone, do you think she'd realized that you and Billy are—"

The elevator dinged, and the doors opened.

"And with that, I will be taking no further questions," Mark said and marched out.

27

AT THE SAME TIME THE EVENING WAS WIND-
ing down at the rooftop bar in Venice, Rick La Rose was
heading home to his Paris apartment thinking of calling it
an early night, too, when his phone rang.

"Hello," he answered.

"Scramble," a female voice said.

"Scramble," Rick said as he initiated the extra layer of
security that would make their call impossible to decipher.
"Who is this?"

"Danielle Verde."

Rick became instantly alert. Not only was Danielle a
well-respected senior agent, she'd been part of the Golden
Hour mission.

"I'm listening," he said.

"Someone tried to kidnap me . . . or kill me. I'm not sure
which."

"When?"

"Forty-five minutes ago."

"You're somewhere safe now?"

"For the moment."

"Tell me what happened."

"Car bomb."

"Your car?"

"Yes."

"That sounds more like they were trying to kill you than kidnap?"

"Not the exploding type of bomb. This one released some kind of gas. Lucky for me, I use an app to remotely start my vehicle, so I wasn't inside as it fogged up."

"That was a smart move."

"I always do it now. I've seen too many people die in the driver's seat."

"Does whoever did this know they didn't get you?"

"They do. Maybe thirty seconds after the gas went off, four men approached the vehicle and broke in. When they realized I wasn't inside, they started looking around to see if I was nearby."

"They didn't spot you?"

"I was watching from a window across the street and ducked out of sight. When I looked back, they were gone."

"You didn't happen to get photos of them, did you?"

"I'm a trained CIA agent. What do you think?"

"Any idea who they were?" Rick thought he knew the answer, but wanted to make sure she wasn't involved in something else that could explain what happened.

"Specifically, no idea. But I'm not stupid. I know someone is coming after all of us who were part of Golden Hour. Unless I'm wrong about that."

"You're not."

"Shit. Please tell me Director Cabot is doing something about this."

"He is."

"Not fast enough, if you ask me."

"He's sent a specialist to root out who's behind this."

"Is this specialist any good?"

"Lance wouldn't send someone he didn't trust to handle the job."

"If Lance says he's okay, then I guess he is," she said and then fell quiet for a moment. "I may have some information that can help him."

"Tell me. I'll pass it on."

"No way. I'm not saying anything over the telephone."

"The line is secure."

"That may be, but it's clear that the people doing this have inside information. That means the Agency has a mole."

"You're not wrong. Lance is looking into that, too."

"Until he's plugged the leak, the only way I'll pass on what I know is in person."

"Okay. I'll contact the specialist and see if I can set up a meeting between the two of you."

"Make it quick, or I'll disappear."

Teddy had been back in Mark Weldon's suite for ten minutes when Rick La Rose called.

"Another one of our agents was just targeted," Rick said.

"Dead?"

"No, she got away. But she says she has information that could help your investigation."

"What is it?"

"I asked, but she said she'll only pass it on in person. She's worried about the mole."

"Rightfully," Teddy said.

"I can't argue with that."

"Has Lance made any progress on that front?"

"If he has, he hasn't told me."

"So, standard Lance behavior."

"You said it, not me."

"Who's the agent?" Teddy asked.

"Danielle Verde."

Teddy's memory of Danielle was that she was a tough-as-nails operative, who did her job well.

"I'll meet with her," Teddy said.

"I was hoping you'd say that. She's currently in Romania and needs to be careful about moving around. I would think she could be in Italy by tomorrow."

"Not Italy, Budapest. I'll be there in the morning."

"That should be even easier."

"Have her leave word with Billy Barnett. He'll be staying at the Ritz-Carlton."

"I'll contact Danielle and send her your way," Rick said and hung up.

From the hotel hallway came the sounds of someone pounding on a door. Not to Mark's suite, but somewhere close by.

After a moment, a stern male voice began yelling, "Mr. Barnett! Open this door right now!"

Teddy headed to the door of his room, ready to give whoever it was a piece of his mind.

"Bianca, I know you're in there!"

Teddy stopped in his tracks. The voice was that of Bianca's ex-husband, Eduardo. Teddy went into his bedroom, where he used his cell phone to call Bianca's room.

"Pronto," she answered.

Making the appropriate adjustments to his voice, Teddy said, "Bianca, it's Billy Barnett."

"Billy! I was hoping you'd call. Are you in your room now? I can be there in minutes."

"I'm afraid I won't be coming back to the hotel. Something's come up, and I've had to go out of town. But you're probably going to want to come up to my room anyway."

"If you are not there, why would I go?"

"I received a call from Mark Weldon. Apparently, Eduardo is outside my door, demanding you come out and talk to him."

"Oddio! I am so sorry. I will take care of the problem."

"Thank you, Bianca. I appreciate it."

"Do not worry about a thing. And, Billy?"

"Yes?"

"The next time you are coming to Italy, be sure to let me know. I'll make sure you see all the sights."

"I'll do that."

Three minutes later, Bianca's voice boomed down the hallway, drowning out her ex's pounding. "Eduardo!" The rest was spoken in rapid-fire Italian, of which no sane person would want to be the recipient.

Soon, the hallway fell blessedly silent.

28

THE NEXT MORNING, THE *STORM'S EYE* GROUP flew to Budapest, arriving a few minutes before 9:30 a.m. From there, a trio of SUVs whisked them through the Pest side of the city to the Ritz-Carlton, near the Danube River.

Though a new Strategic Services detail waited for them outside the hotel, there were no screaming fans to hold off.

"Good job keeping our arrival a secret this time," Peter said to Lizzie.

"I leaked to a few fan sites that we were staying at the Hotel Clark on the other side of the river," she said.

"Sneaky!"

"All part of the job."

As the group entered the hotel lobby, Mark pulled Stacy aside.

"Can you check with the front desk and see if a message has come in for Billy?" he whispered.

"On it," she said.

He'd awoken that morning to a text from Rick awaiting him, confirming that Danielle Verde was on her way to Budapest. She would be traveling under the name of Monique Ortega and should be in the city before he arrived. She'd been told to leave a note for Billy Barnett at the hotel with details on how to contact her.

When Stacy returned, she said, "Sorry, nothing. But I told the desk to call me if something arrives."

"Thanks," he said. "I need one more favor."

He handed her a credit card.

"Is this a reward for having done a great job?" she asked.

"Did you miss the part where I said 'one more favor'?"

"If you give me a reward, I'll be extra attentive, and that would be a kind of favor, wouldn't it?"

"How about this? I promise to buy you a nice memento while we're here."

"My choice?"

"Within reason."

"What do you consider within reason?"

"Three hundred dollars or less."

"Make it five and you have a deal."

"You realize you're trying to extort me to make you do your job."

"If you're asking for a favor, I assume it has nothing to do with the movie or Centurion Pictures. Or am I wrong about that?"

"Fine. Five hundred."

She held out her hand and they shook.

"What's the favor?" she asked.

"Get a room under the name Monique Ortega and tell them she'll be picking up the key later."

Stacy raised an eyebrow. "Why, Mark, is there a girl-friend I don't know about?"

"There is not. And if you want that memento, you won't pursue the subject."

"One room for Monique Ortega coming right up."

Braun glanced up as Jillian entered his office, and barked, "What?"

"I-I-I have something to show you."

"I'm very busy."

"Oh, um, okay. M-M-Mr. Lawrence thought you'd want to see it. But I can come back."

As she turned to the door, Braun let out a resigned sigh and said, "Make it quick."

"Yes, sir." She hurried over to his desk. "H-h-have you heard of the filmmaker Regina Gideon?"

"No. Should I have?"

"Not necessarily. She's made a few indie films and does a lot of commercial work. Sh-she's even been contracted to direct her first studio feature in a few months."

"Good for her. Tell me why should I care, or get out."

Jillian hesitantly laid a photo on his desk. It was a head and shoulders shot of an unremarkable middle-aged man.

"*This* is Regina Gideon?"

"No, sir. This is Roland Turner. He's the script supervisor Ms. Gideon works with on all her projects."

"Ms. Courtois, I don't have time for games. If there's a point to all this, I suggest you get to it!"

She set down a photo of a film set, with several people in it, and tapped on a man half in shadow.

Braun studied the image. There was something about the man that tickled his memory, but he couldn't put his finger on it.

Before he could say as much, Jillian laid down a third photo. He immediately recognized it as the old security cam image of Teddy Fay.

Braun picked up the second and third photos and compared them. The silhouettes weren't exact matches, but they *were* close enough that the intervening years and a bit of plastic surgery could explain the difference.

"Turner is Teddy Fay?"

"I'm not saying that for sure," she said. "I-I'm saying there's a chance he is. I've been looking at everyone associated with the film festival, including people involved in the movies that will be shown. Regina Gideon's latest film will be there."

"And Turner worked on it," Braun said.

"Correct."

He frowned. "Hmmm. I don't know. Maybe there's some resemblance, but . . ."

"I've sifted through hundreds of people, and Turner is the first who even comes close. *And* he's in Europe right now."

That piqued Braun's interest. "Is he, now?"

She nodded. "Gideon is shooting a commercial in Budapest this evening, and she's brought key members of her crew with her, including Turner. They're all registered as attendees at the festival, too. I assume they'll be heading to Berlin after. There's also this."

She laid down a printout of the photo Dieter's team had taken in Venice.

"There's not a lot to work with in this," she said. "So I haven't been able to make a positive ID. Yet, I mean. But if you compare this to the others here . . ."

Braun took a closer look. The guy was wearing a mask and hat, so matching faces was not possible, but his size and shape were basically the same as those of Turner and the old Teddy Fay shot.

"Well, damn," Braun said. "You're right. He's worth checking out."

She wanted to sigh in relief but held it back. "At Mr. Lawrence's suggestion, I've been in touch with a private investigator in California who's ready to look into his life there once I give him the word."

"Tell him to get to work."

"I will," she said.

After she left, he picked up his phone. If it really was Fay, he wanted someone in place to act quickly.

"Mr. Braun," Dieter answered. "What can I do for you?"

———

By five p.m., Mark and the others were back at the Ritz.

"Am I the only one who needs a nap?" Adriene asked, as they crossed the lobby toward the elevators.

"We warned you these things could be a grind," Mark said.

"You did, and you weren't kidding."

"Welcome to the life of a star," Hattie teased.

"I'm not complaining," Adriene said. "Just tired."

Their day had been filled with a series of videotaped

interviews, as well as an appearance by Tessa, Adriene, and Mark on a Hungarian podcast focused on pop culture.

Stacy had hurried ahead to the reception desk when they'd arrived and now rejoined the group. She caught Mark's eye and shook her head. Still no message from Danielle.

Mark hadn't been concerned earlier, but he was starting to feel that way now. As soon as he was alone in his room, he called Rick.

"No sign of Danielle yet," he said.

"Hold on. Let me see if I can contact her." When Rick came back on the line, he said, "I tried several times, but no answer. I don't like this."

"Neither do I."

"I'll keep trying. If she shows up, let me know right away."

A shower and some time spent with his makeup kit turned Teddy from Mark Weldon back into Billy Barnett.

Tonight, Tessa would be filming a commercial for House Dione, a heavy hitter in the fashion industry, for which she was a brand ambassador.

The commercial was being directed by Regina Gideon, an up-and-coming talent who had signed on to direct a film for Centurion Pictures later that year. Since Ben was still in Los Angeles, Billy and Peter would be attending the shoot to touch base with her and watch her in action.

There was a knock on his door as he was pulling on his jacket.

"It's me," Peter called from the corridor.

Teddy exited his room. "Where's Tessa?"

"The production company picked her up thirty minutes ago. I'm guessing she's in hair and makeup by now."

"Lead on."

Another production assistant from the shoot was waiting for them in the lobby.

"Mr. Barrington, Mr. Barnett, I drive for you," he said, taking time to pronounce the English words. "Come."

"One moment," Billy said. He went over to the reception desk.

"May I help you?" a woman manning the desk asked.

"I'm Billy Barnett." He gave her his suite number. "I'm heading out for a shoot and—"

Her eyes lit up. "The commercial with Tessa Tweed and Mari Chen?"

"That's the one."

Mari Chen was a half-Japanese, half-Chinese Australian pop singer who had rocketed to stardom thanks to a talent for writing powerful songs with catchy tunes, which she sang in multiple languages. She was also a House Dione brand ambassador.

"I wanted to go watch," the woman said, "but no one would trade shifts with me."

"If you'd like, I can get Tessa's autograph for you."

Her mouth opened in surprise. "Really?"

"It would be my pleasure."

"Thank you. Could you maybe get Mari's, too?" She lowered her voice to a whisper. "She is my favorite singer."

"No promises, but I'll see what I can do. May I ask a favor of you, too?"

"Of course."

"I'm expecting a woman named Monique Ortega. You're holding a room in her name. When she asks for me, can you please give her the room key and tell her I'll be back later?"

She beamed. "I am most happy to do this for you."

He thanked her and rejoined Peter and the PA.

"Sorry about that," he said. "I'm ready to go now."

"This way," the PA said, then led them out of the hotel.

29

DANIELLE VERDE DITCHED HER STOLEN CAR
five blocks from the Ritz-Carlton Hotel.

There had been several times in the last twenty hours when she'd thought she wouldn't even get it out of Romania, let alone all the way to Budapest. That she had seemed like a miracle.

After her communication with Rick La Rose the previous evening, she'd grabbed a taxi and headed for the airport.

On the drive, she'd purchased a ticket for a flight to Budapest leaving in two hours, thinking she was in the clear.

Everything fell apart after she was in the airport security line. As she and the others plodded forward, she spotted one of the men who'd gassed her car about to go through one of the X-ray machines.

She immediately left the line and headed for the exit. She was almost to the door when someone behind her yelled her name. She sprinted outside and jumped into a taxi that had just dislodged its passengers.

She had the cabbie drop her off in a quiet neighborhood on the outskirts of Bucharest, where she stole the first in the series of vehicles that brought her to Budapest.

She slipped into the Ritz and made her way to the reception desk.

"May I help you?" a female clerk asked.

"I'm looking for one of your guests. Billy Barnett."

"I'm sorry. Mr. Barnett stepped out maybe twenty minutes ago."

"I see. Is it possible to leave him a message?"

"Of course." The clerk hesitated a moment. "Are you Monique Ortega?"

Decades of undercover work kept Danielle from showing the surprise she felt. This was the first time she'd used the alias, and as far as she was aware, the only other people who knew it were Rick, Lance's specialist, and the specialist's go-between she was supposed to contact.

Deciding to take a chance, she said, "I am."

"One moment."

The clerk stepped away for a moment and returned with a small paper sleeve.

"Mr. Barnett wanted me to give you the key card to your room. I do need to see an ID, of course."

"Sure."

Danielle showed the clerk a fake Canadian passport.

"Thank you." The clerk handed her the sleeve. "You're in room three twenty-one. Mr. Barnett said that he would contact you when he returns from the shoot."

"Shoot?" Danielle asked.

Looking excited, the woman said, "Yes. For a commercial staring Tessa Tweed and Mari Chen."

Danielle almost laughed in relief. She had taken "shoot" to mean something entirely different.

"Did Mr. Barnett mention how long he might be?"

"He did not. But if you are interested, you can go watch it yourself. It's by the river. Only a ten-minute walk away."

"Thank you."

She'd been on the run since yesterday. What she really wanted was a hot shower and some sleep. Maybe she could sneak in a short nap before Barnett returned.

Three men entered the lobby from outside as she walked to the elevators. Two of them she recognized immediately. One had been the man she'd seen at the Bucharest airport. The other was Dieter Wenz, a mercenary who'd been involved in many questionable activities over the years but had always somehow evaded blame.

All thoughts of a shower and sleep disappeared. Before the men looked her way, she slipped into the elevator waiting area, out of sight, then hurried into the elevator car when it arrived.

Once in her room, she went straight to the sink and splashed water on her face. After a few deep breaths, her heart rate began to slow, and she was able to think and not just react.

How could Dieter and his companions be here? She was positive no one had followed her out of Romania. And the only people who knew the Ritz was her destination were Rick La Rose, Lance's specialist, and this Billy Barnett person. While she didn't know the latter two, she was sure Lance wouldn't have trusted just anyone on this mission.

That left two possibilities. The first, that Dieter was here for a reason completely unrelated to her. The second and more likely, he was here because Lance's specialist was in the area.

Barnett would need to know about this right away so that he could warn Lance's man.

She found a piece of paper and wrote down what she'd seen and what she knew about Dieter. She then stuffed the paper into a hotel envelope.

She reached for the room phone but stopped herself before lifting it from the cradle. Her first instinct had been to find out which room Billy Barnett was staying in and slip the envelope under his door.

But what if Dieter knew about Barnett, too, and broke into the room? The last thing she needed was for him to find the note.

The clerk had told her Barnett was at a film shoot by the river. The smart play would be to go there and warn him in person.

She left the note on a nightstand, in case she was caught, then headed out.

30

"HOLD CAMERA," REGINA GIDEON SAID.

She jumped out of her chair in front of the monitors—known as the video village—and jogged out to where Tessa and Mari Chen stood on the gravel walkway that edged the Danube River, next to the picturesque Széchenyi Chain Bridge.

This drew new shouts from the fans behind the crowd-control barriers who had descended upon the area in droves when word got out that the shoot featured the two international stars.

Billy and Peter were standing behind Regina's now empty chair, Peter shifting back and forth from foot to foot.

"Are you okay?" Billy asked.

"What do you mean?" Peter said.

"You seem a little on edge."

"Me? No. I'm fine."

Billy put a hand on Peter's shoulder to stop him from rocking. "Are you sure about that?"

Peter looked surprised. "How long have I been doing that?"

"Since a few minutes after we arrived."

"Ugh. Sorry. It feels weird to be on a set and not doing anything." He chuckled. "But I guess you know all about that."

"Excuse me?"

"Well, you *are* a producer. All you do is stand around."

"I may be standing around, but my mind is running a thousand miles an hour, wondering what crazy thing you'll be coming up with next that I'll have to figure out."

"It's called cinematic vision, not crazy."

Billy patted him on the arm. "Keep telling yourself that."

The discussion on the walkway ended, and Regina returned to her chair.

"Roland?" she said.

A middle-aged man who'd been introduced as the script supervisor stepped over to Regina.

"I'm flipping shots two-c and two-d," she said.

Roland made a note on his tablet computer, said, "Got it," and moved back out of the way.

Regina gave a nod to the assistant director, who then raised her bullhorn and said, "Settle, everyone. We're going again."

At the crowd-control barriers, locally hired assistants used their bullhorns to tell the crowds to be quiet.

"How are we looking?" Regina asked her cameraman.

"Camera ready," he replied.

"Roll camera."

"Rolling."

"And action!"

———————

Danielle slipped out of the hotel without seeing Dieter or his men, and headed to the river. Her fear of not being able to find the filming location turned out to be a nonissue. As soon as she reached the Danube, the shoot's bright production lights acted like a neon sign, pointing the way.

A large mob of onlookers stood by the barriers meant to keep them from swarming the film site, and just beyond the barriers several police officers watched over everything.

She cursed to herself.

She had assumed the shoot would draw some attention, but she hadn't anticipated as many people as this.

Turning around and going back to the hotel wasn't an option, however. She needed to talk to Barnett now so that he could pass on the warning.

She slipped into the crowd and began squeezing through the gaps, hoping that she could convince one of the officers to let Barnett know she was there.

———————

Upon arriving at the Ritz-Carlton, Dieter Wenz found a housephone and asked the operator to be connected to Roland Turner's room.

The phone rang until the hotel answering system picked up. Dieter set the receiver back in the cradle. His was a message that needed to be delivered in person.

He approached the reception desk.

"How may I help you?" the man behind the counter asked.

"I'm supposed to meet one of your guests," Dieter said. "Roland Turner. I tried calling his room, but there was no answer."

"Would you like me to try for you?"

"That won't be necessary. He's here to film a commercial, and I'm wondering if he might have mentioned when he'll be back."

The man checked his computer and shook his head. "I'm sorry, sir. He did not leave a message to that effect."

"Thank you anyway."

As Dieter was turning to leave, one of the clerk's female colleagues said, "Are you talking about the shoot with Tessa Tweed and Mari Chen?"

"I believe so," Dieter said. He had no idea if the women she'd mentioned were in the commercial or not, but how many shoots could be happening that evening?

"They're filming by the river." She pulled out her phone and showed him a few photos posted to Instagram from the production site.

"Is this far?"

She shook her head. "Just walk down to the river and you'll see it."

"Thank you. You've been most helpful."

Dieter rejoined Rolf and Andreas, the two men he'd brought with him.

"Any luck?" Andreas asked.

"Not here, but I know where he is." He gave Andreas a

long look. "If we get this done, maybe we can keep your ass out of the fire."

Andreas had overseen the team in Romania who'd failed to take out Danielle Verde. Dieter had pulled him in to help protect him from Braun's wrath.

"You're not going to let it drop, are you? I told you we did everything right."

"If that were true," Rolf said, "then wouldn't you have taken care of Verde already?"

"Like you would have done any better."

"Both of you cool it," Dieter said. "We need to focus on Turner."

"So where is he?" Rolf asked.

"Not far."

They found the shoot and joined the fans by one of the crowd-control barriers. It was farther from the action than Dieter had hoped to be, but with all the fans, the police, and the people working on the shoot, it wasn't like he and his men could do much more than observe anyway.

They needed Turner alone so they could establish whether he was Teddy Fay or not. If the answer was yes, they'd terminate him and leave the boss's calling card.

Dieter pulled out a pair of pocket-size binoculars and scanned the film crew.

For a moment, he thought he spotted Turner standing with a younger man near a table loaded down by several monitors. The man was around the right age and approximately the right height. But when he turned, Dieter saw his face and realized he wasn't Turner.

Dieter scanned the rest of the crew, then smiled when

he spotted Turner, sitting in a chair not too far from the monitors.

All Dieter needed to do now was keep an eye on him, then he and his colleagues could follow him back to the hotel and have a private conversation in the men's room. All very nice and neat.

"Oh, shit," Andreas said.

Dieter lowered the binoculars and saw that Andreas was staring at someone in the crowd, off to the right.

"What?" Dieter asked.

"I . . . I think that's Danielle Verde."

"Verde? Here?"

"Yeah." Andreas pointed. "The woman with the brown and gray hair tied in a ponytail. Gray sweater."

She was about twenty feet away and seemed to be trying to move to the front of the crowd.

"Are you sure?" Rolf asked.

"One hundred percent."

31

DANIELLE WAS A FEW PEOPLE FROM THE
front when someone in the crowd behind her shouted, "Hey,
what the hell do you think you're doing?"

This was joined by a chorus of other displeased voices,
then a quick, muffled "Sorry."

Only the apology wasn't in Hungarian but in German.

She glanced over her shoulder and spotted Dieter and
his colleagues wending their way through the crowd, their
eyes locked on her.

With renewed urgency, she slipped through another
gap, then said, "Excuse me," to a couple standing in her way.

She squeezed between them, then grabbed a man at the
barrier and yanked him out of her way.

"Hey!" he barked. "That's my place!"

She grabbed the top of the barrier and vaulted over it.

"Stop!" a police officer yelled. "You must go back!"

He was close, but not close enough to grab her before she began sprinting toward the film crew.

Tessa and Mari strode arm in arm down the pathway like best friends out for a night on the town, the bridge lit by warm orange lights in the background.

"And cut!" Regina shouted.

"Go again?" the AD asked.

Regina nodded. "It was good, but I want them to try one more thing."

As she headed over to Tessa and Mari, the AD raised his bullhorn and said, "Reset. Going again."

Two makeup artists hurried over to Tessa and Mari and touched them up as Regina talked to the talent.

"I like her," Billy said, referring to Regina. "She knows what she wants."

"She does," Peter said. "I can't wait to see what she creates for Centurion."

Billy's phone vibrated with a text from Stacy.

Just checked with reception. Your friend arrived about twenty minutes ago.

He felt a rush of relief. He hadn't wanted to admit it, but he'd begun to wonder if Danielle had become another Golden Hour casualty.

He sent Stacy a thank-you and slipped his phone back in his pocket just as Regina returned.

"Let's go," she said.

The AD quieted the set.

"Action!" Regina called.

Tessa and Mari began walking again, but before they had gone more than a half dozen steps, a clamor broke out from the crowd of fans.

———————

"Fuck!" Dieter spat as Verde leaped over the barrier.

Around him, the people began shouting encouragement to Verde, as if she was doing what they all wished they'd done.

"Get me a clear shot," he said to Rolf and Andreas.

Verde had not only seen him, but there had been recognition in her eyes. He could not let her tell anyone who he was.

Without a word, his colleagues began pushing bodies out of the way. When they reached the barrier, they stood to either side of Dieter, blocking the crowd from seeing him slip his gun out of his holster and attach a silencer.

It was not going to be an easy shot. If he raised the pistol so he could look down the barrel, everyone around them would see it. And if he crouched down, the people behind him would know something was up.

He took a breath, aimed from his hip as best he could, and pulled the trigger.

The spit of the silencer was drowned out by the noise of the crowd. A beat later, their shouts turned into gasps as Verde was knocked to the ground.

Dieter wanted to take a second shot to make sure the woman was dead, but the police officers running toward her moved in the way.

He couldn't risk staying there a moment longer. "Rendezvous at the train station," he whispered, then he and his colleagues disappeared into the crowd in separate directions.

Billy turned toward the noise coming from the fans. A woman was running toward the shoot with several police officers in pursuit.

He assumed it was a fan who was trying to get to Tessa and Mari, but then he saw her face. She looked terrified, not excited.

A muzzle flashed from the other side of the barrier, and the woman flew forward and smashed onto the gravel walkway.

"Gun!" Billy yelled. "Everybody, down!"

While the crew scrambled for cover, Billy ran over to Tessa and Mari. Their view of the woman had been blocked by the camera and monitors, so they looked confused instead of scared.

"Down!" he yelled.

Tessa grabbed Mari's hand and pulled her onto the ground. When Billy reached them, he positioned himself between them and the shooter. That's when he realized that Peter had followed him.

"I told you to get down!" he said.

"Ben would never forgive me if I left Tessa in harm's way."

"Do you think Hattie would be happy if I let *you* get shot?"

"But I wasn't, so everything's fine."

"Not the point! But never mind. Get down next to them!"

To Billy's relief, Peter did just that.

Billy adjusted his position so he could look in the direction from which the shot had come. While he couldn't see the woman from where he was, he could see that the fans had scattered.

There didn't appear to have been any additional gunshots, though, which meant to him that either the shooter had been caught or had fled.

"Stay here until you get the all clear," he said, then hurried over to where the woman lay, surrounded by three cops.

Someone had rolled her onto her back, and Billy realized she was Danielle Verde. Her sweater was soaked in blood, and her breaths were ragged and uneven.

One of the officers noticed him and said something to him in Hungarian, which Billy assumed was "Get back."

"I know her," Billy said as he knelt next to Danielle.

A younger cop had a hand covering Danielle's wound, but Billy could see he wasn't pressing hard enough. He put his hand on top of the cop's hand and pressed down.

"Like that," he said.

The cop nodded.

"You . . . speak English," Danielle said, her voice so weak that Billy almost didn't hear it.

"Shh," he said. "Don't waste energy."

"I'm looking . . . for someone. Billy Ba . . ." She seemed to fade away for a moment.

"Barnett? That's me."

Her eyes flared with surprise. "You're Billy?"

When he nodded, she closed her eyes in relief.

In the distance, the sound of sirens pierced the night. One of the officers still on his feet ran toward the barrier.

Billy gave Danielle a little shake. "Hey, stay with me. Help's coming."

Instead of saying anything, she moved a hand toward one of her pockets, but she was having a hard time slipping it inside.

"Help . . . me," she whispered.

Billy glanced at the two remaining officers. The one pressing on Danielle's wound was focused on his task, while the other was looking toward the barrier.

Careful not to draw their attention, he slipped his hand into her pocket. The only thing inside was what felt like a credit card. He eased it out, keeping it hidden in his palm, then turned his hand just enough to get a peek at it. It was a hotel key card.

When he looked back to tell her he had it, her eyes were closed again. He tried to shake her awake, but to no avail.

32

BILLY REJOINED PETER, WHO WAS BACK AT
the video village.

"Is she going to be okay?" Peter asked.

"Not sure. She's lost a lot of blood."

Peter nodded at Billy's hands. "I can see that."

Billy glanced down and saw that in addition to the key
card he still held, both his hands were bloody.

"One sec," Peter said.

He retrieved a couple of bottles of water and a handful
of napkins from the craft services table and began pouring
water over Billy's hands. It took all of the first and half of the
second bottle to wash off all the blood.

"Did they catch the shooter?" Peter asked.

"No. And I doubt they will."

"Why not?"

"They were pros."

"How do you know that?"

"Because she was here to meet me."

"Oh," Peter said, getting it now. "About the thing?"

Billy nodded, then pulled out his phone. "Excuse me."

He walked down the path and called Rick.

"Scramble," he said as soon as the station chief answered.

"Scramble," Rick said.

"Danielle Verde's been shot."

"Is she—"

"She's still alive. Or was when the EMTs took her away. I suggest getting protection to wherever they're taking her as quickly as you can. If she survives the wound, the assassin will likely make another attempt."

"I'll call you back."

Billy hung up and returned to Peter, who had been joined by Tessa and Mari. It was then that Billy noticed the crew was breaking down equipment and hauling it away.

"I take it they've canceled the shoot?" he said.

Tessa nodded. "The police shut us down for public safety. I don't think anyone felt up to continuing anyway."

"I know I didn't," Mari said, concern on her face.

"Does that mean you're heading back to the hotel?" Billy asked.

"They're bringing the van around now," Tessa said.

"Mind if I tag along?"

———

Back in his suite, Teddy changed from his suit into slacks and a black pullover, then called Stacy.

"What room is Monique staying in?" he asked.

"Three twenty-one."

"Thanks."

Before he could hang up, she said, "Hey, did you hear all those sirens earlier?"

"I did."

"Do you know what happened?"

"Ask Tessa."

"Why would I—"

"Gotta go. Bye, Stacy."

He was heading for the door when his phone rang.

"Yes?"

"I just got off the phone with Rick," Lance said. "How is Danielle?"

"She wasn't doing great when I last saw her. But you should call the hospital."

"An embassy attaché is on the way there right now."

"One of yours?"

"That's not important."

"Is he or she at least bringing some muscle to keep an eye on her?"

"Unfortunately, he has no muscle at his disposal. Rick is in contact with the local police. They should have some people there shortly."

"Shortly might be all you have."

"Which is why I'm calling you. I'm going to send the men who've been watching over you to the hospital to cover until a team from Paris arrives."

After the night they'd had, Teddy didn't like the idea of his friends being left without protection.

"I have a better idea," he said. "Leave your people at the hotel. I'll go."

"Are you expecting trouble there?"

"I'm always expecting trouble."

"All right. We'll do it your way. I'll have the attaché tell the hospital that we're sending a security specialist, so they'll be expecting you. What name will you be using?"

Teddy gave him a name from one of his sets of false IDs.

"Get there as quickly as you can," Lance said, then hung up.

As much as Teddy wanted to head straight out, he couldn't show up looking like Billy Barnett.

As quickly as possible, he changed into a more generic look, then donned a black wig and a matching beard.

He concealed his shoulder holster under a lightweight black jacket and finished off his outfit with a pair of orange-tinted glasses and a black, logo-free hat.

Satisfied, he headed out.

After making a clean escape from the scene of the shoot-ing, Dieter found a spot down the road where he could keep an eye on the chaos he'd created.

Most of the fans who'd gathered to see Tessa Tweed and Mari Chen had fled the area nearly as fast as he had. Those who hadn't were being questioned by the police.

It wasn't long before an ambulance drove up and several EMTs hurried out. Soon after, they returned with the woman on a gurney.

From their actions, it was clear she wasn't dead yet.

While it was still possible that she would die from the wound, leaving it to chance would be a mistake. There was one person he knew who could quickly find out where the ambulance was taking her. He just needed to be careful in how he framed the situation when requesting her help.

He placed the call.

"This is Jillian Courtois," Jillian said.

"It's Dieter Wenz."

"Mr. Wenz," she said, surprised. "I heard you went to Budapest. Were you able to find Turner? Is he Teddy Fay?"

"That's back burner for the moment. I need your help with something more pressing."

"But aren't—"

"Danielle Verde is here."

"Verde?" Jillian had passed on the information about the woman a few days before and moved onto Fay and the others. "But I thought she was in Romania."

"Not anymore. But keep that to yourself. I'll inform Mr. Braun."

"Okay. What is it I can help you with, then?"

"There's been an incident," he said. "She's being taken to a hospital as we speak."

"Oh my God. How serious?"

"Unclear at this point. Our client would like me to check on her. Can you figure out where she's being taken, and after she gets there, where I might find her?"

"Of course. Where was she picked up?"

Dieter filled her in as best he could without revealing too much.

"I'm on it," she said. "It might take a few minutes, though."

"Minutes are fine. An hour is too long."

"I'll text you the info."

"Thank you."

Dieter hung up, took one last look at the growing collection of police cars, then headed for the train station.

Rolf and Andreas were waiting for him when he got there.

"Any problems?" he asked.

Both men shook their heads.

"Do you think she's dead?" Andreas asked.

"She wasn't when the ambulance took her away."

"Shit," Rolf said.

"What are we going to do?" Andreas asked.

Dieter's phone vibrated. He looked at the screen and saw that Jillian had come through with the info.

He smirked. "What we do is finish the job."

33

LANCE'S ATTACHÉ MET TEDDY IN THE HOSPI-
tal lobby and escorted him to the surgical center waiting
area, where the hospital's director and head of security
waited. Danielle was in one of the operating rooms beyond
the set of double doors that were currently being guarded
by a pair of Budapest police officers.

After the attaché made the introductions, the head of
security said something in Hungarian and held out a badge.

"He says to wear that wherever you go," the attaché
said.

Teddy took it. "Can I go anywhere or does this have re-
stricted access?"

The attaché relayed the question, listened to the answer,
then said, "They would rather you not wander around too
much."

"That wasn't the question."

Lance's man said something to the two Hungarians, then motioned for Teddy to follow him.

Once they were out of earshot, he whispered, "They're not happy that you're here, but strings have been pulled, so they are cooperating. Your badge should get you through any door in the building. All I ask is that you do me a favor and don't abuse it. The last thing I need is for the ambassador to hear about this."

"Anything I do will be necessary."

"I understand, but—"

"*I* understand. No buts."

The attaché let out a breath. "Very well."

"Any update on Danielle Verde's condition?"

"No, but since she's still in surgery, I take that to mean she's still alive."

"Do you have an ETA on when the relief team is expected?"

"Last I heard they should be here by midnight."

Teddy looked at his watch. Just under three hours away. He nodded toward the two cops guarding the surgical center entrance. "Please tell me there are more cops here than just these two."

"I've been informed that these are all that could be spared."

"This is not just a made-up threat. It's very real."

"I get it. I've asked for additional help and will continue to do so, but the Hungarians don't work for us."

Teddy nodded, not liking it but understanding.

After the attaché and the men from the hospital left,

Teddy used his badge to enter the surgical center. Beyond the door was a wide hallway with six doorways running down both sides, each with a number above it.

Two nurses wearing scrubs, surgical caps, and masks exited operating suite 2 and started walking toward him. When they noticed him, they paused, confused by his lack of medical attire.

"Do either of you speak English?" he asked.

The nurse on the left said, "We both do."

"You are not supposed to be in here," the man with her said.

Teddy held up his badge. "Special permission from the director. I'm security for the gunshot victim. Do you know which room she's in?"

"Suite four," the woman said, pointing at a set of doors farther down the hall. "But you cannot go in."

"I'm not planning to. It's not a problem if I stay in here, is it?"

"Not if you do not mind repeating what you told us every time someone sees you."

He smiled good-naturedly. "That, I can handle. Can I ask another question?"

"Yes?"

"Is there a way to find out how the operation is going?"

"I can check for you." She said something in Hungarian to her colleague, then entered suite 4.

The man eyed Teddy up and down. "You are English?"

"American," Teddy said. "And so is the victim. The embassy sent me."

"Ah, I see," the man said, nodding.

Teddy gestured at the doors he'd entered through. "Is that the only way into this area?"

The nurse shook his head. "Is one more that way." He pointed at the far end of the hall. "For, um . . . fire?"

"An emergency exit."

"Yes. This."

The female nurse exited suite 4 and rejoined them. "The bullet has been removed, and the nurse told me the doctor thinks she has good chance."

"Did she mention how much longer it will be?"

"I did not ask this. But I think maybe thirty minutes to one hour."

"And where will they take her then?"

"ICU. Is on same floor as this."

"Thank you. I appreciate the information."

Five minutes after Teddy had headed up to the surgical center, Dieter and his men arrived at the hospital.

As they'd been instructed, Rolf and Andreas remained in the lobby while Dieter headed deeper into the building.

He'd infiltrated medical facilities like this before. He knew if he wore the right outfit, he could go almost any-where. He'd been a nurse and a janitor, but by far the most effective disguise was that of a doctor.

People had no problems approaching nurses or janitors to ask questions or request assistance. A preoccupied doctor, on the other hand, could go almost anywhere without being bothered.

He found a doctors' changing room one floor up. A male

doctor had just finished getting into his street clothes and was closing his locker as Dieter entered. Dieter gave him a nod and continued to the next row to avoid conversation.

As soon as the other man departed, Dieter jimmied the lock on the guy's locker. Not only did he find a doctor's coat inside, but there was also a pair of clean scrubs that would fit him and the man's hospital ID on a lanyard.

After changing, Dieter put his own clothes in an unused locker and sent Rolf a text, instructing him to retrieve them.

He then opened the text from Jillian. In addition to the hospital location, she told him which operating room Verde'd been taken to and provided a link to a hospital map.

He checked the map, memorized the directions to the surgical center, and then left the locker room, acting like the doctor he wasn't.

On the way, he passed an unoccupied nurses' station, where someone had left a tablet computer, identical to the ones he'd seen other hospital personnel carrying. He grabbed it without missing a step. If he hadn't looked the part of a doctor on a mission before, he did now.

He reached the surgical center waiting area a few minutes later and was not shocked to find two cops guarding the doorway to the operating rooms. If anything, he was surprised there weren't more.

He opened the tablet, pulled up a random chart, and looked suitably concerned as he power-walked toward the doors behind the cops.

One of the officers said something to him as he came abreast. Ignoring him, Dieter waved his badge in front of the door scanner. The lock buzzed, and as he expected, neither cop tried to stop him as he pushed the door open and walked through.

———————

At the sound of the lock buzzing, Teddy looked over at the entrance, his hand automatically slipping under his jacket to the grip of his pistol.

The door opened and a doctor took a few steps inside before noticing Teddy.

Their eyes locked, and in that brief second, Teddy knew the man was no doctor but the assassin coming back for a second shot at Danielle.

Seeming to also realize his charade was blown, the fake doctor threw his computer at Teddy like it was a Frisbee.

Teddy jerked out of the way, delaying him from yanking out his gun long enough to allow the man to fly back out the double doors.

Teddy sprinted after him and burst into the waiting room just in time to see the man disappear around a corner into a hallway.

The two cops looked confused but had barely moved from where they'd been.

Teddy pointed at the doors. "No one goes in! Understand?"

One of the cops stared blankly at him, but the other nodded.

"No one!" Teddy reiterated.

The cop nodded again.

Teddy took off in the direction the would-be assassin had gone, but when he reached the hall, there was no sign of the man. What he did see were more than a dozen ways the man could have gone.

He jammed his gun back in its holster and ran back to the cops. To the one who'd nodded before, he said, "You understand me?"

"Yes," the officer said.

"That man was not a doctor. He was here to harm the patient."

The cop's brow furrowed.

Teddy made a pistol with his fingers, pointed toward the operating room, and pretended to shoot.

"Ah, I understand."

"Call hospital security. They can try to stop him. Also"—Teddy pointed at one of the ubiquitous security cameras—"have them check their cameras. Maybe they can find out where he went or if he was alone or not."

The man looked like he only understood part of what Teddy said.

"Hospital security," Teddy said. "Go."

The man said something to his partner, then rushed off in search of a hospital phone.

34

"THANK YOU," JILLIAN SAID INTO THE PHONE,
in English. "I'll authorize the second half of your payment
to be wired immediately."

She hung up and stared at her desk.

The man she'd just talked to had been the private eye in
California who had been doing the deeper background
check on Roland Turner. Given what he'd found, there was
no way Turner could be Fay.

It was both a relief and a gut punch.

While she still didn't know for a fact what Braun had
planned for the names on his list, she had no doubt it wasn't
good. She'd finally googled Alexis Komarov, the Russian
she'd located for Braun a month ago. Less than a week later,
the passenger jet he was flying on experienced a mid-flight
explosion.

The timing was too close to be coincidental.

To think that she had all but fingered Roland Turner as Teddy Fay and had thus potentially signed his death warrant was almost too much to bear.

While she was not glad that Danielle Verde was injured, it at least kept Dieter occupied. She just needed to let him know that Turner was not Fay.

She called him and was sent straight to voicemail. "Mr. Wenz, it's Jillian Courtois. Roland Turner is not Teddy Fay. Call back and I'll give you the details."

She hung up, hoping desperately that he checked his messages.

———————

"It's a no-go," Rolf said. "There are two men in the lobby watching everyone. And where there are two—"

"—there will be more elsewhere," Dieter finished for him.

He, Rolf, and Andreas were at a café three blocks from the Ritz-Carlton. Since dealing with Verde was currently not an option, Dieter had sent Rolf to scope out the hotel. If all looked okay there, he had planned on paying Roland Turner a visit.

Now even that was off the table.

"Wait here," he said, then went outside to call Jillian, and noticed that he had a voicemail from her. Instead of listening to it, he tapped her number.

"Oh, thank God," she said. "You got my message?"

"I saw that you left one, but haven't heard it yet," he said. "Listen, can you find out what Turner's schedule will be for the next few days? That would be a big help."

"That's what my message was about."

"Turner's schedule?"

"No. About Turner. I don't think he is our guy."

"What do you mean? I thought he was."

"I had a private investigator in the States looking into him. His identity is real."

"Teddy Fay could easily create a solid legend for himself."

"Yes, of course. You're right. B-b-but the investigator found more than enough credible evidence, including a half sister, which Fay did not have."

"It could still be faked."

"It's not. Turner is not Fay."

"Well, shit, Jillian. The boss isn't going to like this."

"Oh, um, sh-sh-should *I* tell him?" she asked, sounding very much like she didn't want to do that.

"I'll do it."

"Thank you," she said. "I appreciate it."

"You owe me, though."

There was a long pause before she said, "Okay."

Braun raised his mobile to his ear as he stepped onto the balcony of his penthouse. "Dieter, my friend, tell me the good news."

"There's been a complication."

Braun's grin vanished. One of the things he hated most was a complication, and this project had already had several.

"Explain," Braun said sternly.

Dieter told him what had happened.

"Dieter, I expect you out of all my people to take care of things without any issues."

"I made the best of the situation as it was presented."

Braun usually appreciated Dieter's habit of telling things

like they were, but this time it got under his skin. "I think the words you were looking for were 'I'm sorry, it won't happy again.'"

There was a pause before Dieter said, "My apologies, Mr. Braun."

Braun silently counted to five. It would do no good to get into an argument with Dieter right now. But after this was all done, they would be having a nice, long chat.

"Back to Verde," Braun said, once he had calmed. "This is actually good news. If she was there, and Turner was there, then Turner must be Fay."

"I had thought so, too, but it turns out that's not the case."

"What do you mean?"

Dieter shared what Jillian had told him, then said, "Verde's contact has to be someone else. Someone who probably isn't even Teddy Fay."

Braun wasn't ready to let go of that possibility yet. "Any ideas who she was there for?"

"The man at the hospital who stopped me from finishing off Verde, most likely."

"Did you at least get a picture of him?"

"I wasn't exactly in a position to do so. But I'll asked Jillian to check hospital security footage. If she can get in, she should be able to pull an image of him."

"This is all very disappointing."

"I wouldn't say that."

Braun cocked his head. "Why not?"

"We were here because we thought Turner was Fay. If we hadn't come, we wouldn't have known that Verde showed up."

"I guess that's something," Braun begrudgingly admitted. "Can I assume you'll make another run at her?"

"Yes, but not right now. She's well protected, and we don't want to do something that will jeopardize the rest of the mission. I'll keep you in the loop on our next move."

"Damn right you will."

After the CIA security team relieved Teddy at midnight, he went to the hospital's security department. There, he used security cam footage to retrace the fake doctor's movements from when he walked into the hospital until he escaped through a stairwell emergency exit.

At first, it appeared the man had arrived alone. But a review of the footage from outside the doctors' locker room, where the man had changed, showed another man entering the room a few minutes after the assassin left. When the second man exited, he was holding a rolled-up bundle of clothes.

Teddy rewatched the video of the assassin's arrival and noted that the man who'd retrieved the clothes had entered the lobby a few seconds after the assassin, and in the company of a third man.

The second man received a phone call prior to going to the locker room, and another right before he and his friend left the building. Something that occurred less than a minute after the assassin had done the same.

Teddy pulled screenshots of each man's face and texted them to Rick, then finally returned to the Ritz-Carlton.

Before going to his suite, he stopped by room 321 and used Danielle's key card to enter.

Save for an envelope sitting on a nightstand, the room appeared unused, which meant the envelope had to be what Danielle had wanted him to find. He checked all the cabinets and obvious hiding spots and discovered nothing else. He took the envelope up to Mark Weldon's suite, since that's who he needed to be in the morning.

After reading Danielle's note, he understood why she'd shown up at the shoot. She had seen the same men Teddy had.

Unlike Teddy, however, she knew who two of them were. One was part of the team that had been pursuing her in Romania. She didn't know his name, but she did provide a short description that aligned with the guy who'd remained in the hospital lobby the entire time.

Her description of the second man matched her would-be assassin, and his name she did know.

Dieter Wenz.

Vesna's ex, and Felix Braun's right-hand man.

35

THE NEXT MORNING, TESSA AND MARK WERE
on the set of a morning talk show, sitting across from the
show's hosts.

The assistant director counted down from three on his
fingers, then pointed at the female host.

The woman smiled at the camera and spoke for several
seconds in Hungarian. Her male counterpart jumped in,
and they laughed at a joke neither Mark nor Tessa understood.

The two hosts continued interacting for another half
minute and then turned to Mark and Tessa.

The female host said in English, "Tessa Tweed and Mark
Weldon, thank you so much for joining us today. We are so
very pleased to have you here."

"Not as pleased as we are to be here," Tessa said.

The interview was being conducted entirely in English, the translation occurring via voice-over from a sound booth elsewhere in the studio.

For most of the allotted time, the interview went as expected, the hosts tossing out softball questions about *Storm's Eye* and Hollywood in general, and Mark and Tessa answering with witty anecdotes and behind-the-scenes stories.

Things changed near the end, when the male host said, "Tessa, I hope you don't mind, but I wanted to ask how you are doing after your ordeal last night."

"Oh," she said, caught off guard. "I'm fine. Thank you for asking."

Lizzie had told her and Mark that she requested the interview stick to *Storm's Eye*, since that was the reason they'd been booked, and had been assured by a producer that would be the case.

"For those watching who haven't heard," the man said, "last night there was a shooting in Pest, in the vicinity of a commercial that was being filmed, featuring Tessa and pop sensation Mari Chen." He turned back to Tessa. "Did you see what happened?"

"From where I was standing, I could only see people running around. I didn't even hear a gunshot and didn't know what was going on until later."

"We understand the victim had broken through the crowd barrier and was running toward you."

"I don't know if that's true or not. I never saw her."

Though the host was doing a good job hiding it, Mark could tell he was frustrated that he wasn't scoring the scoop he'd thought he would.

Trying a different tactic, he said, "Mark, did you see any-thing?"

"Sorry, no. I was at the hotel and didn't even know any-thing had happened until this morning."

"Has there been any word on how the victim is doing?" Tessa asked.

"We've been told she underwent surgery last night and has been in intensive care since," the male host said.

"I wish her a speedy recovery," Tessa said.

"Yes, we all do," the male host threw in quickly.

Before he could ask anything else, the female host cut in, "So, what projects are up next for both of you?"

When the interview ended, the male host shook hands with both Mark and Tessa and then left the studio as if he couldn't get out of there fast enough.

As soon as he was gone, his cohost said, "I apologize for my colleague. He is ambitious."

"Don't worry about it," Tessa said. "I was there, so it's understandable that the topic would come up."

"But this was not our agreement."

"No harm, no foul," Mark said.

The woman's brow furrowed. "I'm sorry?"

"I mean you shouldn't worry about it."

"Ah."

Mark's phone vibrated. He pulled it out and saw it was a call from Vesna. "Excuse me. I need to take this."

He moved to a quiet part of the stage and tapped AC-CEPT. "Good morning."

"You look good on TV."

"You watched? Aren't you supposed to be in Berlin?"

"There's this marvelous new technology called the internet. Lets you see things from around the world. Perhaps you've heard of it."

"It rings a bell."

"I thought it might," she said. "You asked me to call you."

Between his late night at the hospital and early morning appointment at the TV station, he'd only had time to shoot Vesna a text, asking her to call at this time.

"I thought you'd like to hear about my evening."

"Your evening? What did I miss?"

"Well, for one, your ex-boyfriend."

"My ex—" She stopped herself. "Dieter was there?"

"In the flesh."

He told her what had happened.

"I'll catch the first flight and be there as soon as I can," she said when he finished.

"I'd rather you stay in Berlin. I can handle things here."

"Are you sure?"

"I am a highly trained agent."

"A *retired* highly trained agent."

"Which means I'm also experienced."

"Or rusty. But if you want me to stay here, I'll stay here. However, if something happens to you, do not blame me."

"I promise. How are things there?"

"Meeting in an hour with a friend who will be helping with surveillance. We should be up and running by this afternoon."

"Reliable as always."

"I do what I can."

"And it's appreciated."

That afternoon, the press tour flew to Zürich, Switzerland, the last stop on their junket before the film festival in Berlin.

On the van ride from the airport to the Baur au Lac hotel, Teddy received a message from Kevin Cushman.

Bad news. Call me.

Kevin was a computer expert known on many online platforms as Warplord924, who had become one of Teddy's go-to sources when his particular skill set was needed. Teddy had asked him to break into BLS's computer system and locate the company's client list.

The conversation was not one to be had in front of the others in the van, so Teddy waited until he was alone in his hotel suite to ring Kevin.

The hacker answered with a mumbled, "Hmmm?"

"Are you sleeping?"

Kevin yawned. "No. Well, maybe."

"What's the bad news?"

"Hold on."

The sound of movement filled the line for several seconds, then came the crisp snap of a soda can being opened and Kevin taking a long drink.

After a smack of the lips, he said, "Okay, that's better."

"The news," Teddy prompted him.

"Right. So, this BLS place isn't fooling around. Their cybersecurity is, like, NSA level."

"If I recall, you've hacked into the NSA before."

"True. But it took me almost a week. I'm not saying

that's how long this will take, but you did say you wanted it ASAP. And I'm guessing that in this case your definition of ASAP and mine aren't going to be the same."

Teddy frowned. He'd been afraid that might be the case. "Can you give me an estimate?"

"No clue, man. I could break through in the next hour, or it might take days."

"Keep at it," Teddy said. "And let me know as soon as you get in."

"Your wish is my command."

The line went dead.

If it took days for Kevin to get Teddy the client list, more agents could die. Plus, there was the very real possibility that even after Kevin hacked in, he might not find it.

Teddy saw only one option.

He sent texts to Peter and Stacy, asking them to come to his suite.

Within a few minutes, they had both arrived and were seated in the suite's living room.

"Anyone want a drink?" Teddy asked.

Peter cocked an eyebrow. "That depends. Do we *need* a drink?"

Teddy considered it for a moment. "Stacy might."

"Do not tell me you're going to need me to cover for you again," Stacy said.

"Your intuition will serve you well in this business."

Stacy opened her phone and studied the screen. "Let's see. This afternoon you have a round of interviews at the hotel. And tonight Billy has the screening at the University of Zürich for *Desperation at Dawn*, with the Q and A after."

Desperation at Dawn was the film that won Peter and Billy a best picture Oscar.

Stacy scrolled up. "Tomorrow, TV interviews in the morning for Mark, a lunch thing, also Mark, and a charity dinner in the evening for Billy." She looked back at Teddy. "Which event are you going to miss?"

Teddy walked over and handed her a glass of wine. "Have a drink."

"Oh, no."

"Trust me."

She took a drink.

"I'm going to miss all of them."

She blinked, then took another drink. "Why?"

"I need to go to Berlin," he said.

"When?"

"Right away."

"But—"

"Don't worry," Peter cut in. "Do what you have to do. We can cover everything."

"Lizzie's going to be *pissed*," Stacy said.

"Which is why I have you," Teddy said.

"Gee, thanks."

"Whatever you're doing, be careful," Peter said to Teddy. "I don't want to have to recast your part in *The Scapegoat*."

"Or find a new producer," Stacy threw in.

Peter shrugged. "Meh. Billy's replaceable. We'll just promote you."

Stacy's eyes lit up.

Teddy shot her a look. "Don't you get any ideas."

"*Moi?*"

36

TEDDY ARRIVED IN BERLIN DISGUISED AS AN unassuming, gray-haired retiree. From the airport, he took the S-Bahn into the city, then the U-Bahn to Potsdamer Platz. By the time he'd exited the station at street level, the sun had started to set.

He sent a text.

I'm here

Less than a minute later, Vesna appeared from around the corner of a building, carrying two cups of coffee.

When she reached him, she looked him up and down and said, "That is not a flattering look for you."

"I feel as if I should take offense, but since that's what I was going for, thank you for the compliment."

"You are welcome."

"Is one of those for me?" he asked, eyeing the coffee.

She lifted the cups. "Caffe latte or Americano?"

"Americano, if you don't mind."

She handed him one of the cups. "Has your hacker friend had any luck yet?"

Teddy checked his email and shook his head. "Still nothing."

"Good. That means we finally get to do something fun."

"We do."

Vesna led him on a circuitous route to the rear entrance of a mixed-use building, several blocks away, then up the service elevator to an apartment on the seventh floor.

"Just so you know," Vesna said. "My friend can be a little prickly."

"As long as he knows what he's doing," Teddy said.

"That, he does."

She knocked three times, paused, then knocked twice more.

The dead bolt clicked and the door swung open, revealing a wiry man with thin brown hair. He gave Vesna a nod, then walked back into the apartment without a word.

"I see what you mean," Teddy said.

He and Vesna entered.

"Is there somewhere I can stow this?" Teddy asked, tapping the handle of his suitcase.

"Since you're paying the bills," Vesna said, "I am giving you the master bedroom, at the end of the hall. You are welcome."

"Your generosity knows no bounds."

"It is one of my best traits, don't you think?"

Teddy put his bag away and returned to the living room.

Vesna was standing near the window where three chairs and a portable table had been set up. The man who'd answered the door was in the chair next to the table, working on a laptop. On the floor around him were several other electronic devices.

Teddy walked over and looked at the twelve-story, modernist building on the other side of the street. It was the reason this apartment was chosen. Occupying its top three floors was the headquarters for Braun Logistics and Security.

"This is Hans," Vesna said, gesturing to the seated man.

"Hello, Hans," Teddy said. "You can call me John."

Hans made no sign that he'd heard anything.

"Hans," Vesna barked.

He jumped and looked at her. *"Ja?"*

"Are you listening?"

"Ja, ja. He is John. I am Hans." He turned back to the computer.

"I swear he's good at his job," Vesna said to Teddy.

"Which is all I care about," Teddy said.

"Hans, can you give us a status report, please."

"I need a moment," Hans said. When he finished what he was doing, he swiveled around to face them. To Teddy, he said, "You are the boss?"

"I am."

Hans gave Teddy the same up-and-down look Vesna had given him when she'd met him. "You do not look like a boss."

"I didn't realize there was a type."

Hans frowned in thought. "Maybe it is good you do not look like one. Can fool many people."

"Hans," Vesna said. "Status report?"

Hans pressed the laptop's space bar, and the screen filled with a four-by-three grid of video images.

He pointed at the top and middle rows. "These are feeds from every side of the building." The feeds were all wide shots from cameras hidden around the perimeter. He then gestured at the bottom row. "Front entrance, parking garage entrance, loading dock, and rear entrance. The last is next to the loading dock."

"No luck getting anything inside the building?"

Hans scoffed, tapped the space bar, and a new set of feeds appeared. This time there were two rows of four. The top row were all feeds from inside the parking garage, while the bottom was split between feeds from the building's main lobby and from inside three stairwells.

"Ground floor on the stairwells?" Teddy asked.

Hans nodded.

"Drones?"

The man pointed up. "I have five on the roof ready to go, when needed."

"Any sign of our people of interest?" Vesna said.

"No sign of Wenz. But Braun left thirty minutes ago."

"Driving himself or chauffeured?" Teddy asked.

"Chauffeured. Black Mercedes-Maybach. I have the license number. When it returns, I'll put a tracking bug on it."

"Only if you can get close enough without drawing attention."

Hans's face screwed up as if the question was ridiculous. "*I* won't be doing it personally."

He picked up a hard-plastic box, undid the latch, opened

STUART WOODS' GOLDEN HOUR

the top, and removed a palm-sized drone. "This will do it for me."

"How does it carry the bug and put it in place?"

"The drone *is* the bug," Hans said. "I fly it under the car and attach it somewhere it won't be seen."

"Huh. I wouldn't mind getting ahold of a few of those. Who makes them?"

"I do."

"Do you take orders?"

"I have an online catalog. I'll send you the link."

"Please do."

"Have you been able to get the blueprints for the building?" Vesna asked.

Hans brought up pdfs of the blueprints. There was a page for each floor, plus several detailed drawings of specific areas.

"Can you show us the BLS floors?" Teddy said.

Hans did so, starting with the tenth floor.

On the top floor was a large office labeled PRESIDENT/CEO. That would be Braun's office.

"Forward that to me, please," Vesna said.

Hans clicked several buttons, then Vesna's phone vibrated. She checked her screen, then forwarded a copy to Teddy.

They spent several minutes studying the camera feeds to familiarize themselves with the building.

"I've seen enough for now," Teddy said. "Why don't we get out of Hans's hair."

Vesna nodded, then said to Hans, "Keep us updated on Braun's movements."

"Sure, sure."

"And let us know if Dieter shows up," Teddy threw in.

Hans waved a hand in the air, dismissing them.

Teddy and Vesna left the apartment and took a stroll around the BLS building, wanting to get a firsthand look at it.

When they finished, Vesna took Teddy to a quiet café, where they studied the blueprints and talked through options as they ate dinner. By the time their plates had been removed, they had a plan for how to sneak into BLS's office, where they hoped to find out which client had ordered the vendetta on the Golden Hour team.

"Still one big question, though," Vesna said.

"Security system," Teddy said.

She nodded.

The blueprints contained a notation that BLS had its own system installed, followed by a fourteen-character alphanumeric sequence and nothing else.

Teddy pointed at the characters. "You're sure this doesn't ring any bells?"

She studied it for a moment, then shook her head. "Sorry. Maybe your friends at the Agency will know."

Teddy grimaced. "I need to think about that."

"Ah, right. The mole."

He nodded. While Lance's people might know what the sequence meant, asking them could alert whoever had been leaking information about Golden Hour. Teddy couldn't risk that.

He did know someone else he could ask, however.

"We've got a big day tomorrow," he said. "Let's go back and get some rest."

"You don't have to tell me twice."

They returned to the flat, and once Teddy was in his bedroom, he called Kevin.

"Dude," Kevin answered. "I told you it might take several days."

"I take that to mean no joy yet?"

"None whatsoever."

"Unfortunate, but that's not why I'm calling." He explained the issue with the security system, then read off the character string.

"Oh, yeah," Kevin said. "That's the system identifier."

"Does that mean you know what type of system it is?"

"Yeah."

Teddy waited, but Kevin remained silent.

"Care to share?" Teddy said.

"It's trouble."

"Is that a brand name?"

"Ha. You're funny. It's a modular system made by a Finnish company with a name that has too many vowels for me to pronounce."

"So, why is it trouble?"

"Next to *top of the line* in the dictionary is a picture of this system."

"Not sure you understand how dictionaries work, but I get what you were going for. Can it be bypassed?"

"No," Kevin said firmly. Then after a beat, he added, "Well, yes, but . . ."

"But what?"

"You need the right piece of hardware and someone who knows how to use it to hack in."

"Where do I get either?"

"Lucky for you, the answer is from me."

"For both?"

"You bet."

"How does all this work?"

"The hardware is basically a souped-up thumb drive. I can talk you through where to install it. Once that's done, it'll give me access to the system, and I can tweak the security settings however you'd like. When do you need this done?"

"We're going in tomorrow night."

"Wow, okay. And where exactly are you?"

"Berlin."

Teddy could hear keys clacking, followed by a curse and more tapping. After another curse, Kevin said, "Uh, more bad news."

"And that would be?"

"The soonest any commercial courier could have it there would be by seven p.m. tomorrow."

"That would be cutting things awfully close."

More typing drifted over the line. "There are some private courier services that could get it there sooner. Basically, a person carrying it on a flight and hand delivering. Yikes. Expensive, though, plus the cost of the flight. Damn, maybe I'm in the wrong business."

Teddy highly doubted that Kevin-the-courier could make anywhere near the amount that Kevin-the-hacker did from the comfort of his basement, but it did give Teddy an idea.

"Are there any flights to Berlin leaving tonight?" he asked. It was barely evening where Kevin was.

Kevin worked his computer, then said, "Yeah. Several, actually. Looks like most have a few open seats."

"Perfect. Book one for yourself."

"What?"

"Send me the details and I'll have someone meet you at the airport when you get here."

"Hold on. I don't do house calls."

"Do you have a passport?"

"Um . . ."

"That's a yes, isn't it?"

"Maybe."

"Grab it, pack a few clothes, and get a move on."

"But . . . but—"

"I realize this is an unusual request, but I think it'll work out best if you're here. And if it helps, I'll make sure you get a bonus."

"But I don't want to go to Germany."

"Your mom is always telling you to get out more."

"How would you know that?"

"That's classified, but I'm happy to call her and see what she thinks about you going on a trip."

"Please don't!"

"Then buy your ticket and get on the plane. Don't worry, you're going to love it."

37

BY 8:30 A.M. THE NEXT MORNING, TEDDY AND
Vesna were in an industrial area on the outskirts of the city,
at a precision tool shop.

The place was run by an acquaintance of Vesna's named
Otto. An older man with a sheepish smile and a disarmingly
friendly demeaner, no one would ever suspect him of running a weapons supply business on the side.

Otto led them to a shipping container in the back lot and
opened the door. Both sides of the container were lined with
floor-to-ceiling shelves.

Otto gestured inside. "Have a look around. If you have
any questions, just ask."

Teddy and Vesna walked down the aisle that ran through
the middle of the box, selecting items from the shelves.
They reemerged with their weapons of choice and a few
other items, like audio bugs, night-vision goggles, and sets
of digital comm gear.

In Otto's office, they settled the bill, then the old man said, "Can I tempt you with some coffee before you go?"

"We'd like nothing more," Vesna said, "but I'm afraid we have a busy day ahead of us."

"You are breaking my heart." Otto placed a hand on his chest, then looked at Teddy. "Every time she visits, it's rush, rush, rush."

"She is a woman in demand," Teddy said.

"Of course she is. It is because she is very good at what she does."

Teddy glanced at Vesna and gave her a small nod.

"Before we go," Vesna said, "we have something we'd like to ask you."

"What is it I can help you with?"

"It's a sensitive matter, and if you'd rather not answer, I understand."

"Now I am intrigued." He motioned for her to go on.

"What do you know about Braun Logistics and Security? More specifically, about its special projects group."

Otto's smile wilted to a flatline, and his eyes grew steely. "Have they offered you a job? Is that why you ask?"

"No. Nothing like that."

Some of Otto's tension eased, but his smile had not yet returned. "The most important thing I can tell you is to not get involved with them."

"That's something you and I can both agree on," she said.

"I know Vesna's reason," Teddy said. "But I would love to know why you say that."

Otto glanced at Teddy as if just remembering that he

was there, then the man turned his gaze to Vesna. "How much do you trust him?"

"With my life," she said without hesitation. She leaned forward and put her hand over Otto's. "He is one of the good ones."

"You swear this?"

"I do."

"I apologize," he said to Teddy. "You know what this business is like."

"Far too well," Teddy said. "And there is no need to apologize. If it helps, our interest in BLS is the exact opposite of wanting to work with them."

A hint of a smile returned to Otto's expression. "Is that so? And how far are you planning on taking this 'exact opposite' interest?"

"To a satisfying conclusion."

That hinted smile began to spread. "It may not be easy."

"Not our first rodeo," Teddy said.

Otto laughed. "I have always loved this expression. So very American."

"You clearly have never been to the Calgary Stampede in Canada."

"I will put it on my to-do list."

"You were going to tell us about BLS's special projects group," Vesna prodded.

Otto sobered, though without the previous tension. "Nothing I know is firsthand, but what I have heard from others. I have no reason to doubt what they say, however."

"Understood," Teddy said.

"It is an off-the-books black ops unit that will take on

any job for the right price. No moral code, you know? Assassinations, kidnappings, business disruptions, it does not matter."

"Do you know who their clients are?"

"Specifically, I do not. But from what I understand, their services do not come cheap, so you can draw your own conclusions as to the types of clients. Is it a client you are interested in or BLS?"

"Both, we think," Teddy said.

"I wish there was more I could tell you, but I have made it a habit not to know what goes on there."

"That sounds like a smart strategy."

"I can give you some advice, if you are interested."

"Please."

"There was a man I knew who worked for Braun. He quit in the middle of a job, which apparently caused some hiccups. For three months, nothing happened to him. Then one night he 'falls' in front of a subway train. No witnesses, and the CCTV cameras covering the platform were conveniently not working. But Braun had to be behind it." Otto paused. "In other words, my advice is to proceed with extreme caution. Felix Braun is not one to be crossed. He has a long memory, and he holds grudges."

Vesna glanced at Teddy. "Anything else?"

He shook his head. "I'm good."

"Thank you, Otto," Vesna said. "We've taken up too much of your time already. I promise that the next time I visit, I'll treat you to lunch."

As she and Teddy stood, Otto said to Teddy, "You heard that, yes? You are my witness."

Teddy smiled. "I will happily testify against her if she tries to renege."

———————

Braun was in the elevator heading down when Dieter called.

"Are you back?" Braun asked.

"Just landed."

"I'm heading to Kurfürstendamm for a meeting. Meet me at Cumberland at one for lunch."

Braun hung up without waiting for a reply.

———————

Teddy and Vesna were heading for the next S-Bahn train back into the city when their phones vibrated at the same time with a text from Hans.

Braun just left the office in his car.

Click here to track him

Teddy tapped the link and a map of Berlin opened on his screen. He zoomed in on the moving blue dot that represented Braun's vehicle.

"I wonder where he's going?" Vesna asked.

They watched the dot travel west, along the south side of Tiergarten park.

When their train arrived, they hopped on board and continued to monitor Braun's progress. It wasn't long before the dot stopped and didn't budge for well over a minute. When it did begin moving again, it only traveled a block and a half and then stopped again. They watched for it to take off again, but it remained where it was.

"I think it's parked," Vesna said.

Teddy nodded and pointed at the building where the vehicle had first stopped.

"My guess is that Braun went inside here, and his driver's waiting for him to come out."

He glanced up from his phone and checked the Berlin transportation map on the wall of the train. "If memory serves, our next stop intersects with a U-Bahn line that passes through that area."

"I believe you're right."

"Interested in a little adventure?"

"I assume that's rhetorical."

38

TEDDY AND VESNA STROLLED DOWN THE
block, talking like two colleagues on a lunch break.

As they passed the parked Mercedes-Maybach, Teddy
glanced at its license plate and gave Vesna a nod, letting her
know it was Braun's car.

They continued walking until they passed the building
where they presumed Braun was, then stopped at a bus stop
nearby like they were commuters waiting for their ride.

While Teddy kept an eye on the building's entrance,
Vesna monitored the tracking app.

Three buses came and went before she said, "It's moving.
Looks like it's going around the block. ETA two minutes."

At the building, a group of people exited and headed
down the sidewalk in Teddy and Vesna's direction. For a
handful of seconds, they blocked his view of the entrance.
When the last of them moved out of the way, Braun was
standing outside with two men.

Teddy took several pictures of him as he conversed with his companions.

"Coming around now," Vesna reported. "Ten seconds."

The Maybach stopped in front of the building. Braun shook hands with the men and then headed to it. As soon as he was inside, the sedan pulled into traffic.

"Back to the safe house?" Vesna suggested.

Teddy's goal in coming here had been to get eyes on Braun, so their little side quest was a success. He checked the time. Kevin should be arriving at the apartment within the hour.

"Sounds like a plan," he said.

They started walking to the U-Bahn station but hadn't even made it a block before Vesna said, "Hold on."

"What is it?"

She was looking at the tracking app. "Braun just stopped in front of Ristorante Cumberland. That's only two blocks from here."

They both watched her screen to see if Braun's vehicle had only been caught in traffic. After half a minute, the car moved again. Then, like it had earlier, it stopped a second time.

"I'm suddenly feeling hungry," Teddy said. "How about you?"

"Famished."

"Italian?"

"Sounds lovely."

At Ristorante Cumberland, Teddy and Vesna were shown to a table in the ground-floor dining room.

"Your waiter will be right with you," said the man who had escorted them.

They each glanced around the portion of the dining room they could see.

"I don't see them," Teddy said.

"Neither do I."

Teddy opened his phone and looked at the restaurant's website. "There are more tables up a floor, including an outdoor patio."

"I'll ask if we can be—"

Teddy cut her off by raising his palm just high enough for her to see. He had the view of the entryway, through which Dieter Wenz had just walked in.

The man spoke to the host, who nodded, then led him up the stairs to the second level.

"Dieter Wenz is here."

She tensed. "If he sees me, he'll come over."

"It's okay. He went upstairs and never looked this way."

"Still, I should leave."

"I agree. Take the duffel back to the safe house. I'll be there soon."

He picked up the bag with the items they'd purchased from Otto, removed one of the audio bugs, then handed the bag to her.

"Don't do anything I wouldn't do," she said.

"So, everything's fair game?"

"More or less."

After she left, a waiter approached the table, looking confused. In German, he asked if something was wrong.

Though Teddy could have answered in kind, he said, "I'm sorry. Do you speak English?"

"Sorry, yes. Your friend, will she be back?"

"Unfortunately, no. She didn't feel well. Upset stomach."

"Ah. Would you like to order now?"

"I don't want to take up a whole table by myself." Teddy set twenty euros on the table. "For your trouble."

The waiter smiled sympathetically. "I hope you can return when your friend is feeling better."

"Thank you." Teddy stood. "Could you directly me to the toilet?"

"Of course. It is upstairs and to the right. You cannot miss it."

"Thanks again."

When Teddy reached the top of the stairs, he proceeded directly to the men's room and locked himself inside one of the private toilet stalls. He synced the bug to a special app on his phone, then clicked the setting that would send whatever the bug picked up to a secure cloud server, allowing him to listen to the file at any time.

When he exited the bathroom into the corridor, he kept his eyes on his phone, like he was checking messages. Two waiters passed quickly by, but neither paid him any attention.

Teddy stopped at one of the windows that looked onto the outside terrace and spotted Felix Braun and Dieter Wenz at a table along the outer edge.

A few moments later, a waiter walked onto the terrace and headed toward Braun's table.

Knowing an opportunity when he saw it, Teddy entered the patio acting like he was listening to someone on his phone and sauntered all the way to the empty table next to Braun's.

While the men were distracted by giving the waiter their orders, Teddy deftly stuck the bug to the underside of the empty table and meandered back to the exit.

Once he was inside, he donned an earbud and checked that the listening device was working.

"I don't like the fact that she hasn't been dealt with yet," one of the men said, annoyed.

"The moment her security detail is pulled off, we'll take care of her," the other replied.

As much as Teddy would have liked to hole up in the men's room and listen in live, the smart move was to get out of there and listen later.

A man brushed past him as he started down the stairs. He was followed by a young woman who was so focused on the tablet computer she was carrying that she nearly collided with Teddy.

Teddy grabbed her arm to keep her from falling, but the tablet wasn't so lucky. It slipped from her hands and tumbled a few steps down before stopping.

"Are you all right?" Teddy asked in German.

She took several quick breaths. "I think so. Thank you."

From the top of the stairs, the man said, "Jillian, let's go. He's waiting."

"Sorry, Mr. Lawrence."

Teddy released her and went down to where the computer had landed. The screen side was up, and on it was an image of the House Dione commercial shoot in Budapest, taken from the fan barrier. It captured a moment not long after Danielle had been shot. She was on the ground, and in the distance Teddy—in his Billy Barnett guise—could be seen hurrying toward her.

He picked up the computer and held it out to the woman. "Probably best to save the Web surfing until you're on level ground."

"Thank you," she said as she took it.

"Now, Jillian," Lawrence ordered.

She gave Teddy a perfunctory smile, then hurried to the top.

39

FORTY MINUTES LATER, TEDDY ENTERED THE
apartment that served as their safe house to find Vesna on
the couch with a washcloth over her eyes, Hans at his chair
by the window engrossed in his laptop, and a large red suitcase sitting in the middle of the living room.

"I take it Kevin made it," he asked.

Vesna lifted one end of the cloth, glanced at him, then
dropped it again. "Fifteen minutes ago."

"Where is he?"

She pointed toward the hallway. "He locked himself in
the bathroom."

"He what?"

"He thinks I killed you and am here to do the same
to him."

"Why would he think that?"

"You will have to ask him that."

"I take it that cloth over your eyes is related."

"Very perceptive."

"What happened?"

"I was sprayed in the face."

Teddy's expression turned concerned. "He maced you?"

"Not mace," she said. "From the taste, I believe it was mint breath spray. Luckily, most of it hit my chin, or I *would* have killed him."

"Were you holding a gun when you answered the door?"

"As one would in our circumstances. I did not, however, wave it in his face, if that's what you're worried about."

"I didn't think you would, but I had to ask. Are you okay?"

"I do have fresher breath. Does that count?"

Teddy went down the hall and knocked on the bathroom door. "Kevin?"

A gasp came from inside, then Kevin said, "You're alive?"

"Very much so. I understand you met my friend Vesna."

"I expected you to be here, so when you weren't, I thought . . . I mean, you should have told me someone else would be here."

"Come on out, Kevin. Everything's fine."

Teddy returned to the main room and was getting a bottle of water from the refrigerator when Kevin entered.

"Welcome to Berlin," Teddy said.

Kevin frowned. "I'd rather be at home."

"And I'd rather be on a beach in Bali," Vesna said, the cloth still over her eyes.

Teddy said, "Kevin, Vesna. Vesna, Kevin."

"Hi," Kevin said awkwardly. "Uh, I'm sorry about earlier."

STUART WOODS' GOLDEN HOUR

"For hiding in the bathroom?" Vesna asked. "Or attempting to blind me?"

"Oh my God. Did it get in your eyes? Are they okay?"

She removed the cloth and sat up.

"Do they look okay to you?" she asked, widening her eyes so the red was unmissable.

"I'm so sorry. I-I-I didn't know who you were."

"Do you mace everyone you don't know?" Teddy asked.

"It wasn't mace. It was—"

"Breath spray," Teddy and Vesna said at the same time.

"We know," Teddy added.

Kevin bit his lip. "I am *really* sorry. I promise, I won't do it again."

"Well, that's a relief," Vesna said.

"There are three bedrooms," Teddy said. "You're in the one with twin beds. You'll be sharing with Hans. Hans, say hi to Kevin."

Hans grunted without looking at them. Kevin grunted back, then cocked his head and walked over.

"Cool setup." Kevin crouched to get a better look at the equipment under the table. "Is that the XC twenty-three twenty-four?" he asked.

Hans looked at him for the first time and smirked. "The twenty-three twenty-four *C*."

Kevin's eyes widened. "Seriously?"

"Seriously."

Kevin reached toward one of the black boxes, but before his fingers reached it, Hans slapped his hand away.

"No touching," Hans said.

"Sorry, man. I don't like people touching my stuff, either." He stood up. "I'll, ah, I'll just get settled in."

He grabbed his suitcase and headed to his bedroom.

"How did things go at the restaurant?" Vesna asked Teddy.

"Let's find out."

Teddy sat beside her and opened the monitoring app. The data from the bug was broken into ten-minute segments for easy listening. He checked the latest segment first and determined that Braun and Dieter had already left the restaurant, so he turned off the bug.

He then played the first audio segment. For a minute or so, there was more talk between Braun and Dieter about the woman they needed to "deal with," which Teddy was sure had to be Danielle Verde. He'd already texted La Rose to make sure the security team continued to protect her.

At approximately the same time Teddy had been exiting the restaurant, the man he'd guessed was Braun said, "Lawrence, what are you doing here?"

"I'm sorry to disturb you, Mr. Braun." The voice was that of the man who'd been on the stairs with the woman Teddy had kept from falling. "Jillian found something that I thought I should show you right away."

"I can't have you just standing there," Braun said. "Have a seat, both of you."

Chairs moved across cement.

"So?" Braun said. "What is it?"

"I-I-I think I found Teddy Fay," Jillian said.

Teddy cocked his head, while Vesna glanced at him, but neither spoke.

"You thought that before when you said Roland Turner was Teddy Fay, so why should I believe you now?"

Vesna reached out and paused the playback. "Who's Roland Turner?"

Teddy started to shrug, but then stopped, his brow knit-ting. "If I recall correctly, there was a Roland Turner on the commercial shoot in Budapest. He assisted the director. Not sure what his actual title was."

"And they thought *he* was you?"

"It sounds like it."

"Does he even look like you?"

Teddy closed his eyes to remember. "Vaguely. About the right age, similar height."

He hit play.

"T-t-to be clear," Jillian said, "I never said he *was* Fay. I said he could be. That's why I continued looking into him."

"So is this new person another 'could be'?" Braun asked. "I don't want to get my hopes up only for you to have made another mistake."

"I didn't make a mistake before," she muttered.

"Technically, this new person is also a *could be*," Law-rence said quickly. "But we're more confident than we were about Turner."

"Who's Fay supposed to be this time?"

"Jillian?" Lawrence said.

There was the sound of movement.

"This man," Jillian said.

Teddy had a bad feeling she was showing Braun the photo that Teddy had seen on her tablet.

"I assume he has a name," Braun said, an edge still in his voice.

"He does," Lawrence said. "It's Billy Burnett."

"*Bar*nett," Jillian corrected him.

Vesna sucked in a surprised breath.

"What makes you think *he's* Fay?"

"This photo was taken at the commercial shoot in Budapest where Danielle Verde was injured," Jillian said. "That is her on the ground, and as you can see, Barnett is running toward her."

"Perhaps he was only reacting to her being hurt," Wenz said.

"If Fay is supposed to be involved in the film festival, Barnett fits the bill," Lawrence said. "He has a film playing there, doesn't he, Jillian?"

"He does. *Storm's Eye.*"

"Good for him," Braun said. "I still don't see how this means he's Fay."

"There's more," Lawrence said. "Tell him, Jillian."

"Um, okay," she said, clearly reluctant. "Barnett is in Europe on a press tour for his new movie. His first stop was in Rome, then he went to Venice."

"He traveled there on the same train Oscar Schmidt was on," Lawrence said.

Except for the distant clink of dishes at other tables, the recording went silent for more than a quarter of a minute.

"He was in Venice?" Dieter asked.

"Yes," the woman said.

"How long?"

"A couple days."

"So, he would have been there when Rick La Rose was." From the way Dieter said this, Teddy thought it was aimed at Braun, not the other two. "Venice, Budapest, and soon Berlin . . ."

"Do you have a better picture of him than this?" Braun asked, sounding excited now.

"We have plenty," Lawrence said. "Show him."

The next minute of the recording was spent discussing the pictures Jillian showed Braun of Billy Barnett from multiple sources.

"And you're sure Barnett is coming to Berlin for the festival?" Braun asked when they were through.

"We are," Lawrence said. "His film will be shown opening night, after which there will be a party to celebrate the commencement of the festival."

After a beat of silence, Braun said, "And how do we get tickets to this event?"

"Jillian can email them on your behalf," Lawrence said.

"Then why are you two still sitting here? Go on. Take care of it."

Chair legs scrapped the floor and steps moved away from the table.

When Jillian and Lawrence had presumably moved out of earshot, Dieter said, "You have that look."

"What look?" Braun said.

"The one you get when you have something on your mind."

Braun huffed. "Do you have locations on the remaining agents?"

"I do," Dieter said.

"Do we have enough men to cover them all at once?"

"All at once?"

"Yes! Did you not hear me? I want to know if we have enough people to hit all the remaining targets at the same time."

"We do. What do you have in mind?"

"We get our teams in place right away, then you and I go to the festival and see if this Billy Barnett is who Jillian thinks he is. If so, we deal with him, then send out the word to terminate the others. Phase one complete." He paused. "That's doable, is it not?"

"Yes, of course. It will leave us a bit shorthanded here for dealing with Barnett, if he *is* Fay."

"You can keep a couple of your best men here and hire as many contract players as you think we'll need. Better?"

"I can make that work." From the tone of his voice, Dieter was not completely happy, but appeared unwilling to argue with his boss.

"Once this Fay and the others are dealt with, we move on immediately to Lance Cabot and Holly Barker. Is your plan ready?"

Dieter nodded. "I think you'll like it."

Teddy and Vesna shared a look.

"As long as there are zero complications, I will," Braun said. "Successfully eliminating the head of the U.S. government and her top spy will be more than enough to convince the Kazakhs to hire us."

"Then I'll make it happen," Dieter said.

Teddy and Vesna listened until Braun and Dieter finished their lunch and left, but the men discussed nothing else of interest.

"So . . ." Vesna said, once the recording was stopped. "That was . . . interesting."

"*Interesting* is not quite the word I'd use."

"Troubling?"

"Better."

"Why would he want to kill your president and your director of the CIA? Were either involved in Golden Hour?"

"Neither were. My guess would be Braun's going after them because they're symbols of the government that greenlit the mission."

"That makes sense, if you're a psychopath."

"Which I'm pretty sure Braun is."

"You may want to warn your CIA friends that their boss and their boss's boss need to watch their backs."

"I'll make the call."

"You may also want to come up with an excuse for Billy missing the festival."

"Perhaps."

She raised an eyebrow. "Perhaps? I was thinking something more along the lines of 'Hell, yes.'" She studied him for a moment. "Don't tell me. You have something else in mind, don't you?"

"More the inkling of something else."

"Care to share?"

Teddy shook his head. "Not yet."

"Then how do you want to proceed for now?"

"Just as we've planned."

40

TEDDY FLICKED THE LIGHTS ON IN KEVIN'S
bedroom and said, "Time to get up."

Kevin flipped onto his side so that his back was to the
door. "Five more minutes."

"You said that fifteen minutes ago." Teddy clapped his
hands loudly. "Let's go, let's go, let's go."

Kevin groaned, flung his legs off the mattress, and sat
up. "What time is it?"

"Eleven p.m. Come on. It's time to get to work."

A few minutes later, Teddy, Vesna, Kevin, and Hans
were gathered in the living room.

"Status on Braun?" Teddy asked.

"He left at nine-thirty," Hans said. "His car drove directly to his residence, and it hasn't moved since."

"Any sign of Wenz?"

"He was here for about an hour between six-thirty and seven-thirty and has not returned."

"All right. Kevin, it's time for you to do your thing."

Kevin opened the messenger bag he'd brought with him and removed a cardboard box about the size of a smart-phone.

"Here you go," he said and handed it to Teddy.

Teddy opened it. Nestled within a bed of foam inside was what looked like a slightly longer than normal thumb drive. He put the top back on and held it out to Kevin.

"What?" Kevin asked.

"Take it."

Confused, Kevin did.

"Let's go," Teddy said.

"Excuse me?"

"You're coming with us."

"But—but why? I can talk you through it."

"Which means there's a higher chance for errors than if you do it yourself. We can't risk tipping them off."

"What if I'm discovered?"

"Didn't you say this could all be done from the communication systems hub on the first floor?"

"Well, yeah."

Teddy clapped him on the shoulder. "You'll be fine."

Grabbing at straws, Kevin blurted out, "I wouldn't hold up well under torture."

"Good to know. Come on."

"But—"

"If anyone gives you trouble," Vesna said, "just spray them with breath freshener. That seems to work for you."

"I said I was sorry!"

Teddy, Vesna, and Kevin sneaked into the BLS building through a rear employee entrance and made their way to the communication systems hub. Vesna made quick work of picking the lock, and in no time they were inside.

The room was the size of a small bedroom and was lined with electronics on racks.

"Your show," Teddy said to Kevin.

It took Kevin a couple of minutes to identify the devices serving BLS's floors and another two to get the modified thumb drive mounted in the correct place. He then plopped on the floor, yanked a laptop out of his messenger bag, and started typing.

As time passed, Teddy began to worry something had gone wrong. But then Kevin said, "Ha!"

"Shh," Vesna said.

"Oops, sorry," he whispered.

"Did it work?" Teddy asked.

"Of course it worked. I now have full control of all the security for floors ten, eleven, and twelve."

"Cameras, too?"

"Cameras, too."

"Good work." Teddy handed out comm gear, then said to Kevin, "You're our eyes. If you see anyone even thinking about heading to wherever we are, you let us know."

"That's a lot of pressure."

"Think of it this way: if we get caught, they'll start looking for whoever helped us bypass their security, and the first place they'll look is this room. So it's in your best interest to stay on top of things."

"Are you trying to stress me out?"

"I'm trying to make you understand the gravity of the situation."

"You know," Kevin said, "now that I'm in their system, I could do everything from across the street."

"The more times we go in and out of the building also increases the chance of something going wrong. Don't worry. We'll pick you up on the way out."

"Can we go now?" Vesna asked. "Or does he need more hand-holding?"

"Knock, knock," Teddy whispered. He and Vesna had just taken the emergency stairwell to the top and were now standing at the door to the twelfth floor.

The lock clicked and Kevin said over the comm, "You're clear."

Teddy opened the door, and he and Vesna stepped quietly into a long hallway.

They were operating under the assumption that Felix Braun kept data concerning BLS special projects clients either on an unnetworked device or written on a piece of paper, such as in a notebook, in his twelfth-floor office.

"Go left," Kevin said. "Then right at the next corridor."

"How many other people on this level?" Teddy asked.

"Three. One in an office nowhere near where you'll be, and two guards at a desk by the elevators."

"Copy."

Kevin guided them to Braun's office.

"Don't touch the door," Kevin warned. "It's locked and alarmed. I'll give you the go-ahead once I have it open."

Kevin had yet to get back to them when Teddy heard a door open somewhere else on the floor, but far too close for his liking.

In a low voice, he said, "Kevin, check the cams."

"What?" Kevin paused, then said, "Oh, shit. One of the guards is heading your way."

"Remember what I said about being our eyes?"

"Right. Sorry. Give me a sec."

Teddy could hear the guard moving down a nearby hallway in his and Vesna's direction.

She looked at him and mouthed, *What do you want to do?*

They'd come prepared to run into trouble like this. In Teddy's pocket was a preloaded syringe that would knock someone out and mess with their short-term memory, and a bottle of additional medication if they were facing more than one problem. Teddy was reaching into the pocket where he'd stored it when the lock to Braun's office clicked.

"Go!" Kevin said.

Teddy eased opened the door and followed Vesna into Braun's office. They stilled just inside, listening to the footsteps in the hallway draw nearer.

Teddy half expected the guard to stop right outside and yank the door open. But he continued on without pausing, his steps soon fading to nothing.

"He's gone," Kevin said a few moments later. "Um, sorry again about not seeing him before."

"Just try not to let it happen again," Teddy said. He glanced at Vesna. "Where do you want to start?"

She looked around. "I'll take the bookcases."

"Then I'll take the desk."

She nodded and they began their search.

The surface of the desk was clear of anything but a monitor, a trackpad, and a keyboard. Teddy tried the drawers. Unsurprisingly, all were locked.

He picked each and checked its contents. The only drawer holding anything remotely interesting was the larger one at the bottom. In it were a few dozen files, but none appeared to have anything to do with the special projects unit.

"Safe," Vesna whispered.

Teddy joined her at one of the bookcases. She had already removed several items from a shelf and exposed a safe that had been hidden behind a sliding panel. On the safe door was a glass touch screen and nothing else.

"It's a Dalby Utra," Vesna said. "First one I've seen in person."

"What do you think?"

"In theory, I should be able to get it open."

"Then give it a go."

From her backpack, she removed an electronic device with several wires hanging from it. As she started to attach the sensors to the safe, Teddy turned to continue searching the room.

As he did, a framed photo on top of the pile of stuff Vesna had cleared away caught his eye. He picked it up and stared at it.

"Forget about the safe," he said.

Vesna looked over her shoulder. "Why?"

"I know who the client is. Or, more accurately, we were wrong. There is no client."

41

THE NEXT MORNING, THE REST OF THE *STORM'S*
Eye press tour crew flew into Berlin and found Ben Bacchetti
waiting for them at the private jet terminal.

"I was beginning to think you weren't going to make it,"
Tessa said to him, after they'd untangled themselves from
their passionate greeting.

"I finally convinced the boss to let me go," Ben said.

"Aren't you the boss?" Adriene asked.

"Sadly, yes. And I can be a real hard-ass when I set my
mind to it."

They boarded a VIP van. As they pulled up to their hotel, a cab stopped behind them from which emerged Mark
Weldon.

Stacy did a double take when she saw him. Forcing a
smile, she walked over to him. "Good morning, Mark."

"Hi, Stacy. How was the flight?"

"No complaints." She lowered her voice to a whisper and said, "You're supposed to be Billy, remember? He's the one with an interview this morning."

"Change of plans. Billy won't be able to make it until the premiere tomorrow night."

"Are you trying to make my life miserable?"

"Not consciously."

"What am I supposed to tell Lizzie?"

"That Billy was unavoidably detained and begs her forgiveness."

"Hmm. So, about promoting me to producer. Can we do that sooner than later and get a new assistant to run interference for you?"

"But you're doing such a great job at it."

Lizzie emerged from the hotel. "Have either of you seen Billy?"

Until that moment, Mark had never seen anyone smile and groan at the same time.

———————

Teddy had barely entered Mark Weldon's suite when the room's phone began ringing.

"Hello?" he answered.

"If you could come to suite ten twenty-one when you have a moment, I would appreciate it," Lance said, then the line went dead.

Teddy had half a mind to ignore the summons.

Last night, as soon as he, Vesna, and Kevin had made it back to the safe house, he'd called Lance but had been put straight through to voicemail.

He'd then called Rick La Rose, who told him that he didn't know why Lance was unreachable.

Now Teddy knew the answer.

Lance opened the door when Teddy knocked.

"Ah, good, you're here. Come in, come in."

As Teddy entered the suite, he saw Stone Barrington standing near the windows.

"Morning, Stone," Teddy said. "Playing messenger again?"

"More like deliveryman this time," Stone said. "Lance found out I was flying here for the festival and finagled a ride."

"Something to eat?" Lance asked, motioning to the dining table where a platter of pastries sat next to a bowl of fruit.

"I'm good," Teddy said.

"Then why don't we all have a seat." After they did so, Lance said, "Apologies for not responding to your message sooner. I take it you have news."

"I know who hired Braun."

Lance leaned forward. "You *know* or you think you know?"

"I know."

"That's excellent news," Stone said. "Who is it?"

"No one."

"I'm not following," Lance said.

On his phone, Teddy brought up the picture he'd taken of the photograph in Braun's office and handed it to Lance. The photo was at least twenty-five years old and showed a middle-aged man in a business suit standing next to a beaming boy who couldn't have been more than ten.

"Is that . . . ?"

"Tovar Lintz, head of the Trust? Yes, it is."

"And the boy?"

"Felix Braun. Tovar Lintz's son."

Lance lowered the phone. "There was no mention of Lintz having a son in his file."

"Braun was illegitimate, and Lintz never publicly acknowledged him. Braun's mother was Lintz's mistress for only a short time. My guess is that their relationship ended when she became pregnant."

"You're positive?"

"Confirmed by three sources." The last of which had reported in just before Teddy had arrived at the hotel, but he saw no need to mention that.

"That should have been in his records."

"That sounds more like a *you* problem than a *me* problem."

"So, Braun has been killing Golden Hour agents as revenge for his father's death?" Stone asked.

Teddy nodded. "He has." He briefed them on all that had happened since Danielle Verde had been shot in Budapest, including that Braun's associate guessed that Billy Barnett was Teddy.

"The idea to leak that you were still alive seems to have worked a little too well," Stone said.

"They *think* they know who Billy is," Lance said. "They don't know for sure."

"What they think is also the truth."

Lance shrugged. "Details."

"That's a pretty big detail," Stone said, then looked at Teddy. "Aren't you concerned?"

"I won't be walking around as Billy Barnett until Lance has cleaned everything up, if that's what you're asking," Teddy replied. He stood. "Now, if you'll excuse me, gentlemen."

"Where are you going?" Lance asked.

"To fulfill my obligations to Centurion Pictures. We have a full schedule today."

"But the mission isn't done."

Teddy shrugged. "My mission was to find out who was behind the Golden Hour deaths. Answer: Felix Braun. You're welcome. I also uncovered a plot to kill the president of the United States and the director of the CIA. You're welcome again. As way of thanks, you can remove Braun and his people from circulation as soon as possible. Now, if there isn't anything else, I can see myself out."

"There is," Lance said.

"And that would be?"

"I believe you are in the best position to neutralize Braun."

"And I believe you have plenty of Agency resources who can handle it."

"Be that as it may, for my people to plan and execute such a mission from scratch will take days at least, if not a week or more. You, on the other hand, already have a handle on the players. Plus, Billy Barnett's presence also provides us with the perfect time-sensitive opportunity."

"And that is?"

"The premiere of Storm's Eye and the opening gala that will follow. You said it yourself. Braun wants to be there."

"With an eye on killing Billy Barnett," Stone said.

"At the risk of repeating myself, the perfect opportunity," Lance replied. "All Teddy will have to do is turn the tables on him." He looked at Teddy. "Well? What do you say?"

Teddy knew what he wanted to say, but the responsibility he felt toward his fellow Golden Hour agents both dead and alive prevented him from doing so.

He grimaced and stood. "Looks like I have some planning to do."

42

THAT AFTERNOON, FELIX BRAUN FEIGNED A
move to the left then juked to the right and swung his fist.

Dieter leaned back just far enough to let his boss's hand
fly past him without connecting.

With an angry growl, Braun followed up with a left
hook. Dieter had anticipated that, too, and had already
danced back a few steps.

Then as his boss reset his stance, Dieter flew forward
and sent one punch into Braun's abs and a second into his
cheek.

If he'd used his full strength, his boss would have been
on the mat, out like a light. Instead, Braun staggered into
the ropes, breathing heavily.

"Maybe we should stop here," Dieter said, not even
sounding winded.

This was their first sparring session since the Golden

Hour revenge plot had gone active, and it was clear Braun wasn't as sharp as usual.

"Not yet," Braun growled. He pushed himself toward the center of the ring and motioned for Dieter to come at him. "Again."

"I think it would be better—"

"Again!" Braun yelled.

Dieter shrugged. When Braun got an idea in his head, he would hold on to it as long as possible—their current operation a prime example.

Dieter bounced back and forth from foot to foot, thinking that if he let Braun land a couple of blows, that should satisfy his boss.

As he took a step toward him, the gym door opened and Braun's assistant stepped through.

"I'm sorry to disturb you, sir," the man said.

Braun whipped around and barked, "Then why did you?"

"You wanted to know when we heard back from the film festival."

"And?" Braun said, still mad but curious, too.

His assistant hurried to the ring and held out an envelope.

Braun lifted his gloved hands. "And how exactly am I supposed to open that?"

"Oh, um, would you like me to—"

"What do you think?"

The assistant opened the envelope and extracted the letter inside.

"Read it," Braun said.

"'Mr. Braun, we received your inquiry about attending

the World Thriller Film Festival opening night screening and celebration. Normally at such a late date, I would be unable to fulfill your request. As luck would have it, we've had a cancellation, and I am happy to inform you that I have set aside four tickets for you and your friends to join us at tomorrow night's festivities.'"

"Excellent." Braun smirked.

"There's more, sir," the assistant said.

"Go on."

"'Given your standing in the business community, I also wanted to let you know about a recently added opportunity in which you might be interested. During the post-screening party, there will be a special meet and greet for individuals considering investing in the film industry. It will be hosted by Ben Bacchetti and Billy Barnett, the producers of *Storm's Eye*, our opening-night film. If this is something that interests you, please let me know right away as space is limited. Sincerely, Constance Mueller, World Thriller Film Festival Director.'"

Braun laughed triumphantly and glanced at Dieter. "Seems things are turning back in our favor." To his assistant he said, "Contact this Mueller woman immediately. Tell her that I would be honored to attend the meet and greet."

"Yes, sir," his assistant said and left.

Braun punched one of his gloved hands into the other and grinned at Dieter. "Now, where were we?"

Twenty minutes later, Teddy was in Mark Weldon's suite with Stone and Vesna, whom he had just introduced, when he received a phone call. He took it in the other room and then rejoined his friends after he was done.

"That was Constance Mueller from the festival," he said.

"And?" Stone asked.

"Braun took the bait," Teddy said.

"Then I guess we have no choice but to go through with this, yes?" Vesna said.

"You took the words right out of my mouth."

43

ON THE OPENING DAY OF THE FILM FESTIVAL,
Jillian headed to work at seven a.m., after tossing and turning through her second night in a row.

It was thoughts of what Braun might do to Billy Barnett—if the producer turned out to actually be Teddy Fay—that kept her from any serious sleep. She knew it wouldn't be good, just as she knew whatever he did to Barnett would be her fault. She was the one who pointed Braun in Barnett's direction, after all.

She'd been so excited when she solved the difficult puzzle that connected Billy Barnett and Teddy Fay. It was a shot of dopamine straight into her brain.

Unfortunately, Lawrence had walked into her office before she had time to think about the consequences of what she'd discovered, and he had wanted to know why she was so happy.

"I found him!" she'd blurted out, then proceeded to show him what she'd learned.

It wasn't until he said they needed to tell Braun right away that she realized her mistake.

Today, as she rode the train, she tried to think of something she could do to try to remedy the situation that wouldn't get her killed. By the time she reached her stop, she had a plan.

When she arrived at her office, she closed the door and woke up her monitor. Using the encryption key Lawrence had given her, she accessed the message inbox.

In addition to the folder that held the messages she had been given access to were several others that were password protected. This would have stymied most people, but Jillian was not most people. The best researchers were also hackers, and she was one of the best of the best.

Within thirty minutes, she had access to all the other folders. There were hundreds of messages from multiple sources.

She performed a keyword search using the name "Teddy Fay" and received hits on a dozen messages. Four of those messages were ones she'd already had access, too, and concerned the rumors of him still being alive.

Interestingly, the remaining eight messages all came from the same source.

She clicked through the messages. Several had documents attached. She opened these.

All were official CIA documents. Most were career summaries of the same people who were on Braun's list.

The only one that wasn't a summary turned out to be the mission report for an operation called Golden Hour. She'd heard the name before. Braun had said it to Lawrence the day she'd been brought up to Braun's office to meet him.

Within the document was a list of the mission participants. It was a match to Braun's list.

She grinned. These messages were what she'd been
hoping to find.

She rolled her head from side to side, rubbed her hands
together, then began trying to see if she could trace the messages back to their sender.

Two hours later, she leaned back, triumphant. The sender
had not been quite as careful as he thought he had been.
Most of the messages were untraceable. Two, however, had
been sent from a personal computer belonging to one Richard Pearson. Ironically, both messages were ones question-
ing when payment would be received.

Breaking into the CIA network took another hour. Once
in, she checked if there were any Richard Pearsons working
for the Agency. Turns out there were two. One was on the
janitorial staff, while the other was a senior analyst special-
izing in European matters.

"You've been a very bad man, Mr. Pearson," she said.

Jillian decided the best person to contact with what she'd
learned would be the person at the top—the CIA's director,
Lance Cabot.

She found an email address for him that appeared to be
for priority matters.

She created a dummy email account and wrote a
message.

Dear Director Cabot:

*Someone in your organization has been selling
information. I've included copies of the
documents that were exchanged. I've done a*

*preliminary track back and the sender appears to
be a person named Richard Pearson. I advise
doing your own investigation.*

*Also, if you have any ties to the film producer
Billy Barnett, please know that his life is in danger,
and advise him not to attend the World Thriller
Film Festival this evening.*

The app she was using would remove all traces of who she was from the email when it was sent.

She was reading through her message to be sure it said what she wanted it to when her office phone rang, the caller ID reading: F. BRAUN.

She looked around nervously, wondering if cameras had been installed in her office without her knowing.

As the phone rang for a third time, she picked it up. "This is Jillian Courtois."

"I need you in my office right now," Braun said.

"Okay, sure. What is this—" She stopped herself when she realized he'd hung up.

She wondered if he knew what she was doing, and whether she should delete the email instead of sending it.

She took a breath to steady herself and hit SEND.

"Oh, God," she whispered as the message disappeared.

She logged out of the app, and then headed for her meeting with Braun.

Somewhere over the Atlantic, Lance's phone pinged.

He'd hitched a ride early that morning on a Strategic Services jet that would be dropping him off in D.C.

The message was from an unknown sender, and he wouldn't have opened it but for the subject line that read: Golden Hour.

He read the note and looked at the attachments.

His search for the mole had not been going well, and now he knew why. Richard Pearson had not been on anyone's list of potential leakers. Lance himself could barely remember what the man even looked like. From what he could recall, Pearson was quiet and unassuming and good but not great at his job.

Lance made a call. "Bailey. It's Lance. There's something I need you to take care of."

Ten minutes later, and less than fifteen after Jillian had hit SEND on her email, someone rang Richard Pearson's doorbell.

His five a.m. alarm had just gone off, and he had yet to pull himself out of bed.

The bell rang again.

"Are you going to get that?" his wife asked without opening her eyes.

"Why me?" he asked.

"It won't be for me. It never is at this hour."

The bell sounded a third time.

"Get the door," his wife said. "They're obviously not going away."

Pearson grumbled and crawled out of bed. After pulling on his robe, he made his way downstairs.

The visitor pushed the doorbell button again.

"Relax! I'm coming!"

When he reached the door, he took a moment to compose himself, then pulled it open and stared in confusion. Standing on his porch was Deputy Director Bailey Robinson, and behind her were four people he didn't recognize.

"Good morning, Richard," the deputy director said. "I apologize for getting you up so early."

"Good morning, Deputy Director. It's fine. I was already awake."

"Oh, good. I was wondering if we might have a word."

"Um, sure," he said, trying to remain calm. "Come in."

He moved to the side and Robinson and two of the people with her entered, while the other two remained outside.

He led them into the living room. "Would you like some coffee? I haven't started it yet, but it shouldn't take too long."

"Thank you, but I've already had a cup," Robinson said. "Shall we sit?"

She motioned Pearson to the couch while she took one of the chairs across from it. Her companions remained standing.

Pearson felt his mouth going dry as he sat, hoping she was just here for his assistance on something urgent.

"What can I help you with?" he asked.

Smiling, she said, "To start, you can tell me when your relationship with Felix Braun began."

"Oh, shit." The words were out of his mouth before he even realized he'd spoken.

"'Oh, shit,' indeed," the deputy director said.

44

FOR THE CENTURION PICTURES CREW, THE
day of the film festival's opening ceremony started with
television appearances by Tessa, Adriene, Peter, and Mark
on three different German networks and the BBC.

Midday was the festival's press luncheon, at which Tessa
and Mark served as the event's MCs. This was followed by a
promotional photo shoot that included Peter, Hattie, and Ben,
and a meeting with a group of twenty fans who had won a
sweepstakes to spend a half hour with the stars of the movie.

By the time they returned to the hotel lobby, it was five-
thirty p.m.

"Well, well, well," a very recognizable voice boomed.
"If it isn't my Centurion Pictures friends."

Action star Tom Norman peeled himself away from the
group he'd been standing with and walked over to join
Mark, Tessa, and the others.

"You really did make it," Tessa said.

"Did you think I was lying about making time to be here?"

"Of course not. But in this business, schedules change on the daily."

"Fair point. But what you didn't know was that I'm the festival's head judge for the films that have entered the competition."

Tessa looked around at the others. "How come we didn't know that?"

"Shh," Tom said, a finger to his lips. "They're not revealing that information until tonight."

"Now I wish we were part of the competition," Peter said.

Tom's eyes lit up. "Peter! I missed you at my premiere."

He and Peter shook hands.

"My apologies. I really wanted to be there."

"No apology necessary." Tom lowered his voice. "By the way, we all know that if you entered *Storm's Eye* no one else would have a chance."

"I don't know about that, but at least allow me to buy you a drink while we're in town."

"That's a great idea," Hattie said. "You two can chat about that project you were thinking about."

"Project?" Tom asked.

"More a loose idea at this point," Peter said.

"If it involves us working together, *I'll* buy the drinks," Tom said.

"Tessa!" another familiar voice called out.

Mari Chen jogged over and gave Tessa a hug. "I'm so happy to see you."

"I didn't think you were getting in until tomorrow," Tessa said.

"Your talented PR rep, Lizzie, was able to get me tickets to the screening and party tonight so I—" She stopped and her mouth fell open. "Oh my God. You're Tom Norman."

Tom looked equally transfixed by her. "You're Mari Chen."

"You know who I am?"

"We *are* working together on the award show at the end of the festival."

"Yeah, but you're *Tom Norman*."

"And you're *Mari Chen*."

To Peter, Mark whispered, "I'm going up to my room before anyone else shows up."

"You mean like Bianca Barone? Because she's sitting in the restaurant right now. I take that back. Looks like she's seen us and is starting to get up."

Mark made a quick exit toward the elevators.

––––––––––

Vesna was waiting in the suite when Teddy entered.

"You're late," she said.

"Blame it on the famous and fabulous."

"Please tell me that's not a fancy way of talking about yourself."

"There was a celebrity traffic jam in the lobby of much more famous people than I."

"I don't know if I've told you this, but your life has taken a strange turn."

"I cannot argue with that, but I wouldn't change a thing. Now, shall we get started?"

"If we must."

"Madam, your makeover awaits," he said and headed into his bedroom.

An hour and a half later, Teddy had transformed the raven-haired Vesna Martic into a strawberry-blonde she'd christened Rita Dane, the two bearing little resemblance to each other.

He'd also turned himself into an Armani-tuxedoed Billy Barnett, with an added component he'd never needed before—a special makeup prosthetic covering the back of his neck that Vesna had helped to apply.

There was a knock at the door, and Billy let Stone in. He, too, was dressed in a tux, his Ralph Lauren.

"Wow," Stone said, upon seeing Vesna. "I would have never recognized you."

"Which is the point, I believe," Billy said.

"If this producing thing doesn't work out for you, you can transfer to the makeup department."

Vesna's transformation had been necessary due to her previous relationship with Dieter Wenz, since there would be no avoiding crossing paths with him that evening.

"Vesna, would you mind if I had a private word with Billy?" Stone asked.

"As long as you don't say anything bad about me," she said.

"Wouldn't dream of it."

"Aren't you a dear." She headed into the bedroom.

Once Stone and Billy were alone, Stone said, "Have you talked to Lance today?"

"No. I've been busy. Why?"

"He received a very interesting email this morning, fingering the mole."

"That *is* interesting. Has Lance acted on it?"

"He has. I understand a full confession is in the works."

"That's a relief. Who sent the email?"

"Unknown, though Lance surmises the sender is someone who works for Braun."

Though Billy had only come in contact with a few of Braun's employees, he had a pretty good idea who the emailer had been.

Vesna stuck her head back into the room. "All right to come back now? Or are you boys still gossiping?"

Billy checked his watch. "Everyone will be in the lobby in a few minutes, so we should get a move on it." He glanced at Stone. "Before we go, hold out your hand."

Billy removed a small cloth pouch and emptied the contents into Stone's palm. There were three items: a box that looked like a thin version of an old-fashioned pager, a dime-sized disc, and a square of plastic on which were several small ovals in a range of skin tones.

Billy picked up the latter and held it beside Stone's ear.

"This should work," he said. He pointed at the third oval in the top row. "It's your earpiece. Adhere it to the end of your ear canal."

Stone placed it where he'd been told. "Like this?"

Billy examined it. The color was almost an exact match, making the earpiece nearly impossible to see. "Perfect." He picked up the dime-sized disc. "This is your mic. It sticks to the inside of your collar and should press against your skin."

While Stone put it on, Billy switched on the black box.

"This is your transmitter. The dial on the side is your volume control. Don't mess with anything else."

He handed it to Stone.

After turning on his own comm set, Billy took a few steps away and whispered, "Test, test."

"Hear you loud and clear," Stone said.

"Then we have a screening to get to."

Since Vesna would be posing as Stone's date this evening, he offered her his arm.

As she took it, she said, "This is already starting off better than most dates I have been on."

"Careful," Billy said. "Stone has a reputation."

Vesna raised an eyebrow. "Good or bad?"

"That depends on who you talk to," Teddy said.

"Or how you define the word 'bad,'" Stone added.

"Forget what I said earlier. This is starting off better than *any* date I have been on."

45

ACROSS TOWN A SIMILAR MEETING WAS OC-
curring in a Braun Logistics conference room. The only differ-
ences were that none of the fourteen men present had altered
their appearance, and only two were wearing tuxedoes.

"If there are any questions, ask now," Dieter said.

He scanned the group, but as he expected, no one
spoke up.

Dieter wished he could have assembled the crème de la
crème of the BLS special projects unit. But per Braun's instructions, they were spread across the globe in position to
terminate the remaining Golden Hour agents as soon as
Braun and Dieter finished dealing with Fay.

The only trusted men he'd been able to retain had been
Rolf, who was the only other person beside himself wearing
a tux, and Andreas, who would be overseeing the others.

The other eleven in the room were made up of a mixed

bag of freelancers. Not ideal, but they were only there as backup and would be unlikely not to see any action.

"There will be zero tolerance for mistakes today," Dieter said. "If even one civilian catches on to what we are doing, the mission is blown. Is that understood?"

This was greeted by a less-than-perfect chorus of *yeahs.*

"Transportation is waiting in the garage." He nodded at Andreas.

"All right, everyone," Andreas said. "Get moving."

He and the others departed, leaving Dieter and Rolf alone.

Dieter handed Rolf a business card with the Trust's logo on it. "Just in case something happens, and we need to act quickly. Otherwise, Braun will use one of his."

Rolf nodded and slipped the card into his pocket.

While Andreas and his team would be stationed outside the event, Dieter and Rolf would be accompanying Braun to the film festival's opening-night event.

Dieter's phone buzzed.

"Yes?" he answered.

"Barnett just left the hotel," his watcher reported.

"Alone?"

"No. With his Hollywood friends."

"You still have eyes on him?"

"He's three vehicles in front of me. On expected course."

"Contact me immediately if there's any deviation." He hung up and said to Rolf, "It's time."

The back door of the BLS Suburban opened, and Mr. Braun climbed in and sat next to Jillian.

She gave him a tight smile into which she hoped he didn't read anything.

That morning, he'd called her to his office and told her that she would be joining him and Dieter at the film festival.

"I want that steel-trap mind of yours nearby, in case something unexpected comes up," he'd told her.

She'd wanted to protest, but she was sure that would have only made him angry, and he would have still insisted she go. So, all she could say was, "Yes, Mr. Braun."

A fashion expert and a makeup artist had been brought in to turn her from her everyday, disheveled self into someone she barely recognized.

Braun looked her up and down. "You look acceptable."

Not knowing how else to respond, she said, "Thank you."

The door opened again, and Dieter and Rolf entered.

"So?" Braun asked.

"The van has been in place for an hour," Dieter said. "Backup team is on its way there."

"And the hit—" Braun paused, glancing at Jillian before he continued. "The teams covering everyone else?"

"I heard from the last of them thirty minutes ago. They're all in position and awaiting your word."

Braun smiled, while Jillian tried to look like she hadn't been paying attention. It took all her will to keep the horror she was feeling from showing.

The van carrying the Centurion group was nearing the opening-night venue when Teddy received a text from Hans.

Braun just left. Dieter and two others with him.

46

"WOW," PETER SAID, LOOKING OUT THE WIN-
dow. "They are going all out."

"The organizers did say they wanted to make a splash," Billy said.

"Why am I suddenly feeling nervous?" Adriene asked.

Tessa put her hand on her friend's. "Just think of it as a reward for all your hard work."

Banners touting the World Thriller Film Festival's opening night lined the road leading up to Berlin's Haus der Kulturen der Welt—House of World Cultures. Many featured images of Mark, Tessa, and Adriene from *Storm's Eye*.

The complex's beautiful main building was lit up by waves of pulsating light. Near the entrance, several spotlights shot their beams high into the darkening sky as a steady stream of cars dropped off their passengers at the end of a red carpet.

From the front passenger seat, Lizzie said into her phone,
"Uh-huh . . . uh-huh . . . Great. Got it, thanks." She hung up
and looked back at the others. "Okay, folks. We'll be there in
about a minute. When we stop, get out in the order we discussed. Congratulations, everyone. This is your night!"

"If we haven't said it already, thank you, Lizzie," Billy
said. "We couldn't have done this trip without you."

"We're not quite through yet, but you're welcome."

The van inched toward the drop-off point.

"How's my hair?" Adriene asked.

"As beautiful as always," Hattie told her.

"I feel like a giant sweat ball."

"Deep breaths," Tessa said. "With me."

Adriene mimicked her sucking air in and pushing it out.
After they'd done this several times, Tessa said, "Better?"

"A little."

"Remember, you're not alone."

"Thanks."

There was only one car in front of them now, and it had
just dislodged its occupants.

As it drove off and the van rolled up to the drop-off, Lizzie said, "Here we go."

She hopped out and opened the side passenger door. A
tidal wave of cheers rushed into the vehicle, making it impossible for anyone to hear anyone else.

Billy stepped out first. As he did, an amplified voice announced first in German and then in English, "Ladies and
gentlemen, the Academy Award–winning producer of *Desperation at Dawn*, and the producer of tonight's world premiere film *Storm's Eye*, Billy Barnett!"

The fans in the grandstands that lined the red carpet roared in excitement.

Billy took a couple of steps down the carpet and waved, garnering even more cheers.

The MC's voice boomed out again, "Composer of the *Storm's Eye*'s score and an Academy Award winner in her own right, Hattie Barrington!"

Adriene came next, beaming and waving, followed by Peter, and finally Tessa and Ben.

They walked down the carpet as a group, stopping several times to pose for photos.

Back at the van, Stone, Vesna, and Stacy exited and headed down the path for noncelebrities.

Teddy and the others reached the platform near the end of the red carpet.

The MC elicited another round of cheers as he reintroduced everyone, then he said, "Film lovers, please welcome the director of the World Thriller Film Festival, Constance Mueller!"

A small woman with a giant smile joined them and waved to the crowd. The MC handed her the mic.

Mueller spoke for several moments in German, then switched to English. "Welcome to the inaugural World Thriller Film Festival! I hope every one of you gets the chance to see one of the wonderful films we will be screening over the next week. And speaking of wonderful, I couldn't be happier that we're opening the festival with *Storm's Eye*, the new film by the magnificent Peter Barrington!"

As the crowd roared, Peter waved and then bowed in thanks.

Vesna's voice came over the comm in Billy's ear. "Braun just pulled up."

Billy's smile didn't miss a beat as he swiveled his gaze to the drop-off point, where Felix Braun was exiting a Suburban. Two men and a woman followed, all of whom Billy recognized.

One of the men was Dieter Wenz, and the other a man who'd been with him at the hospital in Budapest. The woman was Jillian, the person Billy had almost run into on the stairs at Ristorante Cumberland.

Peter's voice boomed out of the speakers. "We are honored beyond words to be chosen to open this wonderful new festival! Thank you so much for inviting us!"

The mic was passed to Tessa. "What Peter said! We're so thrilled to be here!"

Back at the Suburban, a festival worker guided Braun and his party to the alternate path into the theater.

And at the platform, Adriene was thanking the fans for coming out and telling everyone how excited she was.

Hattie came next, sharing a few thoughts on the marriage of film and music, then she handed the mic to Billy.

"I'm not sure how much I can add to what's already been said," he told the crowd. "Thank you for welcoming us to your wonderful city, and to the first of what is sure to be one of the best film festivals in the world!"

The shouts from the crowd reached new heights, while cameras flashed in rapid staccato.

As Mueller made a few more remarks, a beep sounded in Billy's ear. He switched to the comm channel being used by the Strategic Services team helping him deal with Braun and his people and said just loud enough for his mic to pick up, "I'm here."

"This is Strauss," the team leader said. "We've identified twelve hostiles sprinkled around the event perimeter."

Among his conditions to Lance for his continued involvement had been that each member of the Centurion contingent be provided a bodyguard and that a second security team be assigned directly to Billy. He'd further insisted this help come from Strategic Services and not the Agency to avoid the chance of his plans being leaked to Braun. While the mole had been captured, Billy wasn't going to take any chances. Lance had grudgingly agreed to pick up the tab.

"Copy," Billy said.

The MC took the mic back from Mueller. "Thank you all for coming out tonight! And now, it's time for the show to begin!"

Because of their late inclusion, the tickets for Braun's party put them in the back corner of the theater.

This turned out to be a good thing as it allowed them to observe the last of the moviegoers trickle in without drawing attention to themselves.

A ripple ran through the crowd and almost everyone turned their attention to the entrance as a statuesque woman stepped into the theater on the arm of a man a few inches shorter than her.

"She's the movie star, isn't she?" Braun asked Jillian.

"T-T-Tessa Tweed," she whispered.

He had seen images of Tessa in the past, mostly in

advertisements for House Dione and for a brand of high-end cosmetics of which he couldn't remember the name. She was just as stunning in person.

"And the guy with her?"

"Ben Bacchetti, head of Centurion Pictures. They're married."

A second woman entered.

"Adriene Adele," Jillian said, without prompting. "She's in the movie."

Braun had never heard of the woman.

Next came Peter and Hattie Barrington, the film's director and its composer.

The attention of the crowd followed the quintet as they made their way to their seats near the center of the theater.

Braun kept his gaze on the doorway, however, and was rewarded a moment later when four more people walked in.

Beside him, Jillian tensed.

"That's Barnett, isn't it?" Braun said. "The guy in front?"

Though she didn't want to, Jillian nodded.

Braun's gaze narrowed on Billy Barnett. He was a man of indeterminate age, who carried himself with an air of confidence and success. The woman with him was considerably younger.

"Who's his companion?" he asked. "Girlfriend?"

"Assistant," Jillian said.

"That doesn't mean she's not sleeping with him."

"I've found nothing that says they have anything more than a work relationship."

"Too bad." A girlfriend would be a weakness Braun could exploit to get Barnett to reveal his true identity.

"Who are the other two?"

"I believe the man is Peter Barrington's father, Stone Barrington. I don't know who the woman with him is."

Braun focused back on Barnett as he and his assistant walked down the aisle and slipped into the row behind where his colleagues now sat. The director's father and his date followed and took the last two open seats.

A voice came over the speakers. "The World Thriller Film Festival is proud to present Peter Barrington's *Storm's Eye*."

The lights dimmed, the curtain opened, and the Centurion Pictures logo appeared on the screen.

47

THE APPLAUSE STARTED EVEN BEFORE THE FI-
nal shot of the film cut to black and continued through the
entire credit roll. By the end, everyone was on their feet,
whooping and cheering in genuine appreciation.

Billy leaned forward and whispered in Peter's ear, "You
were right. The tweaks you made were just what that scene
needed."

"I don't know. I think maybe—"

"Stop right there," Ben said. "You're not touching another frame."

When the applause showed no signs of stopping, Tessa,
Hattie, Adriene, and Billy stood and waved their thanks,
then they turned as one to Peter and began clapping, too.

Peter rose to his feet, no longer able to keep the smile
from his face. He waved and bowed his head, over and over.

When the adoration finally began to ebb, Constance
Mueller stepped to the front of the theater, mic in hand.

"I don't know about you, but I don't think we could have found a better film to kick things off!"

The cheers and claps resumed for several seconds.

"I've been reliably told the champagne has been chilled and the hors d'oeuvres prepared, so I hope you will all join me as we celebrate this momentous night!"

The party was set up outside in a grassy area that had been transformed into a magical space of sparkling lights and live music worthy of a scene from a movie.

Waiters moved through the crowd carrying trays of appetizers and drinks, while members of a world-renowned circus troupe performed acts of aerobatics on small stages spaced throughout.

Billy had just enough time for a glass of sparkling water before one of the event staff approached him and said, "Mr. Barnett, may I escort you to the meet and greet?"

"Thank you." Billy caught Stacy's attention and motioned for her to join him.

The escort led them to a small events room in the Haus der Kulturen der Welt building. At least two dozen people were already inside, among them Stone and Vesna, and Braun and his female companion.

A waiter approached Billy and Stacy and offered them champagne. Billy took one for appearance's sake only.

Stacy helped herself to one as well but was more than happy to take a sip.

Ben arrived in the company of Constance Mueller. Upon seeing Billy, they walked over.

"I can't thank you both enough for doing this," Mueller said. "It's the kind of thing I want to turn into an essential component of future festivals."

"Our pleasure," Ben said. "And who knows? Maybe we'll discover some production partners."

Mueller did a head count, then said, "I believe everyone is here. Shall we start?"

"Let's," Ben said.

Braun kept his gaze on Barnett as the festival director introduced him and Ben Bacchetti to the room. The two men then spoke for several minutes about the industry and the good and bad of investing in motion pictures.

When they were through, Mueller said, "We'd like to keep this informal, so feel free to approach Ben or Billy with any questions you may have."

Within moments both Barnett and Bacchetti were surrounded by those wanting to learn more.

Braun, Jillian, and a man and woman nearby seemed to be the only ones to hang back.

When the man caught Braun's gaze, Braun realized he was the director's father. Stan? Stewart? He hadn't been paying close enough attention to remember.

"Don't have any questions?" the older Barrington asked.

"I have plenty," Braun said. "But I'd rather ask them of someone who can give me his full attention."

"If you'd like, you can try asking me. I might not know everything, but I should be able to give you some answers."

"You work in the film industry?"

Jillian hadn't mentioned that, but it wasn't implausible. From the little he knew, the movie business was full of nepotism.

"In a way," Barrington said. "I'm on the board of directors for Centurion Pictures."

"Is that so?"

The man held out a hand. "Stone Barrington. You just watched my son's film."

They shook. "Felix Braun. So, you're Peter's father."

"I am."

"Then you already know Mr. Barnett and Mr. Bacchetti."

"I've known Ben since he was born, and Billy since around the time he started working with Ben and Peter. We're here as moral support." He glanced at his date. "May I introduce Rita Dane?"

"A pleasure," Braun said to her. "Are you also in movies?"

She smiled and said in an American accent, "I'm just a friend of the family. I try not to work at all if I can help it. Are you interested in becoming an investor?"

"It's something I'm considering."

"If you'd like," Barrington said, "I can personally introduce you to Ben and Billy."

"I'd like that very much, if it's not too much trouble."

"Not at all."

Once the other attendees started heading back to the celebration, Stone led Braun over to the two producers.

"Ben, Billy, I'd like you to meet Felix Braun."

"Nice to meet you, Mr. Braun," Bacchetti said.

"Please, call me Felix."

They shook hands and then Braun did the same with Barnett.

"How can we help you?" Barnett asked.

They spent the next several minutes discussing the ins and outs of the industry, stopping only when Constance Mueller announced it was time to rejoin the party.

"If you'd like to talk more about this, please give me a call," Barnett said and handed his business card to Braun.

They walked out of the building together. As they neared the festivities, Braun asked Barnett, "I'm curious how one becomes a producer. Did you start off as one?"

Barnett laughed. "Hardly. It was through guns."

"I'm sorry?"

"I started as a part-time gunsmith, refurbishing prop weapons."

"I see. You have a lot of experience in this area?"

"Enough to know which end to avoid." Barnett waved to someone on the other side of the dance area. "Felix, it's been a pleasure meeting you. I hope we can talk again soon."

"I'm sure we will."

As he watched Barnett head into the crowd, Dieter joined him.

"Well?" Dieter asked.

"He didn't come out and say it, but he's Fay all right. I'm sure of it."

48

"THE VAN'S HERE FOR ANY OF YOU READY TO
head back," Lizzie said.

It was midnight, and the party had finally begun winding down.

Tessa raised a hand. "Count me in."

"Me, too," Hattie said. "I've had about as much excitement as I can handle."

"I guess that means I'm going back, too," Peter said.

"And me," Ben said.

"Please tell me we don't have to be up at the crack of dawn tomorrow." Adriene said. Even though she still glowed from the evening, she looked ready for sleep.

"Nothing scheduled until the afternoon," Lizzie said.

"Oh, thank God."

"The sooner my head is on the pillow, the happier I'll be," Stacy said.

"Billy?" Lizzie asked.

"You all go ahead," Billy said. "I promised Constance I'd say goodbye before I left."

"I could send the van back for you."

Before Billy could respond, Stone said, "Ms. Dane and I are staying for a bit longer, too. Billy, you're welcome to grab a cab with us."

"Perfect," Billy said. "I'll do that."

As soon as Lizzie led the others away, Billy said, "Where's Braun?"

"Last I saw, he was leaving with his lady friend," Vesna said.

"Is your ex with them?"

Her expression soured. "Can we just call him Dieter?"

"Whatever makes you more comfortable. The question remains the same, however."

"He and the other man are not with them."

Billy activated the Strategic Services channel on his comm. "Strauss, do you have a location on Dieter Wenz?"

"I do, indeed. He's thirty meters to your right, behind one of the light towers."

"Alone?"

"Yes, and out of sight from your position. His companion is closer to the exit, tucked behind one of the movie poster decorations."

"I've been told Braun was heading out. Can you confirm?"

"He and his date are in the queue waiting for their vehicle."

"It looks like we'll be going with option B."

"Option B. Copy."

"Pass the word. And let me know the moment Dieter or his buddy moves."

"Will do."

To Stone and Vesna, Billy said, "Shall we?"

"Let me check you first," Vesna said.

Billy casually turned his back to her, like he was searching for someone.

After getting a look at the nape of his neck, she whispered, "You're good."

"I see Constance," Billy said, as if Vesna hadn't spoken. "Care to join me?"

"Why not?" Stone said.

They walked over to the festival's director, who was speaking with a pair of women.

When their conversation ended, Billy said, "Constance, I wanted to thank you again for giving our movie the perfect kickoff."

"We should be thanking you," she said. "The film is marvelous."

"Thanks. Will I see you at the panel discussion tomorrow?"

"I wouldn't miss it."

They said their goodbyes, then Billy, Stone, and Vesna headed for the vehicle pickup line.

When they neared the spot where Dieter's colleague was hidden, Billy slowed. "How long until our ride gets here?"

Stone made a show of checking his phone. "Ten minutes."

"Just enough time to use the restroom. You two go ahead. I'll be back in a few."

———————

Rolf's voice came over Dieter's comm. "Barnett is going to the toilet."

"Are the others going with him?"

"No."

"Follow him."

———————

"The man near the entrance is moving out of cover and appears to be following Mr. Barnett," Strauss said over the receivers in Stone's and Vesna's ears.

Vesna let go of Stone's arm.

"Be careful," Stone said.

She gave him a quick smirk. "This is not a word I'm familiar with. I'll see you at the rendezvous point."

Quietly, she headed in the direction Billy had gone.

———————

Moments later, Dieter spotted Barnett walking across the area where the party had taken place. Other than him, the only people present now were festival staff and the caterers removing the last of the food and beverages.

Once Dieter's hiding place was out of Barnett's sight, Dieter strolled out and joined Rolf in pursuit.

Barnett continued to the main building and entered. The two men followed and were in time to see Barnett turn into the men's room.

Silently, Dieter directed Rolf to check the other end of the hallway. Rolf jogged down, then signaled that the area was clear.

Dieter stepped around a corner and called Andreas. "It's going down now. Let the van team know we'll be using the delivery entrance. Get everyone else back to the sedans."

"On it," Andreas said.

"Unidentified van approaching back of main building," Strauss said.

"I believe that'll be my ride," Billy said, voice low.

"The men we've been tracking outside the event grounds are on the move, too."

"Toward the van?"

"No. Back to the cars they arrived in."

"You know what to do."

49

AFTER THE DEBACLE WITH VERDE IN ROMA-
nia, Andreas hadn't expected to be given a prime spot on
any of the other Golden Hour retribution operations. But
neither had he expected he'd be put with the grunts on the
ass end of a job to kidnap some movie producer.

But here he was, making his way back to one of the
three sedans in which he and the others who'd been on perimeter watch had arrived, their reason for being there in
the first place apparently moot.

Andreas reached his vehicle a few seconds ahead of the
others and climbed into the front passenger seat.

Their orders were to follow the van when it left, guarding against trouble Andreas was sure wasn't coming. In
other words, another do-nothing task.

The driver slipped behind the wheel and pressed the
START button.

Nothing happened.

He pressed the button again, but the engine remained silent.

"What the hell?" Andreas asked. "Did you not fill the tank?"

"Of course I filled the tank," the man protested.

"Then what's wrong?"

"I don't know!"

As the driver pushed the button a third time, Andreas twisted around and looked out the back window. The other two cars seemed to be suffering similar problems.

"Oh, shit," he muttered, then yelled, "everybody out!"

Before anyone had the chance to obey, black-clad soldiers slipped from the trees and surrounded the vehicles, their automatic rifles trained on the sedans.

Andreas turned on his radio. "Dieter! Abort! It's a trap!"

Unbeknownst to him, the armed force encircling them had deployed a signal disrupter, preventing any signal from getting through.

All Andreas knew was that the radio was as silent as the sedan's engine.

———————

Teddy washed his hands and dried them.

"Walking out," he whispered.

"Have them in my sights," Vesna replied over the comm.

"I know Dieter's a tempting sight, but don't get trigger happy."

"You really know how to ruin my mood."

Teddy checked himself in the mirror, made sure everything looked as it should, and exited the restroom.

Dieter and his colleague were standing nearby when he entered the hall.

As he started walking past them, Dieter said, "Teddy Fay?"

Teddy purposely put a slight hitch in his step as he continued moving.

"Mr. Barnett," Dieter called. "A moment of your time, please."

Teddy picked up his pace. As soon as he heard the two men rushing after him, he began to run.

Moments later, Dieter's buddy grabbed him from behind to stop him, then swung in front to block the way out. Teddy tried to get by on the right, but the man mirrored the movement.

"Hold on," the man said. "My friend just wants to talk to you."

"I'm afraid I'm rather busy at the moment," Teddy said. "Perhaps we can set up an appointment for another time."

Behind him, Dieter said, "Now works better for me."

As Teddy started turning toward him, Dieter plunged a needle into the prosthetic covering the back of Teddy's neck.

"What are you doing?" Teddy said.

"What do you think we're doing, Mr. Fay?"

"Let me . . ." Teddy staggered toward the man in front of him, as if the drug were taking effect.

"Why are you . . . doing this?" he asked.

Whether Dieter answered or not didn't matter. The question was a code phrase to let Vesna know that the prosthetic had kept the needle from entering his skin.

"You can thank me later," Vesna whispered in his ear.

Teddy's eyes fluttered, then closed as he collapsed onto Dieter's companion.

"Mr. Fay?" Dieter said.

"He's out," the other man said.

Dieter and his friend draped Teddy between them and moved quickly through the building to what Teddy assumed was the delivery area.

He heard an idling engine nearby and the *thunk* of a vehicle door opening. He was then hauled into what he assumed was the van Strauss had reported seeing.

After the door shut, Dieter said, "Go, go!"

The vehicle began to move.

"Where are the others?" Dieter asked as the van neared the venue's exit.

"No idea," the driver said.

The skin on Dieter's arms began to prickle. Before his concern could grow into something stronger, however, three sets of headlights appeared on the road behind them.

He called Andreas.

"Yes?" Andreas answered.

"You should have been waiting at the exit for us. What happened?"

"Sorry. A few of the men were late getting back."

Unfortunately, that was to be expected when working with subpar personnel. "Any other problems?"

After a beat, Andreas said, "Nothing."

"Are you sure?"

This time the answer came right away. "Everything was quiet, just like we thought it would be."

"Good. Proceed as planned and stay alert."

Dieter hung up.

In the back seat of the last of the three sedans, Andreas handed his phone back to Vesna. The delay in meeting up with the van had been due to a combination of making the engines operational again and waiting for Vesna and Stone to reach the vehicles.

"You almost ruined things for yourself," she said, referring to his pause in answering Dieter about problems.

"It's okay," Andreas said. "He doesn't suspect anything."

"You'd better hope that's true," Vesna said. "Now, where exactly are they headed?"

50

DIETER DIDN'T RELAX UNTIL THE FOUR-vehicle convoy reached the gates of the Braun Logistics property, hidden in a forest outside of Berlin.

The driver tapped a remote and the fence rolled out of the way. Once the last of the sedans behind them passed through, the barrier moved back into place.

Originally, the facility had been a base for the Stasi, the East German secret police. Though most of the buildings now were new construction, a few of the originals remained. All were dark tonight, as any employee who might have been present had been given the day off.

The van's destination was one of the legacy buildings, set off a bit from the others.

The unassuming two-story concrete structure hid a multilevel basement where the Stasi had conducted interrogations. Though they weren't used as often now, the lower levels served the same purpose for BLS's illegal activities.

Braun's Mercedes-Maybach was parked near the detainee entrance, but the man himself was not present.

As the van pulled in next to the Maybach, Dieter said to Rolf and the other man in the back, "Get him up."

Dieter hopped out, circled around to the back, and opened the doors.

Between the three of them, they were able to get Billy Barnett outside without dropping him.

Dieter used a key card to open the building's entrance. Harsh fluorescent light spilled out of a short hallway that ended at an elevator.

"Take him to the elevator and wait for me."

While Rolf and the other man did that, Dieter turned to the sedans. For some reason, they'd stopped a good fifty feet away and were still in single file.

If he could have, he would have fired them all on the spot.

He motioned for everyone to get out and create a security net around the building. He then joined Billy Barnett and his men in the elevator and pressed the button to close the door.

Events at the building were relayed to Vesna and Stone via a camera in the lead sedan.

As Teddy was led into the building, Vesna asked Andreas, "What part of the building are they taking him to?"

"Basement, I think," he said.

"You *think*?"

"I don't know for sure. I've never gone down there. I've only heard of it."

"What's in the basement?" Stone asked.

"Interrogation rooms. At least, that's what I've been told."

On the camera feed, Dieter motioned at the sedans for the men he thought were in them to get out and stand guard, then he entered the building. Moments later, the feed from Teddy's mic went silent, all but confirming Andreas's guess that Teddy was being taken to a basement.

Vesna turned on her mic and adjusted the channel to the one assigned to Strategic Services. "We need four people for perimeter watch. The rest meet me at the door in two minutes." She shut off her mic. "Stone, you should probably stay here."

"While I appreciate your concern, I do have a bit of experience in this kind of thing," he said.

"Rescuing someone from an East German spy bunker while taking down those responsible?"

"Perhaps not specifically this. But close enough."

"I can't be held responsible."

"Nor would I ask you to be."

"Fine. But do me a favor and stay toward the back. I don't want to shoot you by mistake."

"That I can promise. I do have one question, though. Does anyone have a spare weapon?"

After getting Stone sorted and asking the other two men in her sedan to put Andreas in the trunk, Vesna approached the van at an angle that would keep its driver from seeing her.

In a crouch, she circled the front until she was right below the driver's-side window. It was open and she could smell cigarette smoke wafting from inside.

She stood, her silencer-equipped pistol pointed at the man's head. "Hello," she said in German. "Don't move."

Either he didn't speak German or he was an idiot. He reached down and came up with a shotgun, clearly intending to use it.

Vesna disabused him of the idea by putting a bullet through his temple.

When she reached the building entrance, Stone and the Strategic Services team were already there. One of Strauss's people had an electronic device connected to the lock sensor pad.

The woman with the device said, "We're good."

Vesna yanked the door open, and she and the others hurried inside.

51

TEDDY WAS CARRIED DOWN A HALLWAY, HIS feet dragging behind him.

"Finally," the familiar voice of Felix Braun said. "Get him inside."

Teddy's handlers maneuvered him through a doorway and into a room, where he was dropped into a chair that didn't move.

"Don't just stand there," Braun said, "tie him up."

Someone grabbed one of Teddy's hands and set his forearm on the arm of the chair. Using the heel of his palm as a base, Teddy adjusted his arm's position so that it was hovering above the chair. He held it there as a cord was wrapped around and tied off. While it appeared to be snug, it wasn't. He did the same with his other arm.

Once that was finished, Braun said, "Wake him up."

A needle pierced Teddy's arm and a jolt of adrenaline

rushed through his system. His eyes opened wide as he sucked in breath.

Across a metal table from him sat Braun. Behind Braun were Dieter Wenz, his buddy Rolf, and a man Teddy guessed had been in the van. The only other person present was Jillian. She was pressed against the wall near the door, looking very much like she wanted to be anywhere else. Teddy could sense no one standing behind him.

"I bet you didn't think we'd be seeing each other again this soon, did you?" Braun said.

"What's going on?" Teddy said, as he began quietly working his arms from their restraints. "Why am I here?"

"Because we have business to discuss, Mr. Fay. Or can I call you Teddy?"

"What?" Teddy's left hand slipped free of the first loop. "My name's Billy Barnett."

Braun smiled. "Sure, you *are* Billy Barnett. But underneath your Billy Barnett façade, you're Teddy Fay."

Teddy's left hand was almost completely free now, and his right was not far behind.

"I have no idea what you're going on about. I don't know who this Teddy person is. But why don't we make a deal."

"What kind of deal?"

"You let me go now, and I won't let anyone know what you've done tonight."

Braun smirked. "Let me get this straight. You're saying you'll give us a *pass* if we let you walk away?"

"Exactly that," Teddy said, both of his arms now free. "I won't say a word."

Braun glanced at Dieter. "What do you think, Dieter?"

"I think he's lying," Dieter said.

"I couldn't agree with you more. But we need to remember, it's all people like him can do." Braun focused back on Teddy. "Let's stop playing games, shall we? We both know who you worked for and what you did."

"I work for Centurion Pictures."

"You *work* for the CIA."

"I guarantee you, I don't work for the CIA."

"You worked for them when you killed my father."

A click came over the comm in Teddy's ear.

"Your father?" Teddy dropped all traces of fear from his expression. "You mean Tovar Lintz? The same man whose efforts contributed to the deaths of thousands?"

Braun stared at him, looking like he could hardly believe what he was hearing. "You . . . you admit it? You're Teddy Fay?"

"Like you said, let's stop playing games."

———

Minutes earlier, Vesna, Stone, and the Strategic Services team had rappelled down the elevator shaft and landed softly on top of the elevator car at the bottom.

The trapdoor in the ceiling was quickly found and opened.

Vesna went through first and dropped softly into the car. Strauss and one of his people followed.

Once they had the doors pried open, the others came through the hatch.

As soon as Vesna stepped out of the elevator, the audio feed from Teddy's mic went active. From Stone's reaction, he was hearing it, too.

They moved down the hallway until they reached a

door with the number one painted above it. Muffled voices from the other side matched the voices coming over the feed.

As Braun was telling Teddy that he knew Teddy worked for the CIA, Vesna tested the door handle. As expected, it was unlocked.

In the room, Braun said, "You worked for them when you killed my father."

Vesna clicked her mic to let Teddy know she and the others were there.

Braun laughed, deep and loud.

Teddy merely looked at him blankly.

"Of all the people associated with Golden Hour, you were the one I'd wanted to eliminate the most. Since you were dead, I thought that chance had been denied me. But here you are in the flesh. I have never been so pleased to be wrong in my life."

"I'm happy for you," Teddy said.

"You should be. I've worked hard to reach this point."

Teddy shrugged skeptically. "Have you really?"

"The fact that you're sitting in a room from which you will never leave alive is proof of that."

"You say *fact*. I say unlikely possibility."

Braun tutted. "Try to delude yourself however you want, but we both know how this will end."

"I'm going to have to disagree with you about that, too."

"I would think an intelligent man like yourself would be able to work it out on your own. But if you wish to play ignorant, I'm happy to spell it out for you. Tonight, Operation Golden Hour officially comes to an end."

"Is that so?"

"I have assassins in place near all the remaining agents associated with your vile mission. As soon as you're eliminated, they'll finish everyone else off."

"Thanks for sharing, but you appear to have misunderstood what I meant when I said I disagreed with you. I'm not the one who doesn't understand how this will end."

Braun snorted. "You just don't know when to give up, do you?"

"It's not in my nature."

"Nothing you can do about it, I suppose. Fine. Think what you will. That won't change what's about to happen to you."

"I want to make sure I have this right. You kill me, then give your assassins the word and they kill the rest of my team. And *then* you go after the director of the CIA and the president of the United States. Or will you wait a bit before you attempt to kill them?"

Braun's mood darkened, but he kept his mouth shut.

"I just ask because I'm curious," Teddy said. "If you don't want to share, that's fine. It's never going to happen anyway because they already know."

"What are you talking about?"

"It's what you and your buddy Dieter talked about at lunch the other day. Or don't you remember that?"

The first signs of concern flashed through Braun's eyes.

"The director and the president have already been informed of your intentions."

Braun's sneer returned. "Nice try, Teddy. Nothing you say is going to change your fate. All you're doing is delaying the inevitable."

"Am I? Perhaps you should check in on those assassination teams you think you have on standby."

Braun stared at him for a few seconds, then looked back at Dieter. Dieter pulled out his phone and started making calls. Each time he hung up without anyone answering.

Braun whirled to face Teddy. "You son of a bitch! What have you done?"

"My job."

52

BRAUN FLEW AROUND THE TABLE, HIS EYES
glued to Teddy's. As soon as he was in range, he sent a fist
flying at Teddy's cheek.

Anticipating it, Teddy leaned back and turned his head
so that Braun's hand only brushed his skin. Before Braun
had a chance to pull his arm back, Teddy was on his feet.

He moved behind Braun, grabbed the man's wrist, and
yanked it behind Braun's back.

Dieter, Rolf, and the other man pulled out their guns,
but with their boss between them and Teddy, they didn't
have a shot.

"Let go of me!" Braun said, struggling to break free.

Teddy shoved the man's arm higher, eliciting a shout of
pain. "A little help, if you don't mind," he said.

"What?" Braun asked.

The request had not been directed at him.

The door was shoved inward and Vesna and several Strategic Services personnel swarmed in. Their guns swept the space and landed on Dieter and his colleagues, who were now pointing their pistols at the new arrivals.

"Drop your weapons!" Vesna ordered.

"You drop yours!" Dieter countered.

Knowing this was her chance to do the right thing, Jillian flung her clutch at Dieter's head. He flinched to the side, bumping into the guy next to him, both of their pistols moving off their targets.

Vesna and three members of the Strategic Services team rushed them.

Two gunshots went off, the sound deafening in the small room.

Braun used the distraction to lurch out of Teddy's grasp. Instead of running toward the entrance Vesna had used, he raced to the wall that had been at Teddy's back and through a second door Teddy hadn't realized was there.

Teddy sprinted after him.

———

Vesna went straight for Dieter and knocked the gun out of his hand.

A gunshot went off nearby, followed instantly by another.

Dieter took a swing at Vesna. She stepped back, out of the way, and pointed her weapon at him. "I *will* put a bullet in you if you try that again!"

The desperation on his face twisted into confusion. "Vesna?"

She hadn't disguised her voice. "Hello, Dieter."

"What are you—"

"On your knees, hands behind your head, or I'll start putting holes in you. On second thought, that sounds like a better idea."

Dieter dropped to his knees and laced his fingers behind his head. Once one of the Strategic Services people had zip-tied Dieter's hands together, Vesna looked around.

The man with Dieter who she didn't know was in a similar kneeling position. Dieter's buddy Rolf was sprawled on the floor, however, with a hole in the center of his chest that hadn't been there before.

That accounted for one of the bullets. The second had hit one of the Strategic Services team in the arm. He was being attended to by one of his colleagues and didn't appear to be in serious distress.

"Where's Teddy?" Stone asked.

Vesna spun around, looking through the room, but both Teddy and Braun were gone.

"Shit," she muttered, seeing the second exit. She pointed at a man and a woman from Strategic Services. "You two with me. Stone, can you keep an eye on things here?"

"Of course."

Vesna and the two agents she'd picked left in search of Teddy and Braun.

Teddy raced after Braun, down the narrow hallway that ran behind the interrogation cells.

Braun yanked open the door at the end and passed through seconds before Teddy did the same.

Beyond was a stairwell. Teddy followed Braun to the top and through a door that led out of the building.

As Teddy exited, a voice shouted, "Halt!" and three of the people on perimeter duty closed in on Braun, their rifles aimed at him.

One noticed Teddy and momentarily focused his weapon on him. When he realized who Teddy was, he moved his sights back to Braun and said, "Mr. Barnett, are you all right?"

"I am," Teddy said.

The stairwell exit opened again and Vesna rushed out with two more security personnel. They brought their weapons to bear on Braun.

Teddy walked over to the man and smiled. "As I said, you were the one who didn't know how this was going to turn out."

53

THREE HOURS LATER, TWO UH-60 BLACK
Hawk helicopters descended toward a field on the former
Stasi base.

"Time for me to go," Vesna said.

Teddy, Vesna, and Stone were standing near the interrogation building. She preferred that the CIA remained unaware of her involvement in the operation.

"Thank you," Teddy said. "This would have been a lot
harder without your help."

"Obviously."

They hugged.

"Take care of yourself," Teddy said. "You know how to
reach me if you ever need my help."

"Stone, a pleasure," she said and shook Stone's hand.

He smiled. "I couldn't have asked for a better date this
evening. If you ever make it to New York, perhaps we can do
it again."

"Perhaps we can."

As the first helicopter touched down, Vesna gave them a wave and disappeared into the night.

After both aircraft had settled on the ground, Rick La Rose hopped out of one and led a troop of special forces soldiers over to Teddy and Stone.

"Mr. Barnett, sorry we couldn't get here sooner," he said. "Stone, good to see you again."

"Hello, Rick," Stone said.

Rick looked around. "Where's John?"

"John?" Stone asked.

"The specialist Lance sent. I met him in Venice."

"He had obligations elsewhere and said he'd be contacting Lance directly," Teddy said.

"Then I guess we'll take the prisoners off your hands, and you can be on your way."

"One thing," Teddy said. "The woman's name is Jillian Courtois. I think she became wrapped up in something bigger than she realized. I'm under the impression she has some pretty impressive skills. If you handle her correctly, she could be an asset. You should also mention to Lance that she's the one who emailed him."

Teddy had confirmed this with her after everything had gone down.

"Email?" Rick asked.

"He'll understand."

"Then I'll let him know."

54

FOR THE NEXT WEEK, THE FESTIVAL WAS filled with films, panels, meet and greets, and parties. The final event was the awards ceremony. Trophies for the best actors, writers, documentaries, shorts, and the like were handed out.

Near the end, the MC's voice announced, "Ladies and gentlemen, once more, film star and head judge for the inaugural World Thriller Film Festival, Tom Norman, and joining him, musical sensation Mari Chen!"

Tom and Mari walked onto the stage to the cheers of the packed crowd and headed for the Plexiglas podium rising out of the floor, front and center.

When the shouts and whistles finally faded, Mari said, "Wow! Thank you!"

Someone in the audience yelled out, "We love you, Mari!"

"I love you, too!" She made a heart with her thumb and index finger and thrust it toward the audience.

The crowd cheered again, and many returned the gesture.

Mari beamed and then glanced at her copresenter. "Sorry, Tom."

"We love Tom, too," someone else yelled.

Tom grinned. "Back at you!" Someone else started to shout something similar, but Tom held up a hand. "You are all too kind, but if we let this go on any longer, the festival will have to pay overtime to the crew."

The crowd laughed.

"Mari and I are here right now for a very special reason," he said. "Tonight, we've been celebrating the award winners of those films entered for competition. But there have also been several excellent, noncompetition films screened over the last week."

He listed several of the titles, then said, "One in particular caught the attention of both fans, judges, and festival staff."

"In a special committee session," Mari said, "it was decided to present the first of what we hope will be many World Thriller Masterpiece awards, to be given to films that the festival believes will stand the test of time."

Tom said, "Tonight, we are honored to present that award to . . ."

He and Mari leaned toward the mic and said together, "*Storm's Eye*, directed by Peter Barrington, and produced by Ben Bacchetti and Billy Barnett."

Thunderous applause filled the auditorium as Billy, Peter, and Ben rose from their seats.

"Let's all go," Billy said.

Tessa and Adriene stood, but Stacy and Lizzie did not.

Billy pointed at them. "You, too."

Stacy said, "But we didn't—"

"You're part of the team. Let's go!"

They grinned and joined the group as it piled onto the stage.

Mari and Tom congratulated everyone, then handed the award to Ben.

Ben immediately passed it to Peter and motioned him to the mic.

"To call this unexpected would be an understatement," Peter said. "Which is lucky for you, because it means I didn't prepare any remarks." A wave of laughter crossed the room. "Thank you to Constance Mueller and the entire World Thriller Film Festival staff. You've created a fantastic event."

The room broke out in applause. At first, a trickle of people stood, and soon everyone was on their feet.

Once the clapping started to die down, Peter said, "Making films is all about the people you work with, and I couldn't ask for a better group both behind the camera and in front. Thank you, everyone!"

Tessa said a few words, then Ben, and finally Billy was pushed forward.

"I echo what my colleagues have said, and would only add, what a crazy week this has been. Oh, and don't forget to tell everyone you know to see *Storm's Eye!*"

Later, while celebrating with his friends at the closing-night party, Billy received a text from Lance.

Congratulations on your award. And you have to admit,
I was right. Your trip was the perfect cover. Let me
know if you'd ever like to help us out again.

"Everything all right?" Stacy asked.
Billy blocked Lance's number, then smiled. "It is now."